‖‖ ‖ ‖‖‖‖‖‖ ‖‖ ‖‖ ‖‖‖ ‖‖‖‖‖‖‖‖ ‖‖‖‖ ‖ ‖‖

⟨ **W9-BWQ-174**   ?017

PRAISE FOR THE TUCKER MYSTERIES

Child Not Found

"Daniel is more than generous with the violence, guilt, tweets, craft brews, and compassion."—*Kirkus Reviews*

"[An] enjoyable if complex third book of murder and mayhem with a ... satisfying whirlwind of a resolution."—*Publishers Weekly*

"The third Tucker outing features a gripping plot and engaging characters who are sure to satisfy readers of Vincent Lardo, Joseph Finder, and John Hart."—*Library Journal*

"By any measure, [*Child Not Found*] is a terrific book. It's got a gripping plot, characters so real you can feel them, and a narrative voice that grips you by the heart and won't let go. A terrific read!"—John Gilstrap, author of *Friendly Fire* and the Jonathan Grave thriller series

Corrupted Memory

"Compulsively readable ... Against a meticulously detailed Boston background, the likable but undisciplined Tucker lurches from one crisis to the next."—*Publishers Weekly* (starred review)

"Crisp writing, an engaging plot, and well-drawn characters make this ... a corker of a mystery. Fans of Boston crime writers Dennis Lehane, Jeremiah Healy, and Hank Phillippi Ryan will delight in picking up this new series."—*Library Journal* (starred review)

"A fast-paced crime thriller with an engaging narrator, quirky characters, and explosive secrets ... 4 stars."—*Suspense Magazine*

"Excellent and suspenseful."—*Crimespree Magazine*

"A taut novel of high tech and high drama played out against a backdrop of family dysfunction and government intrigue."—Reed Farrel Coleman, *New York Times* bestselling author of *Robert B. Parker's Blind Spot*

SPRINGDALE PUBLIC LIBRARY
405 S. PLEASANT
SPRINGDALE, AR 72764
479-750-8180

"[A] soulful hero."—*Kirkus Reviews*

Terminated

"A lively debut."—*Kirkus Reviews*

"A smart novel with plenty of witty asides, slam-bam action, and it doesn't flinch from depicting sexual violence."—*The Boston Globe*

"Ray Daniel has nailed it. Nailed the story, nailed the writing, nailed the whole clever, original and quirky deal. An authentically riveting thriller, with wit and skill and a voice you can't forget. Terrific."—Hank Phillippi Ryan, Anthony, Agatha, Macavity, and Mary Higgins Clark Award-winning author

"[A] smart, snappy, suspense-filled entertainment that knows just when to ratchet up the action, just when to turn the plot, just when to twist the knife. And more than that, it's filled with fascinating characters, snarky humor, and some sharp social observations, too. You'll read far into the night and come away with two things: a deep sense of satisfaction and sweaty palms from turning the pages so fast."—William Martin, *New York Times* bestselling author of *Back Bay* and *The Lincoln Letter*

"Ray Daniel delivers a fast moving and engaging story with fully-blown characters, biting wit, and sparkling dialog. Terminated is a terrific debut novel. There is a new kid in town who deserves a wide audience."—Gary Braver, bestselling and award-winning author of *Tunnel Vision*

"Ray Daniel not only delivers a suspenseful, twisty, action-packed yarn, he's created an everyman hero named Tucker who will linger in the reader's consciousness long after the final page is read. A terrific debut for a promising new series."—Steve Ulfelder, author of *Wolverine Bros. Freight & Storage*

"Ray Daniel knows what he writes and has written a winner."—Mike Cooper, award-winning author of *Clawback*

205 S. PLEASANT
SPRINGDALE, AR 72764
479-750-8180

HACKED

A TUCKER MYSTERY

RAY DANIEL

MIDNIGHT INK
WOODBURY, MINNESOTA

SPRINGDALE PUBLIC LIBRARY
405 S. PLEASANT
SPRINGDALE, AR 72764
479-750-8180

Hacked: A Tucker Mystery © 2017 by Ray Daniel. All rights reserved. No part of this book may be used or reproduced in any manner whatsoever, including Internet usage, without written permission from Midnight Ink, except in the case of brief quotations embodied in critical articles and reviews.

First Edition
First Printing, 2017

Book format by Bob Gaul
Cover design by Ellen Lawson
Editing by Nicole Nugent

Midnight Ink, an imprint of Llewellyn Worldwide Ltd.

This is a work of fiction. Names, characters, places, and incidents are either the product of the author's imagination or are used fictitiously, and any resemblance to actual persons living or dead, business establishments, events, or locales is entirely coincidental.

Library of Congress Cataloging-in-Publication Data
Names: Daniel, Ray, author.
Title: Hacked / by Ray Daniel.
Description: First edition. | Woodbury, Minnesota: Midnight Ink, [2017] |
   Series: A Tucker mystery; #4
Identifiers: LCCN 2016047687 (print) | LCCN 2016055163 (ebook) | ISBN
   9780738751108 (softcover) | ISBN 9780738751818
Subjects: LCSH: Hackers—Fiction. | Murder—Investigation—Fiction. | GSAFD:
   Mystery fiction.
Classification: LCC PS3604.A5255 H33 2017 (print) | LCC PS3604.A5255 (ebook)
   | DDC 813/.6—dc23
LC record available at https://lccn.loc.gov/2016047687

Midnight Ink
Llewellyn Worldwide Ltd.
2143 Wooddale Drive
Woodbury, MN 55125-2989
www.midnightinkbooks.com

Printed in the United States of America

SPRINGDALE PUBLIC LIBRARY
405 S. PLEASANT
SPRINGDALE AR 72764
479-750-8180

For Carl my honorary father,
who has no use for all this "Internet stuff."

#THANKS

It takes the work of one village to keep me from making a fool of myself and the faith of another village to make my writing life possible. I'd like to recognize just a few of the many villagers in my life.

Karen Salemi lives in both villages. She is my cheerleader, my coach, my editor, my wife, and my best friend. Tucker exists because of her help and unwavering support.

Eric Ruben and Terri Bischoff believed in the Tucker books (and me) from the beginning. We're up to four books because of their commitment to the series.

Jay Shepherd offered his outstanding copy-editing skills and also provided his much appreciated hashtags of wisdom.

Thanks to Dr. Brian Breed of UMass Amherst for helping me get the Latin right.

We artists sometimes need an energy boost, and Kay Helberg is always there with a cheer, a hug, and a reader's view of the story.

Dan Less has made himself the official Ray Daniel photographic chronicler. Thank you, Dan, for coming to my events and capturing my fleeting, but bizarre, facial expressions.

Thanks to my early readers Tom Fitzpatrick, Tim McIntyre, as well as all of the above villagers. Stories in novels only exist when a reader sees them. Thank you all for giving me the reader's perspective.

The only thing a writing life can guarantee is the opportunity to be with other writers. Thank you to all my writing friends for making this journey so much fun! #LOL!

AUTHOR'S NOTE

All Twitter handles that appear in this book are fictitious except for @TuckerInBoston, which is run by the bot who writes for Tucker. Any relationship to existing Twitter or IRC handles, either now or in the future, is unintended and coincidental.

ONE

THERE IS NO RAGE like Internet rage. Whether the source is a Facebook friend who calls your political views "childish fantasies," a Twitter follower who says your New England Patriots are "filthy cheaters," or some anonymous asshat who refers to the song that got you through the tough times as "derivative pop sell-out crap," the incoherent, obsessive rage is the same. You could even imagine killing someone.

I was feeling that rage as I sat at a kitchen table in the North End and clicked through Maria's porn-infested Facebook account.

"The phone won't stop ringing, Tucker," said my cousin Adriana, Maria's guardian.

"The bastard posted those pictures on all her friends' walls," said her wife Catherine.

"The other parents are calling Maria a degenerate."

"The other parents are idiots," I said. "A ten-year-old doesn't post this stuff."

"That's what I told them," said Adriana.

"When we weren't falling over ourselves apologizing," said Catherine.

I'm a computer guy—not a "my PC has a virus" computer guy, but an actual computer security consultant who will look at your network and tell you how the hackers can break in. Truth be told, I don't do a lot of it. I had a disastrous separation from my last employer, and they gave me ten million dollars in exchange for my signing a nondisclosure agreement. I could have sold the story for more, but I didn't want to talk about it.

Despite my standing as an honest-to-god software engineer, my friends and family still call me when their computers act up. In this case, Adriana called me just after she got the first outraged parental phone call.

I clicked through Maria's Facebook account. "You were lucky," I said. "They usually lock you out of the account when they do a life ruin."

"What's a 'life ruin'?" asked Adriana.

"This is a life ruin. You get the password to someone's Facebook account, then wreak havoc in their name. You message porn to their mom, change their relationship status, and start fights with their coworkers."

"Who does this sort of thing?"

"Bored dweebs."

I went to work, first changing the password to keep the bastard from returning, then posting a general apology that, sadly, would be seen only by those who hadn't already blocked Maria. Finally I started removing the porn from people's walls.

Next to me, Adriana made a list.

"What's the list for?" I asked.

"Apology phone calls. We're going to be making a lot of them."

"Phone calls?"

"Just keep cleaning."

I continued, downloading each picture in case we could use it as evidence, then deleting it. Most of it was lesbian porn. Women in bed, women on lawns, women on porch swings. In fact, the entire collection consisted of lesbian porn. Not one guy.

The phone rang again. Catherine picked it up. "Yes. I know. We're sorry. We're fixing it." She hung up. "Who would do this?"

"Usually it's someone random," I said. "But in this case I think it's somebody who knows Maria."

"Why do you say that?" asked Adriana.

I looked from Adriana to her wife, Catherine, then pointed at the collection of pictures. "See any guys?"

"Oh," said Adriana.

"Exactly," I said. "Somebody knew that Maria has two moms."

"This is a hate crime," said Catherine.

"I don't know that—"

"What would you call it?"

"Some mean friend of Maria's playing a prank."

"Maria!" Adriana yelled, causing me to jump. "Get in here!"

We waited. Fifteen feet separated the kitchen from Maria's bedroom down the hall. No response. I cleaned the last bit of porn off Maria's page.

"Maria!" Adriana was edging into hysteria. "You get in here right now!"

This was not helping. I grabbed my jacket.

"Where are you going?" asked Adriana.

I left the kitchen, walked down the hall, leaned on Maria's bedroom door. The ten-year-old girl with jet-black hair sat in a little desk chair, clutching a stuffed eggplant to her chest, eyes red, morose. Back in the kitchen a skirmish had broken out between Catherine and Adriana over the definition of a hate crime.

"Want to get a coffee?" I whispered.

Maria sniffled, then nodded.

"Grab your coat."

She grabbed her coat and I opened the front door. Adriana appeared in the kitchen door. "Where are you going? She's grounded!"

I looked at Maria, then back at Adriana. "We're getting coffee."

I pulled the door shut and we ran down the stairs.

TWO

MARIA AND I STEPPED out onto Cleveland Place in the North End. Cleveland Place is a wide alley that connects to a narrow street, which connects to another narrow street, and so on past the Old North Church. Maria had moved here with her aunts a year ago.

We walked down Prince Street, past dying piles of snow that had refused to succumb to the recent equinox. Winter in Boston doesn't give up without a fight. Still, the Sox were playing again, the Boston Marathon was set for Patriots' Day on Monday, and even this cold spring day was above freezing.

Maria maintained her silence. I assumed that the recent invasion of her Facebook account and the hysterical response of her friends' parents had shocked her. Truth was she'd been a quiet kid for the past year, life having knocked the stuffing out of a rambunctious tween. As a software engineer who's worked with his share of introverts, I try to respect the silence of others, figuring that people talk when they're ready. I don't always succeed.

We turned at Hanover Street and headed for the only place where we went for "coffee," Caffe Vittoria. Her dad's old hangout.

Nick the barista waved a hello. "The usual for you guys?"

I looked at Maria, who nodded. "Yeah, Nick. Thanks."

We sat in the front of the restaurant behind a floor-to-ceiling window and watched people bustle along the street. At one time Sal had run his business from this spot, but that was a long time ago.

Nick brought us the usual. Two biscotti to share, one chocolate, one almond, an espresso for me, and a hot chocolate for Maria.

I drank the espresso. "Any idea how that guy got your password?" I asked.

Maria slurped hot chocolate. "I was stupid."

I waited. Maria bit into the chocolate biscotti. She always started with the chocolate.

"Stupid how?" I asked.

"I don't want to talk about it."

"That's fair. Nobody wants to talk about how they were stupid."

Maria drank more hot chocolate.

"But I want to find out who did this to you."

"It doesn't matter."

"Of course it matters. It was a terrible thing to do. The guy should be punished."

"Why do you say he's a guy?"

"It's always a guy."

Maria bit into the almond biscotti. Chewed, swallowed. "You promise not to be mad at me?"

"Yeah. It's not your fault."

"I told him my password."

"You told who your password?"

"The guy who said he worked for Facebook."

"Did he send you a direct message?"

"Yeah. He said hackers were trying to break into my account and he needed to fix it. He asked me for my password."

"Seriously? You fell for that?"

"You said you wouldn't get mad at me."

"I'm not mad at you."

"You promised."

"I'm *not* mad at you. I'm—I'm mad at the asshat who stole your password."

I bit the almond biscotti. I like to start with the almond because otherwise the chocolate takes over your mouth and ruins everything. Maria would learn that in time. Drained my espresso. Got up. Asked Nick for another. I had thought the walk would vent some of my spleen, but it hadn't done the job. Got my espresso, paid, sat down next to Maria.

"Why you?" I asked.

"Huh?" said Maria.

"Why would somebody target you?"

Maria shrugged. "I dunno."

"Is somebody mad at you? Maybe somebody from school?"

Maria shrugged again.

"Because," I said, "this is bullying."

"Don't call it bullying," said Maria.

"Why not?"

"Because if you call it bullying, it becomes this whole big thing, and there are police, and the principal, and then you're a snitch and everyone hates you."

"Looks like somebody hates you now."

"That's better than *everyone*."

"So who hates you?"

Maria stood, pulled on her coat. "Can we go home now?"

"Sure," I said. "But, Maria … "

"Yeah?"

"I'm going to find out who did this whether you help me or not."

Maria pushed through the glass door, led me back into the street. She stayed a step ahead of me, heading toward Prince Street. I caught up, tapped her shoulder with the backs of my fingers. She reached for them. We held hands and walked, swerving around pedestrians living their own lives.

It had been more than a year since the events that had brought her to live with her aunts, Adriana and Catherine: a year of The-First-Withouts. The first Easter without her parents. The first birthday without her parents. The first Christmas without her parents. Adriana, Catherine, and I had been united in a sort of protective tribe, making sure Maria knew she wouldn't live through those milestones alone.

Still, the retreat had come. Whether it was a young girl's typical transition into the angst of the tween years, or a reaction to her new life, we didn't know. We just knew that she'd spent a lot of time in her room, binge-watching videos on the computer, giving her homework scant attention, and rarely laughing.

"Nice day," I said.

Maria took in the gray sky and raw chill. "It's cold."

"The marathoners will like it, though. They hate the heat."

"Hmm."

"You know who did this to you, don't you?"

"I don't want to talk about it."

"You shouldn't let him get away with it."

Maria pulled her hand from mine. Crossed her arms. Just like a grown-up. When did that happen?

"It doesn't matter," she said.

"It does matter."

Maria didn't answer. Apparently it didn't matter to her.

We turned right and left through the brick streets, back to Cleveland Place, and climbed the steps to her apartment. Adriana and Catherine sat in the front living room, pecking on laptops. They looked a question at me. I shrugged. Maria took off her coat, wordlessly closed her bedroom door behind her.

"So?" asked Adriana. "What happened?"

"We shared some biscotti," I said.

"And?"

Maria opened her bedroom door. "Why can't I log into Facebook?"

"I changed the password so you wouldn't get hacked again."

"What's the new password?"

I glanced at Adriana. She gave her head a tiny shake. Then a nod toward Maria.

Great. Give me the dirty work.

"What's my password?" asked Maria.

"Honey," I said, "you're too young for Facebook."

"What's my password?"

"You don't have a password anymore," I said.

Adriana stepped in. "But you can get back on when you're thirteen."

"You took away my account?"

"Technically," I said, "that hacker you're protecting did that."

"This isn't fair!"

Catherine said, "You are too young, and that's the end of it."

Maria's face shattered into a crinkled mash of sobbing. She turned, slammed the bedroom door behind her, and wailed, the sound carrying through the door, twisting my heart.

THREE

THE WAILING IN MARIA's room slowed, then quieted. I tapped on her door, peeked inside to see her sleeping in a crumpled pile of bedclothes.

"She's passed out," I said.

"Just as well," Adriana said. "She needs the sleep."

I stretched. "Me too. I'm heading home."

"No, you're not."

"Why not?"

"C'mon."

The three of us moved to the kitchen, where Adriana poured out some wine and opened a freshly delivered pizza box. "Let's get to work."

"Work?"

Adriana produced the list of names she had been compiling as I had been removing porn. "We need to make apology calls."

"Can't we just write letters? 'Dear Mrs. Smith, please accept our apology for the picture of women having sex on a porch swing.'"

"You read from Maria's Facebook friend list and I'll check this list of people we cleaned up. I want to make sure we apologize to everyone who got porn."

"Can't you and Catherine do this?"

"Get to work."

I got to work. Maria had blessedly few Facebook friends, owing to the fact that most of her real-life friends were not allowed on Facebook, and to the fact that several must have unfriended her. We'd have to figure out another way to apologize to them.

"Carter," I read off the Facebook friend list.

"Check," said Adriana, marking her list.

"Fellini."

"Check."

"Georgiani," I read.

"I told you so," Adriana said.

"What?"

"I told you so."

"What did you tell me?"

"I told you that Maria was too young for Facebook."

"Really, we're going to go back to that fight?"

"This is your fault."

"This isn't my fault. This is some hacker's fault. Is Georgiani a check or not?"

"Check."

I read another name from the screen. "Harris."

"Check. Do you know how goddamn sick and tired I am of you being the fun uncle?"

"I'm not her uncle. I'm her cousin."

"Whatever! You know how sick I am of this?"

"Of what? Incaviglia."

"Check. I'm sick of you being the one who she runs to whenever I have to discipline her. Like today. She gave away her password, I grounded her, and you decided she should get a fucking biscotti."

"She was distraught." I looked back at the screen. "Jones."

"You think I couldn't see that?"

11

"Did you get Jones?"

"Yes, I got Jones! Don't change the subject."

"I'm not changing the subject. She was already down. Why kick her some more?" Another name. "Laramie."

"Check. I wasn't kicking her. I'm raising her."

"So am I."

"That's bullshit. Does she live with you? Does she spend any time at that man cave you've got over in the South End?"

"Yes, she does."

"Right." Adriana made air quotes. "'The sleepover.' You take her there, play a movie, eat some popcorn, call it parenting."

"It is parenting."

"It is *not* parenting. I'm parenting. Catherine is parenting."

"Leave me out of this," Catherine said.

Adriana turned to Catherine. "Leave you out? You didn't ask for any of this. You didn't ask to be a parent."

"I'm happy to help."

Adriana turned back to me. "Lesbian couples are supposed to be immune from surprise children."

"Look. None of us expected our role."

"Your role hasn't changed. You were the happy uncle before, taking her sledding and—"

"Don't start with that."

"Yeah, let's just drop everything that makes you uncomfortable. Poor Tucker."

Catherine said, "Can we just get back to the names?"

I read off the friends list. "Mathews."

Adriana said, "Check."

"Olinsky."

Adriana slid her pencil down the sheet. "Not here. Did you miss it?"

I brought up a page for Gustav Olinsky.

"Gustav?" asked Adriana.

"Rough name," I said.

"You should know, Aloysius."

"Har. Har. This page is mostly blank."

"No porn?"

"No nothing. He only has ten friends. Is he in Maria's class?"

"I haven't heard of him. Let's just move on."

We moved on. Worked our way through the rest of Maria's friends, checking each against whether or not they had received porn. They all had. Some had seen the porn before I could remove it, prompting reactions from "LOL" to "gross" to parents apparently taking over the keyboard to launch into a tirade against Maria through the pictures' comment sections. Now that the pictures were gone, Maria's page had gone silent.

This brought me back to Gustav. Why had he been spared a flurry of woman-meets-hammock photographs? What made him special? I looked through his page: nothing and more nothing. He'd had a birthday recently. Three kids had posted birthday greetings on his wall. One was Maria. She had written *Happy Birthday, Gutso.*

Gutso?

I looked back at Gustav's profile picture. His round face looked back at me. I found a picture of Gustav standing in the Public Garden where his bulk blocked out most of a passing Swan Boat.

Unable to find anything more on Gustav's page, I opened Maria's private messages and read the chain of outraged screeds. Parent after parent had taken this opportunity to demonstrate that it took a village to raise a child and that, for them, Facebook was that village, and Maria was that child.

In the real world, none of these parents would have had the guts to tell Maria to blow her nose, but in the Facebook world they got to beat their judgy chests at a little girl who'd made a mistake.

I scrolled down the list, happy that we hadn't allowed Maria back onto Facebook, happy that she didn't have to see any of this. I skipped over message after message until I saw an interesting one at the bottom next to Gustav's fat little face.

I'm sorry.

FOUR

I leaned back in my chair, drained my wine, and read the cover of the Regina Pizza box. The cover told the story of the Oldest Pizza House in New England. New York had nothing on Regina.

I flipped the box open and surveyed the pie chart inside. The chart told the sad tale that six-eighths of the pizza had been eaten. Adriana, Catherine, and I had eaten two slices each. Maria had refused to leave her room.

I reached for a slice. Adriana slapped my hand.

"Ow!"

"That's for Maria."

"Both of them?"

"She's going to be hungry. Don't be a pig."

I poured some more wine. "One for the road."

"Road? What road?"

"The road back to the South End."

"You're not going back to the South End until we finish these phone calls."

"Seriously? Tonight?"

"Yeah, tonight. We're calling every parent and apologizing."

"But it's seven o'clock. They're going to be cleaning up after dinner."

"Yeah, then they'll be watching TV and going to bed. When do you want to call them? Midnight?"

"I don't want to call them at all."

Catherine handed out three lists. "It's only eight calls each."

"What do I say?"

"Don't be a baby," said Adriana. She took her list and retreated to the living room. Catherine took her list and headed for the bedroom. That left me in the kitchen alone with my phone, a bottle of wine, and forbidden pizza. I poured a little more wine into my half-full glass. Drank it back to half. Dialed the number next to *Carter*. A guy picked up.

"Hello, Mr. Carter? My name is Aloysius Tucker."

"Who?"

"Aloysius Tucker."

"Never heard of you."

"No. No, you wouldn't have."

"What kind of name is Aloysius? Is this a joke?"

"I'm Maria's cousin."

"Maria? Maria who?"

"Maria Rizzo."

"I don't know any Maria Rizzo."

A woman's voice screeched in the background. The receiver got muffled, probably pressed to a chest. A bass-and-treble discussion ensued, sounding like an argument between two adults in a Charlie Brown cartoon. The phone was unmuffled.

"Maria Rizzo?" a woman said. An angry woman.

"Uh, yes. I'm her cousin."

"Your cousin is a horrible little girl."

"I think *horrible* is a bit strong."

"After what she did?"

"It wasn't her. Someone hacked her Facebook account."

"Facebook account? What do I care about her Facebook account?"

"What I mean to say is, she didn't put the porn on Michael's page."

"Michael? Michael isn't on Facebook."

I looked at my computer screen, at Michael Carter's profile picture. "Um. Maybe he never told you?"

"Michael's not on Facebook, and he doesn't look at porn. He's ten years old."

I decided not to argue that point. "I was just calling to apologize."

"For Facebook porn."

"Uh, yeah. Maria's really sorry."

"Is she really sorry for making Michael cry in class?"

"Huh?"

"Is she sorry for calling him an 'asshat' during his science presentation?"

"I'm sure she is."

"Don't call here again." The old-fashioned handset clattered as Mrs. Carter smashed it into an old-fashioned cradle.

Asshat? Where did Maria pick that up?

Fellini next. Dialed the phone, got the mom, introduced myself.

"Your cousin is a degenerate," said Mrs. Fellini.

"To be fair, her Facebook account was hacked."

"Sure. Hacked, my eye."

"What's that mean?"

"Hackers can't guess a password on Facebook. She gave someone her password."

"Yes … because …"

"Aha! I knew it. She got some older kid to put porn on poor Stella's Facebook page."

"No, she didn't know—"

"Lesbian porn, no less. That's disgusting."

"Hey, listen—"

"Why are you calling?"

17

"To apologize."

"Why aren't her parents calling?"

I paused a beat. Told her. That shut her up for a second.

"I knew that," said Mrs. Fellini.

"Then why did you ask?"

"Why isn't one of her moms calling?"

"We split up the job."

"What are you? Like the father?"

"No, I'm—" *What am I, anyway?*

"Because I think she needs a father."

"Thanks for your advice."

"She's been terrible. A real brat."

"And so she needs a father to straighten her out?"

"She called Stella fat. She body-shamed her."

It was my turn to be shut up for a second.

Mrs. Fellini continued, "She used to be such a nice girl."

"She's been through a lot."

"I know," said Mrs. Fellini. "Good night. Thank you for the apology."

"I *am* sorry."

"I hope you can get her what she needs." Mrs. Fellini closed the call.

She used to be such a nice girl.

Adriana's voice rose from the living room. "Still, we are sorry."

Catherine's muffled voice wafted out of the bedroom. "She called him a what? Oh my God."

I looked at my list. Georgiani was next. What fresh insight would the Georgianis provide? I called. Learned that Maria had put a bug in their Isabella's milk. Called Harris. Learned that Maria had called little Wade a "retard."

Incaviglia, Jones, Laramie, Mathews. Each had a tale of horror regarding Maria. Five were sure she'd put the porn there herself and

18

just blamed a hacker. Two more said that she needed a father. All agreed that Maria used to be very nice, but not anymore.

Maria's door remained closed. Maybe she was asleep. Maybe she was plotting some other prank. Maybe she was crying. A dark shadow of failure filled the room. Adriana, Catherine, and I were failing, but it seemed to be mostly me.

I focused on the claim that Maria had put the porn there herself. That she hadn't been life ruined, but had decided to ruin some lives. Her refusal to help me find her hacker gave me pause. Could she have done that? Found the porn, put it up all over?

There was only one way to know for sure. Find the hacker myself, or find that there never was a hacker.

Adriana's voice rose in the living room. "Because it's important! When? Nine o'clock? Fine."

Adriana stalked into the kitchen. I drank down a slug of my wine. The pizza looked like cardboard.

"Don't drink too much," she said.

"Why?"

"You don't want to have a hangover in the morning."

"What's in the morning?"

"We're going to see Gustav's mother."

FIVE

A JET SCREAMED LOW over our heads as Adriana and I exited Wood Island station. I looked up, counted the rivets on its wings, watched its wheels spin in slow, wind-driven anticipation of their landing. The wheels puffed white skidmark smoke as they touched down on the runway.

"They just keep coming," I said, pointing at the next plane lining up to assault us.

"Yeah, loud," Adriana said. "Figures Gustav would live in East Boston. Just perfect."

We crossed Bennington, took a right toward Swift as another plane roared overhead. A cool wind blew off the ocean behind the airport, while low gray clouds scudded across the sky. April in Boston.

"She said she lives on Swift across the street from a car dealership. I don't see a car dealership."

We reached the corner and found a little parking lot filled to the brim with ten cars. One end of the lot held a small office with a neat sign: JIM'S AUTO SALES.

I said, "That's—"

Another plane bombed over us.

Adriana pointed across Swift to a lonely Cape house. "That must be the Olinsky place."

Like most of the houses in East Boston, the Cape wore aluminum siding, protection against the cost of ocean-inflicted repainting. Its two second-story windows and big living room window formed a sad face, the slanted roof forming two worried eyebrows.

We crossed Swift, climbed steps on the side of the house leading to the entrance. Rang the bell.

"Coming!" a voice called from inside.

The door opened and a woman wearing a yellow-and-black reflective Hertz jacket answered. Short and wide, with black hair framing her round face in wisps of gray.

"Mrs. Rizzo?" she asked Adriana.

"Ms. Rizzo," Adriana answered.

"And you're Mr. Rizzo?"

"No," I said, "Tucker."

"Mr. Tucker?"

"Just Tucker is fine."

She looked from one of us to the other, perhaps calculating the web of events that had created this odd couple.

"Well, come on in. You might want to leave your coats on. I can't afford to heat the house in the spring." She turned and led us past a plastic folding table set as a dining room and into the kitchen. "I made coffee."

"Thank you," said Adriana.

"Only way to stay warm some—" An airplane roared overhead. She looked up at the ceiling. "Lots of planes today. I need to get Massport to buy me some soundproof windows."

Mrs. Olinsky poured us the coffee. We sat around a small kitchen table and looked at each other. Adriana gave me a kick under the table as she flicked her eyes from me to the woman.

Adriana was a big talker right up until it was time to do the big talking.

"Um—Mrs. Olinsky, do you know about Facebook?"

"No. I don't have time for that computer stuff. Gustav likes it."

We'd hit the defining communication challenge of our age: how to explain Facebook to someone who didn't use it. Was it like a message board? E-mail? A yearbook? What? Mrs. Olinsky helped me out. "Ms. Rizzo here says that Gustav did something bad on it. What could he have done?"

"The kids—" A train on the nearby Blue Line rattled past, making its own racket. I continued. "The kids use Facebook to talk to each other. They connect up as friends, and then"—a plane roared over—"they can post pictures for the others to see and comment on."

Adriana said, "Adults use it too, and you can play games on it. Also follow movie stars."

This time I gave Adriana a kick. *You're not helping.*

Adriana glared at me. I glared back.

Mrs. Olinsky brought us to the uncomfortable point. "And so what?"

"Somebody pretending to be Maria posted porn on Facebook under her name. It made her look bad."

"I know. Victoria Incaviglia told me about Maria's filth."

"Maria didn't do it."

"How do you know?"

"She wouldn't."

"She's a nasty little girl. Why wouldn't she do it?"

"What are you talking about?" Adriana said.

"She's a bully. Gustav comes home crying because of her."

Again.

"She is not."

"That's why I had to laugh when you called me and asked to come over. I couldn't believe you had some complaint about Gustav. You have a hell of a nerve."

Adriana sat in rare silence. A plane roared over.

I waited until it passed. "You know we're not Maria's parents, right?" I said.

"Yeah, I know," said Mrs. Olinsky. "Her father was some sort of crook. Probably deserved what he got."

"I wouldn't say that."

"Of course you wouldn't say it. You're probably a crook too. You think that scares me?"

Adriana said, "Nobody is a crook. We just want to talk about what someone did to Maria."

"Did to Maria? She's the one who put porn on the Facebook."

"She didn't do it."

"You helicopter parents make me sick."

"What's that supposed to mean?"

"Did I go to your house when Maria called Gustav a fat pig?"

"No."

"I let Gustav fight his own battles, let him get tough, learn how to take it from bullies."

"Maria's not a—" Another plane, then footsteps on the floor overhead.

Mrs. Olinsky said, "It's even worse when the bully is a girl and he can't punch her."

"I'm sure Gustav is a sweet kid," I said. "He sent Maria a private message telling her he was sorry."

"Damn right he's sweet. That girl called him fat, named him Gutso, invited him to a play date, and sent him to the wrong address. After she did all that to him, he still told her he was sorry for what happened to her. I would have laughed in her face."

There was a bang overhead. Mrs. Olinsky looked up. "I told him not to tip his chair back."

I followed her eyes. "Who?"

"My oldest, Peter."

Here was a chance to bond. "How old is Peter?"

"Twenty."

"That's great."

"Why? You think he's too old to live with his mother?"

"No, I just think it's nice that he's still around for you."

"You're wrong. He's too old to live with his mother."

"I'm not here to—" Airplane.

"He just sits up there on that stupid computer."

I sipped my coffee. Listened to a train rattle by. "Is he close to Gustav?"

"Sure. He's his brother."

"Did Gustav ever complain to him about Maria?"

"What are you asking?"

"Somebody hacked Maria's account."

Mrs. Olinsky narrowed her eyes. "Are you accusing Peter?"

I stood. "Thank you for your time, Mrs. Olinsky."

Adriana looked up at me in surprise. "What?"

"We appreciate your telling us about Maria's behavior."

Mrs. Olinsky stood. "It's hard raising kids."

"Don't I know it," I said.

"Don't *you* know it?" Adriana said. Then to Mrs. Olinsky, "He doesn't do anything."

"Single mom, huh?" said Mrs. Olinsky.

"No, I have—"

"Me to help her," I said. "Let's go, Adriana."

"At least you've got your boyfriend," said Mrs. Olinsky to Adriana.

"He's not my boyfriend."

"Let's go, honey." I led the way out of the kitchen, leaving Adriana nothing to do but follow.

After a fast walk through East Boston, Adriana and I stood on the Wood Island platform, waiting for a train to take us home.

"What was that?" asked Adriana.

"I think I got what I needed," I said.

"What?"

"A twenty-year-old guy who lives at home with his mother and spends all his time on the computer."

"You're profiling him?"

"There is a type."

"What are you going to do about it?"

A plane roared over as a train entered the station. The noises combined into a high-decibel assault. The train rolled to a stop, the doors whooshed open, and we found seats inside.

"So," said Adriana, "are you going to do anything?"

"I'm going to find out if he did it."

"How?"

I had a plan. It was nasty, but Adriana wouldn't understand how nasty and I didn't want to explain.

"I'll handle it," I said.

SIX

BOSTON HAS TWO ENDS, a North End and a South End. It once had a West End, but urban renewal destroyed it in the 1960s. The cozy streets and brick tenements that had been gentrified into prosperity in the North and South End never had a chance to flourish in the West End. Instead, developers evicted the tenants, bulldozed their homes, and put up high-rise apartment buildings. All that's really left of the West End today is a sign on Storrow Drive that says, IF YOU LIVED HERE YOU'D BE HOME NOW.

I had left Adriana's place in the North End and was heading for my home in the South End when I remembered that the Boston FBI office sat between the two. I pulled out my Pop-Tart-sized Android phablet and called my buddy, Assistant Special Agent in Charge Bobby Miller.

"You in the office?"

"Yeah."

"I've got some dirty pictures for you."

"Then come on up."

I had crossed Government Center, another monument to urban renewal, and had gone on up. I now watched as the Internet rage overtook Bobby Miller.

"Motherfucker!" he said.

"Exactly," I said.

"Did Maria see these?"

"Yeah, she saw them, and so did all her little Facebook friends."

"Isn't she too young for Facebook?"

"Don't you start."

Bobby flipped through a few more pictures and said, "You know who'd like to see these? Mel." He yelled into the hallway, "Hey, Mel! Get in here and check out these pictures!"

Mel: perfect name for a guy who'd love to see porn.

Bobby made eye contact with someone behind me. "Tucker, meet Mel Hunter."

I turned, expecting to see the sweaty lips and fishy handshake of a porn-lover. Instead I saw the black hair and curvy suit of an FBI agent—a fresh-faced, female FBI agent.

She stuck out her hand. "Special Agent Hunter, Mr. Tucker."

Bobby said, "Mel is just out of Quantico."

I shook, noting the warmth of Mel Hunter's hand and the confidence of her grip. "You can call me Tucker."

She said, "You can call me Special Agent Hunter."

"Okay."

"You two wanted to show me some dirty pictures?"

"How did you know they were dirty?"

"Because Bobby was looking at them."

Bobby said, "Nice." He told her the story of the pictures.

Special Agent Hunter flipped through the woman-on-woman action, her eyes flitting around each picture before looking at the next. She seemed to be looking at the pictures without looking at their subject.

"Yeah," said Hunter, "these are in the database."

"Database?" I asked.

"Our porn database," Bobby said.

I said, "Why not keep them in a folder like normal people?"

"We'd lose the indexing," said Hunter.

"What indexing?"

"You know those websites that track currency?" asked Bobby.

"No."

"Those ones where you take a buck from your wallet, put the serial number into the site, and it tells you where your money's been."

"They have those?"

"Yes."

"Cool."

"The FBI does the same thing with porn."

"You do?"

"Yeah," said Special Agent Hunter. "We originally wrote it to help with child-porn investigations. Then we expanded it. We web-crawl all the porn sites, download the porn, and store it in a database. Then we can track where it's appeared on the web and who posted and commented on it."

"Isn't that spying?"

"Spying shmying," Bobby said.

"It's really just collating public data," said Hunter.

"But if we do get a warrant for some terrorist's computer, we can use the porn to make connections to other people," said Bobby. "Porn is a universal tracking system."

"But it only works for men," I said.

"Exactly," Hunter said. "It's a great filter."

"That's creepy on so many levels."

Hunter tapped on her phone. "Yup. Found them. They were on 4chan.org."

Bobby asked, "On that /b/ thing?"

"Yeah."

Bobby said, "Figures."

"The 4chan/b/ board?" I said. "Gross."

"Yup," said Bobby. "The anus of the Internet."

In 2003, an unassuming student named Christopher Poole got a lesson in the law of unintended consequences. The fifteen-year-old Poole created a website called 4chan.org that let users anonymously post images to the Internet and discuss them. He had imagined that it would be used for anime. He was mostly right, and wildly wrong.

The site provided a variety of discussion boards. Poole named the discussion board for anime 4chan.org/a/, and the board for video games 4chan.org/v/. But as in fairy tales, one board was different from all the other boards, a chaotic board without rules or reason. This was the random board: 4chan.org/b/.

Imagine a website where images that generate a long string of comments and replies float to the top of the message board, while ignored pictures drift down and disappear from view. Next, imagine that you're a lonely kid who's desperate to post an image that will keep people talking. What will you post? It probably won't be kittens in a basket. Unless, of course, the basket were on the Niagara River and the kittens were about to go over the falls. You could also post naked pictures hacked from a celebrity's phone, an uncensored picture of a gruesome suicide, or unique porn.

4chan.org/b/ really was the anus of the Internet.

"Those pictures were all on 4chan?" I asked Hunter.

"Yup. They were posted two days ago. I can trace them back further if you want."

"The timing's right. Maria got hacked yesterday. Can you see who downloaded them?"

"No. That *would* be spying."

"I just don't see how little Gustav got pictures like that."

Bobby asked, "Who's Gustav?"

"Gustav Olinsky is Maria's classmate. He apologized to Maria for the hack. I think his brother Peter might be involved."

Hunter and Bobby exchanged a glance.

"What?" I said. "You know a ten-year-old named Gustav Olinsky? He on the most-wanted list?"

Bobby looked at his watch. "Don't we have a meeting, Mel?"

Hunter pulled out her phone, glanced at it. "Crap, you're right."

"Yeah, Tucker. We've got to get going."

"We'll look at those pictures for you and see if we can find anything."

"Yeah, absolutely. You know the way out, right?"

With that, Bobby and Hunter skedaddled out of the room and down the hall.

I stood in the empty office.

What just happened?

Pulled out my phone. Tweeted:

@TuckerInBoston: That #awkward moment when you clear a room.

SEVEN

GEOGRAPHICALLY, THERE ARE TWO Bostons. One is "original Boston," which is the Boston the settlers landed on in 1630, and the other is "landfill Boston," which actually makes up most of the city. Back Bay, Logan Airport, and big chunks of the North End are parts of landfill Boston, created by filling in mudflats.

Milk Street is part of original Boston. The birthplace of Benjamin Franklin, the little street had undergone transformation after transformation as the city churned and even burned around it. Today Milk Street sits in the Financial District, where captains of finance chart the course of our mutual funds while high-tech start-ups sputter to life in incubators.

My buddy Huey coded in one of those incubators. Huey and I had worked together at MantaSoft a hundred years ago. Since then, I had taken an enormous severance package and MantaSoft had closed its New England office. Huey had been cast off, but had landed well. A prodigious feat for a man of his size.

I stepped into Max's Deli Cafe and saw Huey looming over a Formica table next to the window. I waved, got myself a chicken soup with a gigantic matzo ball, and brought it over to Huey, who had already gone through almost half of a Dagwoodesque sandwich piled high with luncheon meats.

Huey had always been a large man, a guy who could fill a small office. Yet when motivated, either in playing Ping-Pong or saving my ass, he could be surprisingly nimble.

He took a big swig of Diet Coke. Burped a greeting. "Hiya."

"Hello to you too," I said. "One sec." I took a picture of my soup. Put it up on Twitter.

`@TuckerInBoston: That's a big ball! #lunch`

"You're still on Twitter?" asked Huey.

"Yeah, I like it."

"You're still not on Facebook?"

"No, but that's a good thing. Now we have something to talk about."

"What?"

"We can catch up on each other's lives."

Huey shoved part of his sandwich into his considerable maw, washed it down with Diet Coke, and followed that up with a pickle. "Why aren't you on Facebook?"

"I don't like it. I like it even less now."

"Why?"

I told him about Maria.

"Why is she on Facebook? Isn't she too young?"

"Another quarter heard from."

"I mean, kids don't do Facebook."

"They don't?"

"No. It's for old people."

"What do kids do?"

"A lot of Snapchat and Yik Yak. A lot of texting. A lot of emoji."

"How do you know?"

"My company is going after the young market. I get all this research."

I took a spoonful of soup, then attacked the matzo ball, averting my eyes as Huey jammed the two-fisted half sandwich into his mouth and took a bite. He looked like an orca eating a beach ball.

"I want to catch the guy," I said.

"Why?"

"Make him apologize."

"Hmm … How is Maria taking it?"

"She's mostly upset about being banned from Facebook."

"They banned her?"

"No, we banned her."

"You and your cousin?"

"Yeah."

Huey took another bite. Chewed and cogitated. "Must be tough with no parents."

I poked at my matzo ball. "You'd think the parents at her school would get that."

"Get what?"

"That she's gone through a tough time. That maybe it's not the worst thing if Maria is mean to their precious pumpkins. They could cut her some slack."

"Maria's being mean?"

"Just kid stuff. Called one kid an asshat. Called another one Gutso."

"'Cause he's fat, right?"

"Um … right."

Huey sipped his Coke. Took another bite of his sandwich. Looked out the window.

"You're not saying she deserved it, are you?"

"I'm not saying anything," said Huey, continuing to look out the window.

I changed the subject. "How's your sandwich?"

"How's your soup?"

"It's good."

"Just like Mom used to make?"

"My mom was Italian. She made gravy, not soup."

"Oh."

More silence.

"I think I know who did the life ruin," I said.

"Yeah?"

"The older brother of one of Maria's classmates."

"The fat one?"

"Um, yeah."

"And you want to make this brother apologize."

"Yeah."

"To the mean girl who called his little brother fat."

"Did she deserve to be cyberbullied?"

"Did the fat kid deserve to be called fat?"

"No, but it's not right."

"It's kids, Tucker. Stay out of it."

"The older brother is twenty. That's not a kid."

"Barely not a kid."

"He needs to grow up."

"And you want to expose him? Maybe dox him?"

"Doxing" or "getting the documents" on someone is like outing them, but with nicknames. You find out their real name and tell everyone, ruining their anonymity. It has the same effect on hackers as crosses do on vampires.

"Dox him?" I said. "I don't even know his nickname. I need to know his nickname before I can expose who's behind the nickname."

"But then you'd dox him."

"Maybe. I'll admit, unmasking a guy is a shitty thing to do. Still, he deserves it."

Huey shook his head.

"What?"

"This is how people get hurt."

"C'mon. He just gets another nickname."

"So do you want him to apologize, or do you want to dox him?" I crossed my arms. "Look, are you going to help?"

"I think you have bigger problems."

"Like what?"

"Like a mean little girl who wasn't mean a year ago."

"Look at who's the parenting expert now."

"It sure isn't you."

I stood. Picked up my half-eaten soup. Threw it in the trash. Walked back to Huey. "I don't need this bullshit."

"Could you sit down?"

"We're doing our best, you know."

"I know. I know. I'm sorry."

I sat. Watched Huey take another bite of sandwich. "When did you get so wise?"

"I just have some experience with getting bullied."

"Yeah, I guess. I'm sorry."

"Not your fault. You were probably one of the popular kids."

"Me? I was a nerd."

"That's changed?"

My stomach growled. I wished I'd kept my soup. "Probably not."

"Have you ever heard of PwnSec?"

There's all sorts of ways for words to get into English. In the case of "pwned," a kid tried to type an instant message to another after winning a video game. He wanted to say "I owned you!" but mistyped and got "I pwned you!" Suddenly, English had a new word that rhymed with *owned*.

"What's the Sec stand for?"

"Security."

"I get it. Pwn the security guys."

"Yeah. So a few hackers got together and made this little club called PwnSec. Someone with the nickname Eliza wrote a manifesto about how they were going to take it to the Man."

"And did they?"

"No. They suck. They mostly do life ruins."

My phone rang. A Boston number.

"Mr. Tucker?"

"Yeah."

"This is Ms. Marks from the Elcott School."

"Okay."

"We need you to come down here. There's been an incident."

EIGHT

I CLIMBED THE CONCRETE steps to the door of the Elcott School. Adriana stood on the landing at the top, waiting for me.

"You should have gone inside," I said. "It's cold."

"Not alone," she said.

"Where's Catherine?"

"One of us has to work."

"That's okay. We're in this together, right?"

"If you say so."

We entered the school at a staircase. The old-school smell of varnish and paint met us as we climbed stairs worn down by a century of little feet. The hallway to the office sported bright graffiti-like paint and paper decorations. Maria sat on a bench outside the office with a woman sitting next to her. The woman had light brown skin, pearls, and a gray jacket. She stood, stuck out her hand.

"I'm Assistant Principal Marks," she said.

We all shook. Made introductions. Maria watched.

"Please step into my office."

We stepped into her office and sat in front of her desk, Maria between Adriana and me. She hadn't said a word.

"You mentioned an incident," I said. "Maria seems okay."

"Are you okay, Maria?" asked Ms. Marks.

"Yes," said Maria.

Ms. Marks kept looking at Maria as she spoke to us. "Apparently, Maria has been using her social media account to spread pornography."

"That's ridiculous!" said Adriana.

"We've had several complaints," said Ms. Marks.

"Yes, we know about this," I said. "She was life ruined."

"What?"

"Someone broke into her Facebook account and did this to her."

"Did this to her?"

"Yes. It's cyberbullying."

"According to the other parents, Maria was the one engaged in cyberbullying."

"We called them and apologized."

"This is on top of Maria's other bullying."

"Other bullying? What other bullying?" I said.

Adriana looked at her hands.

"Maria, what—"

Ms. Marks broke in. "Maria has been sent home with several Think About It Forms."

"Think About It Forms?"

"Yes. Three TAIFs. The last two were sent home. And Maria called Ms. Rizzo in front of a staff member. I have all the paperwork here."

I had never seen anything called a Think About It Form, but then again, I wasn't really her father. Adriana continued to stare into her lap, as if she were the one being disciplined. Maria maintained eye contact with Ms. Marks.

"Mr. Tucker, as one of Maria's guardians, you should have seen this form." She handed me a sheet of paper.

"I'm not one of Maria's guardians," I said, taking it before she changed her mind.

Maria's neat penciled handwriting answered questions.

What did you do? Please be specific. Start with I.

I called Gustav fat.

What was wrong with what you did? Who did you hurt? How did you know you hurt them?

I made Gustav cry.

What problem were you trying to solve? Did you want attention? Did you want to be left alone?

I wanted to be left alone.

I looked up at Ms. Marks. "She wanted to be left alone?"

"Yes, she wrote that. But it seemed to me that she copied the answer."

"Maria, why did you call Gustav fat?"

Maria shrugged. Adriana sat back in her chair, crossed her arms.

"Can we talk without Maria here?" I asked.

"Maria, please go wait on the bench."

Maria got up, eyes down. She opened the office door, stepped out, and closed it behind her.

"You know she's been through a lot," I said.

"We've all been through a lot," said Adriana. "Now this."

"I recognize the situation, Mr. Tucker."

"Please just call me Tucker. I hate being called mister."

"I would rather keep this formal," said Ms. Marks.

"Fine."

"Maria is too young for Facebook."

"We've had this conversation in our house," said Adriana, glaring at me.

"Even Facebook says she's too young. Their policy is thirteen years and older."

"She's precocious," I said.

"That does not make her thirteen, Mr. Tucker."

Even with my father's honorific, she made it sound like I was the one sent to the principal's office.

"Okay, well, she's off it now, so let's move on."

"Light dawns on Marblehead," muttered Adriana.

"What?"

"Nothing."

"We need to talk about consequences," said Ms. Marks. "This is a serious offense."

"Consequences?" I said. "She didn't do anything. She's the victim here."

"The real victims here, Mr. Tucker, are the children who were exposed to age-inappropriate content. And their parents, some of whom had to explain the pictures."

"It was just a porch swing."

Ms. Marks held up her hand, traffic-cop style. "Let's not get into details."

"It was *not* Maria's fault. Gustav's brother did it."

Ms. Marks and Adriana stared at me.

"What?" Adriana said.

"Do you have proof?" asked Ms. Marks.

"No. Not proof as such."

"Then why would you say that?"

"He's a twenty-year-old man who lives with his mother and spends his day on the computer."

"And so this makes him a hacker."

"He had motive."

"If you had been reading the TAIFs we sent home, and if you knew about all the times we didn't fill one out, you'd know that half of Maria's class has motive."

"Why?"

"I hate to label, but she is a bully."

"Chip off the old block," said Adriana.

"Me?" I said.

"Not you. I mean my brother, Sal."

That sunk in. Sal was out of the picture, but he'd taught his child well.

"Mr. Tucker, Ms. Rizzo, Maria needs to see there are consequences for her behavior."

"She … was … tricked," I said, slowly so it would sink in. "It's not fair to punish her."

"We don't punish."

"No, you consequence."

Ms. Marks gave me a cold stare.

"She's a kid," I said.

"Yes. You should have thought of that before you allowed her on Facebook."

"The other kids were on Facebook too."

"Mr. Tucker, stop. This was Maria's account. She gave away her password and her classmates were hurt. She is suspended."

"For how long?" asked Adriana.

"The rest of the week."

"This is crazy," I said. "And unjust."

"And for Maria's own good," said Ms. Marks. "This needs to blow over. Next week is school vacation. In ten days, everyone's emotions will have settled down and she can start over."

"Start over what?"

"Start over by being nice to her classmates."

"But what if—"

"Also, she should go back to counseling."

"Counseling?" I asked. "What counseling?"

"Her grief counseling."

I turned to Adriana. "Maria was in counseling?"

"Yes," said Adriana. "Six sessions."

"Only six?" asked Ms. Marks. "Why only six?"

"That's all our insurance covered," said Adriana.

"Insurance," I said. "You should have come to me if you needed money."

"We don't want your charity."

"It's not charity! It's—"

Ms. Marks stood, stuck out her hand. "Good day."

"But—"

Adriana stood as well. Shook. "Thank you, Ms. Marks."

"But—"

"Shake her hand, Tucker. We're going home."

I shook Ms. Marks's hand. Did *not* say thank you.

We gathered up Maria.

"What happened?" asked Maria.

"You're suspended," said Adriana.

Maria's face crumpled for the second time in two days. The tears started. She cried the whole walk back.

Peter was going to pay for this.

NINE

THE STATE OF AN Italian family can be divined by looking at the dinner table. A heaping pile of gravy-smothered spaghetti, supported by sides of meatballs and sausages, Caesar salad, Parmesan cheese, and a dessert of green Italian cookies tells you that all is right with the world.

We were eating Fenway Franks and canned baked beans.

Adriana sat at one end of the table, Catherine at the other, Maria and I across from each other on the long sides. Maria absentmindedly poked at a pile of beans, eating them one at a time using a spoon. I nibbled a hot dog, put it down, had some beans. Decided they tasted like tiny kidneys, stopped eating. Adriana had cleaned her plate and was reaching for another hot dog.

"You're stress eating," said Catherine.

"Yah think?" said Adriana.

"Getting fat isn't going to help."

"Are you saying I'm fat?"

"These are really good hot dogs," I said.

"Shut up, Tucker."

"I'm just saying, maybe I'll have seconds too," I said, forcing a bite.

"Don't take her side," said Catherine.

Maria burst into tears, jumped off her chair, and ran to her room.

We chewed in silence.

"Maybe I should open another bottle of wine," I said.

"Yeah, because getting drunk will make this so much better," said Catherine.

"Can't hurt."

I went to the pantry, pulled a bottle of chianti out of the cabinet, worked the opener. Walked back to the table, placed the bottle on the table, and sat. Adjusted the chair, raised the bottle. Glanced at Adriana.

"Sure, why not," she said, pushing her glass at me.

I filled her up. Catherine waved me off. I filled my glass and drank half.

"So what do we do now?" I asked.

Adriana said, "What do you mean?"

"We can't just let this stand."

"The suspension?"

"Yeah."

"We're going to do exactly that," said Catherine.

"Let it stand?"

"Yes."

"But it's unjust!"

"How is it unjust? Maria gave away her password, got life ruined, and exposed a bunch of kids to porn. On top of it, she's been a bully."

"That's horseshit."

"No. It's not," said Adriana. "The principal—"

"Assistant principal."

"Assistant principal was right. Maria has filled out a ton of Think About It Forms. She has been to the office over and over."

"What did you do about it?"

Adriana looked at me, something hateful brewing behind her eyes. "What did *I* do about it?"

"Yeah."

"What did *you* do about it?"

"I didn't know about it."

"How convenient."

"What's that supposed to mean?"

"You sit out there in your man pad while Catherine and I raise Maria, and then you judge the job I'm doing?"

"I'm not judging. I'm just asking."

"Fuck you."

We drank our wine. Stared at the pile of hot dogs. Adriana reached for one, brought her hand back, and slugged some wine instead.

"On the bright side," said Catherine, "at least now Tucker will get to spend some time with Maria."

"What?" Adriana and I said.

"This week."

"What about this week?" I asked.

"Maria is suspended, so she's not going to school."

"Right," I said. "I know what suspended means."

"I have a job. Adriana has a job. You don't have a job."

"Hey, that's right," said Adriana. "That takes a load off my mind."

"What does?"

"You can stay here for the rest of the week and watch Maria."

"I can't do that."

"Why?"

"I'm busy."

"Busy doing what? Bingeing *Battlestar Galactica*?"

"I need to prove that Peter did the life ruin."

"No, you don't," said Adriana.

"Just drop it," said Catherine.

45

"I'm not going to just drop it. That kid owes Maria an apology. He owes you two an apology also."

"Let's just get through the next few days," said Catherine. "Just accept the suspension, get through it, and let everything cool down."

"I am *not* letting Peter get away with this. Justice has to count for something."

"Maybe it did," said Catherine.

"What justice?"

"Karma, then. Maria has been a little bully, and the universe responded."

"'The universe' didn't respond, Catherine. Peter Olinsky responded."

"Says you."

"That's why I need to prove it."

"All right, enough of this," said Adriana, standing. "Tucker, are you going to help us or not?"

I drank my wine.

Adriana said, "You were all pissy because the judge appointed Catherine and me guardians and left you out."

"Because I was single."

"And apparently, because he saw right through you."

"Saw through me?"

"Saw that you're still a child."

"Fuck you." I sat back in my chair, crossed my arms, and stared at the pile of beans.

Adriana started cleaning plates, banging them into the dishwasher. Catherine pursed her lips, stood, and started to help Adriana.

The boiling rage that had churned in me since I saw the porn on Maria's Facebook page continued to course through me, setting off an upset stomach and an aching head. The year of First-Withouts had been a trial for all of us.

I blew anger through puffed cheeks. It caught Adriana's attention, who glanced at me but said nothing. Nothing more needed to be said. We had all said enough. What's worse, she was right. I had bitched about not being named a guardian, and the judge had been right to give Maria to a married couple—an *employed* married couple.

I closed my eyes, blew out a few more puffs of adrenaline. "Okay," I said.

"Okay?" asked Adriana.

"You're right. I'll take care of Maria this wee—"

Maria came bolting around the kitchen door and jumped into my lap. "Yay! This will be so much fun!"

Adriana rolled her eyes. "Some consequence."

I said to Maria, "You're going to have to keep up with your schoolwork."

"Yes, I will!" She threw her arms around my neck, hugged me hard.

I patted her back and thought again, *Peter, you are going to pay.*

TEN

THE NOTION OF BEING "on time" is a myth propagated by the perpetually late. In reality, it's impossible to hit the absolute perfect moment to be *on time*. One is either early or late.

I prefer early, so at 7:55 the next morning I knocked on Adriana's door, travel mug in hand and backpack on my back. Adriana opened the door wearing an unbuttoned blouse and a skirt turned a quarter around from the front.

"I thought I said eight," she said.

"This is almost eight."

"Just come in."

I came in and set up shop in the kitchen while frantic last-minute commuter activity happened around me, with Catherine and Adriana making lunches, putting the finishing touches on their looks, and getting ready to run out the door.

"Where's Maria?" I asked.

"She's sleeping late. Make yourself at home," said Adriana. "And no television for her. She's being punished."

"What?"

"Gotta go!"

She and Catherine bolted out the front door, leaving me in a quiet house. I made a cup of coffee, found one of Catherine's scones in a tin, and sat down to do some online sleuthing. Much as he didn't want to help me dox Peter, Huey had given me a clue to start looking. I began searching for the hacking group PwnSec.

We think of hackers as loners, guys (or mostly guys) who sit in front of their computers all day engaging in mischief or learning how to engage in more mischief. If you don't count the times that the hacker collective Anonymous has inspired real-world protests, the generalization is often true. Hackers don't see much of each other, but they chat a lot.

When hackers meet on the Internet and love each other very much, they go to a chat room and create a hacker club with a clever name. PwnSec was such a club, combining the word for beating someone in a contest (pwning them) with an abbreviation for *security*. Apparently PwnSec thought they would pwn a lot of sec.

"Tucker, what are you doing?" Maria was up.

"I'm looking for people on the Internet."

"Like with dating?"

"No. Not like with dating. What do you want for breakfast?"

It turned out that Maria wanted pancakes. I fished through the unfamiliar kitchen, found the ingredients, and whipped up some pancakes with chocolate chips as a favor to Maria. I'm not a fan of candy for breakfast, but then again I'm in my thirties.

As Maria ate her breakfast, I started searching Twitter for signs of PwnSec. They were easy to find; in fact, they screamed for attention. The @PwnSec account spewed links to manifestos, plans, and—

"I'm going to watch TV," said Maria.

"Your mom said no TV," I said, looking at my computer screen.

"What?"

I turned to Maria. "No TV."

"Why?"

49

"It seems you're being consequenced for letting your Facebook account get hacked."

"What?"

"You are being punished."

"This is bullshit!"

"Hey! Language."

"You say it."

"I'm an adult with a potty mouth."

"I'm a kid with a potty mouth."

"Kids aren't allowed to have potty mouths."

Maria slid out of her chair and headed for her room.

"What are you going to do?" I asked.

"Use my computer. If that's okay."

"Yeah, it's fine."

Maria stomped down the hallway to her room. Just before her bedroom door closed she got in one last "Bullshit!"

Well, that was a bad start.

I went back to Googling PwnSec. They had a pathetic track record. While they were good at recruiting others to take part in denial-of-service attacks, team efforts that overwhelmed websites, they rarely initiated an activity. They were vocal about the #GamerGate battle on Twitter, which mixed a call for ethical standards in video-game journalism with a heavy dose of misogyny. But they didn't—

"I'm bored." Maria stood by my side.

A tweak of irritation rippled through my stomach.

"Don't say you're bored. Only boring people get bored."

Maria climbed in my lap. "But I *am* bored."

"You must be able to find something to do. You have all those toys in your room."

"They're boring."

"Please, honey. I'm trying to do something."

"You're supposed to be watching me."

"I am watching you."

"I'm bored!"

"We'll go out for lunch, okay?"

"What about until then? You said I can't watch TV."

"No, no TV."

Maria jumped off my lap. "This is such bullshit!"

"Hey!"

She stomped back down to her room. Slammed the door.

I went over to Twitter and looked at PwnSec's account. They had ten followers, which was pathetic. A group of any—

I started wondering what Maria was doing in her room. Got up, walked down, knocked on the door, opened it.

Maria sat in front of her computer, transfixed.

"Whatcha doin'?"

"Computer," said Maria.

I walked around her computer and looked at the screen. A cartoon llama was having a bad day.

"I thought your mom said no TV."

"I'm not watching TV."

"Netflix is TV."

"No, it isn't TV. You said I could use my computer."

Screw Adriana and her arbitrary rules.

"You're right. It's not. Enjoy."

I went back to my computer, back to the PwnSec Twitter page. With only ten followers, anything in the feed had to be useful. I wrote a little script that listed the followers in the order they'd joined. Got a list of names: Eliza, Runway, Tron, Metalhead, etc. Some of these had to be on PwnSec. Now I had to—

"Tucker, I'm hungry," said Maria.

I looked up at the wall clock. It was 1:30. I had coded through lunch.

"Let's get lunch," I said.

SPRINGDALE PUBLIC LIBRARY
405 S. PLEASANT
SPRINGDALE, AR 72764
479-750-8180

We walked over to Neptune Oyster, where Maria devoured a lobster roll while I chowed down on fried clams and tartar sauce. Comfort food *di mare*.

We finished lunch and walked back to the apartment, where I coded while Maria continue to watch the adventurous llama's hijinks. By the time Catherine showed up to relieve me, I had a pretty good handle on PwnSec.

Let the doxing commence.

SPRINGDALE PUBLIC LIBRARY
405 S. PLEASANT
SPRINGDALE, AR 72764
479-750-8180

ELEVEN

I UNLOCKED MY CONDO door, stepped inside. Put my laptop bag on the kitchen counter. Pulled my last Mayflower Winter Oatmeal Stout out of the refrigerator. While I was happy to see the relatively mild winter go by the boards, I'd miss the Oatmeal Stout.

"Hey, boys," I said to my roommates as I poured the beer. I examined its dark color and creamy head. "See you in November," I said to the stout and took a long drink. Made a mental note to pick up some Mayflower Spring Hop Ale.

I love living in a place that has all four seasons.

Click and Clack, my hermit crabs, slept in their tank. The crabs, like all things in my life, had maintained a comfortable stasis over the past year, going about their crabby routines without regard to the passage of time.

I sat on a barstool at my kitchenette's counter. This put me in the dead center of my space, living room at one end and bedroom at the other. I considered calling Caroline Quinn for a date, but it was late and I was bushed. I opted for some solitude instead. Time for supper.

I steamed some leftover eggplant parm, opened my laptop, and continued my doxing of PwnSec. I'd discovered a lot. PwnSec seemed to have four main members: Eliza, Runway, NotAGirl, and Tron. Their Twitter traffic, pronouncements, and threats to the general welfare of society generated a constant stream of self-congratulatory traffic, yet little real action. The only thing they seemed to be good at was life ruins.

Eliza generally spoke for the group, writing posts and tweets that tried to equate the shaming of a young woman with a takedown of the nation's power structure. The tweets often linked to pictures on 4chan.org/b/. The pictures usually featured a topless young woman with a shoe perched on her head. The "shoe on head" is the Internet way of saying, "I surrender!"

Runway was PwnSec's own little life-ruin wrecking ball. His favorite trick was to post live-chat logs of his attacks on Twitter:

@Runway: You're sorry now, aren't you, bitch.
@HeartBaby: Why are you doing this?
@Runway: You know why. Your boyfriend let us know.
@HeartBaby: I don't have a boyfriend. Give me back my e-mail!
@Runway: You hurt him pretty bad.

These conversations eventually got around to Runway demanding a topless picture of the girl with a shoe on her head. Runway also posted these to Twitter with the hashtag #missionaccomplished.

The other PwnSec members spent their time doing minor hacks on websites, encouraging others to join in on denial-of-service attacks, and occasionally engaging in their own life ruins.

The results got PwnSec the attention they craved. Friends of the women lambasted PwnSec on Twitter, launched into flame wars with them, threatened to turn them in to the police. The hue and cry reached a crescendo when a student at UMass Amherst committed suicide after an online attack. PwnSec disavowed responsibility for the death.

@Eliza: We didn't kill her.
@UMasster: Sure. #RememberSue

@Eliza: She had mental problems. No normal person suicides over a life ruin.

@UMasster: Keep telling yourself that. #RememberSue

I looked up from my computer. My eggplant parm sat untouched on its dish, having cooled and congealed into something that looked more like a genetic accident than a dinner. Wallowing around in the Internet left me with a case of free-floating anger and a touch of self-loathing. If you wanted to believe that there is no judge and there is no justice, the Internet was the place for you. It wasn't the place for me.

I picked up the phone and called Huey. "These PwnSec people are pieces of shit."

"Yeah, I guess," said Huey.

"You guess?"

"There's worse."

"There's always worse. You still don't want me to dox these guys?"

"I didn't say that I didn't want you to dox them. I said that this kind of stuff always gets people hurt."

"Maria was suspended from school because of them."

"Why do you say it was them?"

"Gut feeling."

"You do what you have to do, Tucker. Just leave me out of it."

"These guys nee—Wait, I have another call coming through."

"Take it. I'm hanging up."

"You let her watch TV!" Adriana screeched over the phone.

It took a moment for my brain to click back from the Internet to the real world.

"Did you hear me?" she asked.

"I did not let her watch TV."

"You let her watch it on her computer."

"That's not TV," I said, stealing Maria's argument.

"You are as bad as she is."

"Listen—"

"Worse! You're supposedly an adult."

"Yes, well, supposed adults don't get screamed at over the phone."

"I asked you to do one thing."

"Yes. Stay home with her. I did."

"And no TV."

"That's two things."

"You couldn't back me up on that?"

"I did back you up, but I wasn't going to ruin my day for you. What's she supposed to do without a computer?"

"I don't know. Her homework?"

"What homework? She's not going to school."

"The teacher sent some home."

"She can do it now."

"There's too much. She's going to have to do it tomorrow."

"I'm taking her out tomorrow."

Silence. I imagined Adriana fuming. Finally she said, "You're what?"

"I'm taking her out somewhere."

"Where?"

"I thought we'd take in a cockfight, then cruise the Combat Zone."

Adriana held the phone to her chest and started yelling muffled things at Catherine. Then started in again, apparently with a new strategy. "This is no good for her."

"What?"

"She misbehaves and you reward her?"

"She's not misbehaving."

"What do you call bullying the other kids and getting suspended?"

"I call it working shit through."

Mumbles from Adriana.

"She's had a rough year," I continued. "Everything's gone to hell for her."

"Taking it out on other kids is misbehaving."

"Taking it out on other people is what Sal would do. She's doing her best with what she's been taught."

"Hmmph."

"You're doing the same thing. There are a lot of apples that didn't fall far from the Rizzo tree." I paused. "Switching subjects, I've been looking into the guys who hacked Maria."

"For Christ's sake. Drop it!"

"They're really bad people. She's not the first."

"And she won't be the last."

"I'm telling you that one of them is Peter Olinsky."

"Where are you taking Maria tomorrow?"

"Haven't decided. When I do, I'll let you know."

Adriana broke the connection. I tossed the phone down, walked over to the kitchen cabinet that held my liquor, and examined my options. Noah's Mill bourbon with its 114 proof beckoned.

"Yes," I said. "You'll do nicely."

TWELVE

I'M A FACEBOOK ESCAPEE. A few of us have fled the big blue status machine, and I don't know one who has ever said, "Boy, I miss being on Facebook."

I have friends on Facebook. They tell me, "Oh, Tucker, you just don't *get* Facebook." I get Facebook just fine. Facebook is like being at a continuous drinking session with your pals down at the bar where one of them says something stupid and everybody argues about it all night.

"Tom Brady is the best quarterback in the history of everything."

"No, he's not!"

"Yes, he is. I'll prove it..."

"Here's a picture of a funny cat."

Then you all throw up on each other—figuratively—if not always literally.

Compared to that, Twitter is like a cocktail party. You say something witty, people chuckle, they give you a golf clap, sometimes they take you aside with a direct message and say something short— 140 characters short. Following someone on Twitter is the same as walking up to a group at the cocktail party and giving someone your attention.

I fled Facebook because I wanted to be left alone after my wife died. I stayed off Facebook because I realized that trying to keep yourself private with Facebook's byzantine privacy system is like trying to catch rainwater in a colander.

Twitter is pretty simple. You tweet something and everyone following you sees it. You put someone's handle at the beginning of a tweet and only those following the both of you see it. Direct messages are private. That's it. That's the whole system.

Facebook is not simple. You post something and only your friends can see it, unless you made it public, or unless you tagged a friend, or unless a friend tagged you, etc., etc., etc. Same for comments. Your political buddy posts something outrageous, so you call him a misanthropic ignoramus. That comment, which you thought was private because you weren't paying attention to the little audience icon, is actually visible to the world. Keeping things private on Facebook requires a level of paranoid diligence that most of us cannot muster.

I sat in front of the computer, drank high-proof whiskey, and logged into Maria's Facebook account. I wasn't going to post anything in her name—that would be creepy—but I was going to invoke my white-hat status as a hacker and fish around her friends' accounts. Gustav Olinsky was, amazingly, still Maria's friend. Then again, Gustav had only ten friends, so I could see how he'd be slow to unfriend her. Gustav's brother, Peter, was one of Gustav's friends, a Guy Fawkes profile picture among Gustav's handful of schoolmates and cool adult relatives.

I clicked on Peter's Facebook account. Peter wasn't Maria's friend so I could see only his public information. To his credit, Peter ran a tight ship. I couldn't see much. His friend list was hidden, a trick he should have shared with Gustav.

Peter had not made any public posts and had hidden most of his photos. He must have thought himself safe, but he had probably never checked to see what his public page looked like. As it was, he missed one of the many Facebook privacy loopholes and doomed himself.

Facebook profile pictures are, obviously, public. They're your face to the world, and so the world gets to see them. And by default, the world gets to see every profile picture you've ever chosen, because each time you change it you create another public post that says, "This person has changed their profile picture." Then all your friends get to like it and comment.

Peter, for his part, used several profile pictures before he'd chosen the Guy Fawkes mask. His previous profile pics showed an older version of Gustav with cherubic cheeks and a body that had clearly never seen the inside of a gym. They all featured Peter sitting in front of his laptop camera. Peter sitting in front of his laptop camera wearing a baseball cap. Peter sitting in front of his laptop camera holding a cat. Peter sitting in front of his laptop camera sticking out his tongue. And then, a year ago, the Guy Fawkes mask.

The post that announced the change to the Guy Fawkes mask had thirteen likes and five comments. Four of the comments were variations of "LOL." But the last comment, from an Earl Clary, was key.

`Yes! Yes! Yes! Runway is in the house!`

If Peter had been paying attention he would have deleted that comment, and perhaps given Earl a slap in the back of the head. But he hadn't been paying attention, and now I had proof that I was right. Runway was Peter Olinsky.

I poured another shot of Noah's Mill high-proof elixir.

It was time to end things with Peter.

THIRTEEN

IN 1988, BACK WHEN a four-year-old Mark Zuckerberg was considering preschool options, a programmer named Jarkko Oikarinen wrote a program that presaged Facebook, Twitter, and every variation of chats, messengers, and hangouts.

The Internet Relay Chat, usually called the IRC, brought real-time chat to those who had agreed to connect their computers to this new "Internet" thing. The simple system allowed you to communicate anonymously with a tiny but growing circle of Internet chatters.

Today the Anonymous collective used IRC chat rooms to plan operations such as bringing down the Scientology web server by flooding it with page requests, or showing up at a protest wearing Guy Fawkes masks.

I'd finished my second pour of Noah's Mill and had poured another when I decided to fire up an IRC client of my own and go stalking through the channels looking for Runway and PwnSec. Images of the porn on Maria's Facebook page, the fights with Adriana, and the disdain on the face of the assistant principal charged my rage battery as I launched the software.

I went over to the Anonymous website and opened up their IRC web client, just to see if Runway was logged in. If he was, then I had a few private chat words ready for him. I used my old handle, Rosetta.

I searched the server, found that Runway was sitting in the channel, and started stalking the conversation. It was like eavesdropping on the kids sitting in the back of the school bus.

```
Runway: <Pokes Tron>
Tron: What? What? What do you want?
Runway: Nothing. Just seeing if you were doing
anything.
Tron: Watching porn.
Runway: Any good?
Tron: Meh.
NotAGirl: Rosetta just signed on!
Runway: Who's Rosetta?
NotAGirl: You are such a newfag.
Epomis: He wrote the Nappy Time Virus
```

One little virus, and you're infamous.

```
Epomis: Hey Rosetta.
```

Busted. So much for stalking.

```
Rosetta: Hey.
Epomis: You haven't been around for years.
Runway: He's gotta talk to someone about porn.
Tron: Ha!
```

I sent Runway a private message.

```
Rosetta <private>: Hey Runway.
Runway <private>: Yeah?
Rosetta <private>: We need to talk.
Runway <private>: About porn?
Rosetta <private>: About you doing a life ruin
on Maria Rizzo.
```

Runway <private>: What do you care?
Rosetta <private>: I care.

My cell phone rang.

What the hell?

The evening had gotten away from me. It was eleven, and my glass had somehow emptied itself again. I answered the phone, left it on speaker so I could type. "Do you know what time it is?" I asked.

Bobby Miller said, "Yeah, it's eleven."

"What time zone are you in?"

"Boston."

"Then what the hell are you doing calling me at eleven?"

"I don't know. What the hell are you doing poking around on the Anonymous server?"

I glanced at my screen. Runway had not answered me. "How did you know?"

"Mel told me."

"Mel? You mean Special Agent Hunter? How did she know? Are you guys spying on me?"

"No, we're not spying on you."

"Really? Because creepy phone calls in the middle of the night suggest that you're spying on me."

"Listen, Rosetta—"

"See? See, that. That's spying. You just doxed me."

"I didn't dox you. If I was going to dox you, I'd put your contact information all over the Internet."

"How did you guess my nickname?"

"You've had that nickname for years."

"How did you know that?"

"Mel."

I need to figure out Special Agent Hunter.

Bobby continued. "In fact, she says that 'Rosetta' should keep a low profile. Something about some invaded web servers?"

"That was years ago, Bobby."

"Don't shoot the messenger. I'm just repeating what I heard."

"Why are you watching me?"

"Just get off the server."

Runway <private>: Forget it, oldfag.

Rosetta <private>: You owe her an apology.

Runway <private>: What?

Rosetta <private>: She got suspended from school.

Runway <private>: That's why they call it a life ruin, idiot.

Bobby repeated, "Tucker, get off the server."

"I'm busy."

"Get off now. We'll talk about it tomorrow."

Runway <private>: Got nothing to say?

Rosetta <private>: Fuck you.

I said, "Bobby, I'm not getting off the server until this asshole admits what he did to Maria."

"Whoa, whoa. What asshole?"

"Runway. The asshole who hacked Maria."

"Trust me and get off that server now, or I can't help you!"

I'd never heard Bobby sound desperate.

Rosetta <private>: Gotta go.

I moved the mouse up and pointed at the little window-closing X.

Runway <private>: Buh-bye, oldfa—

I told Bobby, "All right, I'm off. You happy?"

Bobby said, "You're shouting."

"I'm on a speakerphone."

"You're drunk."

"That too."

"Let's talk tomorrow. Mel and I will buy you dinner."

"Not breakfast?"

"Go sleep it off. I don't want to watch your hangover." He broke the connection.

Sleep it off.

Going to bed at a reasonable hour is *not* sleeping it off. It's just going to bed. And there would be no hangover; just sleep until about ten and it works out. I abluted and hit the sack.

My alarm went off at 6:30 a.m., hangover clanging in my skull.

I had to go watch Maria.

FOURTEEN

MARIA STOOD NEXT TO me, squinting up at the spire of the tall building. The Uber car drove off toward Storrow Drive while I gave the driver five stars from my phone. The hangover had finally subsided to an ignorable background buzzing.

"What is it?" she asked.

"It's the Museum of Science!" I said, flourishing my hands. "Ta-da!"

"Looks boring," said Maria.

I frowned and walked past a huge chunk of granite and around a hexagonal pile of basalt. "C'mon."

Maria looked up at the spire, then after the Uber car.

I stopped. Waved an impatient wave. "C'mon, let's go."

Maria slumped her shoulders, stomped in my direction. "This is going to be boring."

I sat on a petrified log, patted the spot next to me. "We need to talk."

Maria stood eyeing the log and blocking the path, forcing a hook-nosed guy in a suit to skip around her to avoid knocking her over.

"Sorry," I said to the suit. "Maria, say you're sorry. Get out of the way."

"Sorry," muttered Maria, climbing onto the boulder.

"Look, I'm not taking you to my favorite museum if you're going to be a pill all day."

"This is your favorite museum?"

"Yes. My dad used to take me here a couple times a year."

"Why?"

"He liked science. He wanted me to like it too."

"And you want me to like it? Sounds boring."

"It gave me time to talk with my dad. I didn't see him much."

"Auntie Adriana says he was a terrible person."

Ouch.

"It's complicated," I said. "It's always complicated."

"Did he make you look at these rocks?"

"He didn't *make* me do anything, though I have a picture of him and me sitting on this one. It wasn't my favorite thing at the museum, but I liked it."

"What was your favorite?"

"I could show you."

"Okay."

Maria hopped off the petrified log and headed for the museum entrance. We stepped into the lobby, a vaulted combination of granite and glass sporting banners that exhorted us to innovate and transform. Model airplanes hung overhead while the names and dates of scientists from Archimedes to Pavlov adorned three-story granite slabs.

I operated a kiosk, got us tickets to the museum and a couple of special exhibits, then got in line behind the guy in the suit to show our tickets and get our hands stamped. Ahead, through an enormous plate-glass window, the Charles River twinkled in the April sun while duck boats plied its waters.

"Let's go to your favorite place," said Maria.

"You don't want to go to a favorite place right away," I said. "You want something to look forward to."

"Where do you want to go?"

"C'mon, I'll show you something embarrassing instead."

We entered the Blue Wing, which I still thought of as the West Wing. A long rectangular building with a three-story open floor plan, the Blue Wing presented live science shows, exhibits on modeling, and on the bottom floor, an exhibit on the history of computers.

Maria pointed at a hulking cabinet. "What's that?"

The sign read *VAX-11/780*.

"That is a computer from a long time ago," I said. "It wasn't even as powerful as your iPad."

"What did they do with it? Go on the Internet?"

"There was no Internet."

"Then what did it do?"

"A lot of calculations. It could play games like tic-tac-toe."

"That's lame. Is that what you said was embarrassing?"

"No," I said, approaching a glass case. "This is embarrassing."

The case contained a single plastic three-and-a-half-inch floppy disk, the reason we'd come to the museum. I hoped that the floppy would build trust between Maria and me. I'd share a secret with her, and maybe she'd feel comfortable talking to me about her world. The sweet girl I'd known for years had turned into a bullying machine in the past year. The reason was obvious: her parents were gone. But I needed her to talk to me if she was going to get past it. This floppy disk was the key.

"What's that?" she asked.

"It's a floppy disk."

"It looks like a save button."

"Yeah. That's where you saved your work back when we had floppy disks."

"Not on a flash drive?"

"They didn't have flash drives back then."

"And that's what's embarrassing?"

"No. You have to read the sign."

Maria read, "*A floppy disk containing the Nappy Time Virus.*"

"Yup."

"What's that?"

"Read some more."

Maria read that the Nappy Time Virus brought down a big chunk of computers on the Internet.

"Who's Rosetta?" she asked. "It says someone named Rosetta wrote the virus. Rosetta sounds bad."

"He wasn't bad," I said. "He made a mistake."

"Did they catch him?"

"No."

"Then how do you know?"

I knelt next to Maria. "Can you keep a secret?"

"Yeah?"

"A real secret. A secret that you can't tell anyone, not even your friends."

"Can I tell Adriana and Catherine?"

"Yes. They know the secret." Or at least Adriana did.

"What's the secret?"

I leaned close to whisper into Maria's ear, looked over her shoulder. Saw the guy in the suit, the one who had almost tripped over her—same hooked nose—standing on the other side of a gigantic tire trying to be inconspicuous, trying not to show that he was peeking through the center of the tire and looking at us.

"What secret?" Maria asked again.

I stood. He ducked back behind the tire. I took hold of Maria's hand.

Maria pulled her hand free. "You were going to tell me a secret."

I crouched down again to whisper in Maria's ear, and to keep an eye on Hook Nose. He walked from behind the tire, studiously examining the dinosaur exhibit on his way toward the exit.

"Here's the secret," I whispered. "I am Rosetta."

Maria squealed, "You *are?*"

Everybody in the Blue Wing turned and looked toward the source of the sound.

"Shh! It's a secret, remember?"

"How did you write it?"

"It's complicated. But remember, you can never tell anyone that I'm Rosetta."

"Why not?"

"It's impolite to tell secrets."

I looked up and around. Hook Nose was nowhere in sight. The adrenaline that had surged when I realized we were being followed sloshed around, nestled in my lower brain, and turned into anger. I considered options. My instinct was to wander around until I saw this guy, chase him down, confront him—all impossible with Maria in tow. Another option was to ignore him. He didn't want to be seen and would probably just stay hidden and follow us. He'd report back that we were at the museum.

We had a third option.

"You know what?" I told Maria. "Let's go see my favorite thing."

"Okay."

We left the Blue Wing, passing a model of a gigantic mosquito and a kinetic sculpture that clanged as balls rolled down tracks and fell through space.

I led Maria to the base of a spiral staircase, and took the staircase to the lobby. I caught Hook Nose scurrying out of sight around a corner toward an exhibit of stuffed animals. Led Maria toward the exhibit, knowing that Hook Nose was trapped. I found him, his back turned to me as he carefully examined a moose at the end of the cul-de-sac of exhibits.

I pointed at a model of Earth to distract Maria. "Pretty big globe!"

"Is that your favorite thing?"

"No."

"Good."

I led Maria up stone steps under a fossil of an ichthyosaur to reach the second level. I could have taken the elevator, but we would have been harder to follow. I could have taken Maria to see the tamarins, sure that she would have marveled at their little faces and hands. Maybe I would, after I'd sprung my trap. Instead, I continued to climb, saying loudly, "It's on the third floor!"

There was little on the third floor. We reached the level, turned, and walked into the library, a large, wide room filled with books and reading tables, all lit by plate-glass windows that looked over the Back Bay, providing the city's best view of that landfilled wonder of the nineteenth century.

"Here we are," I said to Maria, pointing at my favorite thing.

"Bees?"

We sat behind a rectangular glassed-in beehive. Inside the glass, a vibrating world of bees churned across a narrow honeycomb, feeding young, cleaning cells, and attending to the queen. I pointed out a small window where the hive connected to the outside world.

"You can see them coming and going out here."

Maria watched them for a moment. "Is this really your favorite thing?"

"Yes," I said. It actually was. I also liked that it hid us from the library's front door.

"What are they doing?" Maria asked.

I pointed at a bee dancing near the entrance. "That one has found some flowers."

"How do you know?"

"The dance, it tells—"

Hook Nose walked past us quickly, searching for us in the library. I stood, stepped in behind him.

He saw me at the last instant. Spun.

"You suck at this," I said. "Worst tail ever."

I had no plan for what he would do next. The library was empty. It was always empty; that was one of the reasons I'd led him here. I didn't want a big public spectacle, a chase through the museum, or easy access to backup. I wanted to talk where his handler, if he had one, wouldn't see us do it. I expected him to sputter, to claim ignorance, to threaten to call the police. I didn't expect what he actually did.

"Why are you following us?" I asked.

Hook Nose raised his hands to my chest and shoved me hard, back toward Maria. She screamed as I caught myself and pirouetted around her. Then, while I was trying not to crush Maria, he ran out through the library door, down the steps, and was gone.

FIFTEEN

MARIA AND I RETURNED to the Cleveland Place apartment, closed the door, looked at each other, sighed, and went about our business. She to her room, me to the kitchen. I fired up my laptop and poured myself a glass of wine.

I considered calling my friend Jael, a good friend, private investigator, and retired Mossad assassin, in that order. But calling Jael and saying, "Some guys were following us" is akin to saying, "Unleash the kraken," and I wasn't quite sure it was time to activate that side of Jael. The guy seemed harmless enough, and unusually inept.

I drank my wine, checked Twitter, and saw several new followers. I had no idea why anyone followed me. All I did was wander through life and share the occasional observation. I scrolled through the list of new followers, filtering out the ones that promised me ten thousand new followers for six dollars (not really wanting followers all that much). I followed back the ones who were real. One popped out: @PwnSec.

Really. Looks like I got someone's attention.

I clicked on the little icon and followed @PwnSec back.

Following someone allows them to send you a private direct message. Usually this results in you getting some ridiculous machine-generated drivel thanking you for the follow: "Thank you so much for the follow, I look forward to hours of fun and mutual enlightenment as we dialog... buy my music and/or book." But in this case, the direct message I got was a little more precise:

`@PwnSec <private>: Rosetta, leave us alone.`

Interesting. I replied.

`@TuckerInBoston <private>: All I want is an apology for Maria Rizzo`

`@PwnSec <private>: We're telling you to leave us alone.`

`@TuckerInBoston <private>: Make me.`

It probably wasn't the response they were expecting. Popular culture has turned hackers into omniscient and unstoppable demons, the windigos of the Internet. The pros can do some damage. This bunch of kids could not.

Their attack came pretty quickly on my Twitter feed.

`@PwnSec: We announce that @TuckerInBoston is really Rosetta. #doxed`

The response was just as quick.

`@Epomis: Hey @Pwnsec. No shit, Sherlock. #doxed #lame`

At least I had one person on my side.

I was about to follow @Epomis when the door to the condo opened.

"Tucker, I'm home!" Adriana called through the house.

I walked to the kitchen doorway and saw Maria's bedroom door open. Maria flew out, wrapping her arms around Adriana.

"We went to the Museum of Science!" Maria said.

"That's wonderful," said Adriana, pulling off her jacket and hanging it on the coat hook.

"And a man followed us, but Tucker fought him off."

Adriana looked at me, eyes going from wide and happy to narrow and angry. "What?"

"'Fought him off' is overstating it," I said.

"Really?"

"Why don't you get settled and I'll tell you what happened."

"Why don't you tell me what happened right now?"

I turned back into the kitchen.

Adriana followed me. "So? What happened?"

"Maria summed it up. I took her to the museum and some guy in a suit was following us."

"And you fought him off?"

"I confronted him. Asked him why he was following us. He ran away."

"Who was he?"

I shrugged.

The front door opened. "I'm home!" called Catherine.

"In here," called Adriana. "Tucker was just telling me how he got in a fight today."

"What?"

Now there were two of them in the kitchen. Adriana recounted my story.

"Seriously?" said Catherine. "We asked you to watch her for one day."

"Actually for one week," I said.

"Yes, and you got only two days into it before screwing it up."

"I didn't screw it up. I don't see how this is my fault."

"Of course it is," said Catherine, "unless everyone has a guy in a suit following them."

"Yeah, but I don't see—"

"You never see," said Adriana. "That's the problem."

"Look, if you don't like how I'm watching Maria, then just tell me."

"I am telling you."

"Okay, well, thanks for the feedback."

"And I'm telling you that we're done with this experiment."

"What experiment?"

"You acting like a dad."

"What are you talking about?"

"I think you need to go back to happy-go-lucky uncle," said Catherine.

"Yes," said Adriana.

"What's that mean?"

Adriana walked to the front door, to the coat hooks. She pulled my coat off and handed it to me. "Your services are no longer required."

I took my coat, picked up my laptop. "I have to go to dinner tonight anyway."

"No. I mean not required at all. I'm taking over suspension duty."

"You said you had to work."

"I'll call in sick."

I looked from Adriana to Catherine and back. "What, so I'm out?"

"You're not out," said Catherine. "We'll call you when things settle down. We'll have dinner."

"Don't call us, we'll call you?"

"It's not like that."

I pulled on my coat, opened Maria's bedroom door. She had been listening. She looked up at me, stricken.

"I'll see you later, kiddo," I said.

Maria said in a small voice, "I'm sorry. I shouldn't have told."

"Not your fault."

I turned from Maria, left without saying another word. Thought it instead.

Fuck this.

SIXTEEN

THE KNUCKLEHEADS WHO TORE down the West End in the name of urban renewal didn't know the first thing about renewing the urban. Big politics and big money don't turn a neighborhood around. The only thing that's been proven to work is a generation of young people bearing a funny name.

The yuppies renewed my South End neighborhood in the eighties and nineties, wading into the heroin dens and gang-ridden streets, dragging with them builders, painters, high property values, and fern bars. I now lived a block from Walnut Street, whose biggest claim to fame had been getting featured in a book in which an idealistic young couple gave up on the place and fled to Newton.

The yuppies were gone now, the members of that generation being no longer young nor upwardly mobile. They had been replaced by the hipsters, who now took on new neighborhoods, and the hipsters had decided to turn Jamaica Plain into the coolest place on Earth.

After I had gotten Maria home, Bobby called to tell me that he and Special Agent Hunter wanted to talk to me about Runway. He and I now sat in a bookstore-cum-tapas bar named Tres Gatos. The small amalgamation had been nestled inside a Victorian house: restaurant in the front, bookstore in the back. Bobby and I sat at a black bar, drinking beer and eating warmed olives. A black guitar sporting the words *Take me to Tres Gatos* hung from the wall, while vinyl records and old books decorated the dark wood of a painted fireplace mantle of what must have been the house's formal dining room.

"What's with the vinyl records?" Bobby asked.

"I have no idea," I said. "They're either before my time or after it."

Hunter walked through the front door, approached Bobby, and tapped him on the shoulder. "You're sitting in Ron's seat."

"What?"

Hunter pointed at a nameplate attached to the bar in front of the seat. It said *Ron MacLean*. "It's his seat. You'll have to get up if he comes in."

"I'll take my chances, Mel."

"Suit yourself." Hunter climbed onto the stool next to Bobby, kitty-corner from me. Took an olive, chewed on it, produced a pit, and placed it in a little pit bowl.

The bartender stepped up. "Hey, Mel. The usual?"

"Thanks, Brett."

"Agent Hunter," I said.

"Special Agent Hunter," she said.

"Am I the only person in the world who calls you Special Agent Hunter?"

Hunter fixed me with a gaze. "No. All my suspects call me that."

"Suspect? Suspected of what?"

"You tell me, Rosetta."

Bobby said, "Hold on, Mel."

Hunter said, "You should call me Special Agent Hunter in front of Tucker."

"I'll call you Special Agent Hunter when you do something special."

"You're disrespecting me in front of a suspect."

"No," said Bobby, "you're disrespecting my friend in front of me."

I said, "Do you guys need some alone time? I could go look at vinyl."

"Shut up," said Bobby.

At least *our* relationship hadn't changed.

Bobby continued, "What were you doing in that chat room?"

"I don't think I'll answer that," I said.

"Just a friendly conversation," said Hunter.

"Talk about disrespect. You think I'm an idiot."

Bobby raised his hand. "Mel, let me handle this."

The bartender brought Hunter a glass of white wine. "These guys bothering you?" he asked her.

"Nothing I can't handle," I said.

He gave me a hipster scowl and turned away. I drained my beer, gnawed a warm olive, and spit the pit into the plate. "Why were you guys spying on me?"

"We were *not* spying on you."

"So then why the phone call?"

"We're working on another case."

"Seriously? By lurking on the IRC chat? You going to put some kid in jail?"

"We're not chasing kids, Tucker. We're retrieving some information."

"Yeah? What information?"

Hunter broke in, "You're not going to tell him, are you, Bobby?"

Bobby winced. "I am going to ask for his help."

"But he's Rosetta! You know? *The* Rosetta?"

"Yes, I know."

"The one we studied in Quantico."

I ate an olive. "Who says I'm Rosetta?"

"Did you write the Nappy Time Virus?"

"Not that you know," I said.

"See? He practically admits it. He probably brought down PayPal."

"Rosetta didn't bring down PayPal."

"Cut the Rosetta shit, okay?" said Bobby. "Jesus, I hate nicknames."

"She started it."

Bobby slugged his whiskey back.

"Any good?" I asked.

"Yeah."

I made a twofer motion. The bartender poured us each a Nikka Coffey Grain Whiskey. Bobby got a little more than a shot; I got a little less. Never tweak your bartender.

Hunter asked, "So what *has* Rosetta brought down?"

"The Tunisian government."

Hunter said nothing. Bobby spit an olive pit into his hand.

I continued, "Not the whole thing; just the website."

"That's espionage."

"Arrest me."

Hunter reached for something—handcuffs, gun, wallet?

Bobby said, "Enough."

"But—"

"Enough, Mel! We're not arresting Tucker."

"But—"

"If arresting Tucker were valuable, I would have done it years ago. As it is, he does slightly more good than harm."

I raised my whiskey. "Here's to being marginally good."

Bobby ignored me. "We have bigger fish to fry and you know it," he said to Hunter.

Hunter crossed her arms, stared at her wine. Almost pouted. I felt bad for her. She was trying to prove herself, and I wasn't helping.

I pushed the olive dish toward her. "Olive?"

No response.

"In the name of peace."

Hunter took an olive. "Did you really bring down the Tunisian government's website?"

"Sure."

"Why?"

"It seemed like the thing to do. You know, Arab Spring and all that."

"How did you do it?"

"Nothing you didn't study in Quantico."

We ordered supper. Let the funky ambience of the little restaurant settle over us.

I decided to break the ice. "Is this your happy place?"

"Yeah, I guess so," Hunter said.

"It's a good one."

"Thanks."

"So why were you guys spying on me?"

"We were not spying on you," Bobby said. "We're on a case."

"What kind of case?"

"Runway stole some information."

"Secret?"

"Confidential."

"Confidential? Since when do they send the FBI after confidential information?"

"Since now."

"So why were you watching me?"

"I told you. We were watching Runway."

"Why?"

"When he stole the information, he left a trail."

Hunter said, "We've traced his IP address."

"Pretty sloppy of him," I said.

"Hackers screw up all the time."

"They're like other crooks," said Bobby.

"How so?"

"They're not as smart as they think they are."

"Good thing I'm not a crook."

"And yet ... " said Bobby. Hunter laughed into her hand.

I asked, "So what do you want from me?"

"Just leave Runway alone until we get what we want."

"I don't know if I can do that, Bobby."

"Seriously?"

"He's really hurt Maria. I just want an apology."

"How are you going to get that?"

"Threaten to dox him, then video the apology."

"Do you know who he is?"

"Maybe. Who do you think he is?"

Hunter said, "You're not going to tell him, are you?"

"No," said Bobby.

"You might as well tell me," I said. "Confirmation can't hurt any-thing."

"I just said I'm not telling you. You'll fuck everything up."

"No, I won't."

"Forget it," said Bobby. "You get him *after* we do."

"Fine," I said. Drank my dram of whiskey. Got up, left the bar.

Next stop, a place I rarely went.

SEVENTEEN

LIFE IS FULL OF simple rules that avoid disasters. For example: never guess that a woman is pregnant, order all hamburgers medium well, don't eat the yellow snow, and never, ever drink and post things on the Internet. If you've drunk a few tumblers of whiskey, do not go onto Twitter or Facebook and tell the world how you think it should be run. You'll read it the next morning and realize that drunk you is not half as clever as he thinks he is, and he's a jerk.

An addendum to that for hackers is, never drink and join an IRC chat.

I sat at my kitchen counter, refilled my whiskey glass, silenced my phone, and logged into the IRC chat as Rosetta. The chat software announced my presence and the anons noticed me immediately.

```
Epomis: Welcome back, oldfag.
Tron: I looked you up, Rosetta.
Rosetta: Yeah?
Tron: Righteous resume!
Rosetta: Just horsing around.
Epomis: You logged in twice in two days. What
brought this on?
```

Rosetta: Lack of closure.
Tron: ??
Runway: He means me.

I had noted that Runway was logged into the channel, but didn't know if he was paying attention. I guess he was.

I sent him a private message

Rosetta <private>: All I want is an apology.

Rather than keep things between us, Runway decided to bring our little dispute into the public.

Runway: Rosetta wants me to apologize for a life ruin.
Tron: Did you do it?
Runway: Yeah, but she's a dumb slut.
Rosetta: Hey!
Runway: The dumb slut is all unhappy because I put up pictures of her lesbo moms.
Rosetta: Those were not her moms.
Runway: Yeah, her slut moms aren't hot enough to post. Little man-hating bitch is probably in training.
Rosetta: Jesus, Runway, she's 10 years old.
Tron: You life ruined a ten-year-old, dude?
Runway: Yeah but she's a nasty little whore.
Tron: LOL!

The whiskey kicked in.

Rosetta: It's nothing to be proud of, you jackhole.
Runway: Listen to the oldfag whine.
Epomis: I would be careful, Runway.
Runway: Or what? What's the oldfag going to do?
Rosetta: I'm going to ruin you, that's what I'm going to do.

Runway: Ha! You're funny. You can't do anything to me, you fucking dinosaur.

Rosetta: Don't count on it.

Runway: You going to go crying back to Maria? Tell her I wouldn't apologize?

Rosetta: This is going way beyond Maria.

Runway: Puleeze. Besides, everybody knows you're an FBI spy.

I said to Click and Clack the hermit crabs, "Can you believe that Bobby blew my cover already?"

Rosetta: That's bullshit.

Runway: Yeah? I Googled you.

Rosetta: Everyone Googles me.

Runway: No. I Googled the real you.

Tron: Dude, you doxed Rosetta?

Epomis: Try to keep up, Tron.

Runway: And the real you is good buddies with the FBI. It was in the newspaper. All about your wife?

Rosetta: Stay away from that.

Runway: Your wife got slashed, dude.

Rosetta: I said stay away from that.

Runway: And the FBI helped you get away with it.

Tron: No shit! That's sick!

Rosetta: I caught the guy who did it.

Runway: Sure. Your fall guy.

Rosetta: I swear to God, Runway, you're gonna burn.

Tron: Rosetta, did you do anything to her first?

A little something snapped deep in my gut.

Rosetta: What do you mean "anything"?

Runway: I'll bet he did. I saw the pictures. She was hot.

Tron: Man that's just cold. You murdered your hot wife? Who would do that?

Rosetta: I did NOT MURDER MY WIFE!

The ALL CAPS were slipping out.

Runway: Hee. Hee.

Rosetta: I'm going to fucking cut your head off.

Epomis: Careful, Runway, Rosetta's got the skills to dox you.

Runway: Yeah we already doxed him.

Epomis: We?

Runway: PwnSec.

Tron: You doxed a murderer? Badass! Do it here! I didn't see the other one.

Adrenaline surged into my blood. My fingers twitched and shook, mashing around the keys. A little voice in my head said *Log out! Log out!* but I told it to shut up. There was no way I was going to let this little shit get away with it.

Rosetta: Go ahead, you FUCK! Do it. See what happens.

Tron: Uh-oh, Rosetta comin' in hot!

Runway: I'm gonna teach you something, Rosetta. Maybe get your slut friend Maria to apologize.

Rosetta: I'm waiting, fuckhead.

Runway: You want me to dox you here?

Rosetta: You don't have the balls.

Toto, the dog in the Wizard of Oz, has the honor of doing the first recorded doxing. Toto ran to the wizard's little box and pulled back the curtain—and suddenly the Great and Powerful Oz was revealed to be a little old man in a black suit and a pompadour. Oz's power disappeared as soon as everyone knew who the real person was behind the curtain.

Those who troll the anonymous chat room feel the same way. As long as you don't know who they are, they've got power. They can puff themselves up, make themselves look like giants, but as soon as you reveal who they are, you show them to be a kid sitting in a bedroom under a *Matrix* poster.

Runway thought he was about to unleash hell.

Runway: Here it is. Rosetta, the wife murderer and FBI spy, is really named Aloysius Tucker.

The chat room went silent as people digested it and Googled my name.

Epomis: Yeah, no shit, Runway. Everybody knows that.

Tron: I didn't know that.

Epomis: That's because you are the newest of newfags.

It was my turn.

Rosetta: Hey, Runway.

Nothing.

Rosetta: Was that your best shot?

The chat stream had frozen, all attention on Runway and me.

Rosetta: Here's my shot…Peter.

Tron: Oh shit.

Epomis: Yup. Saw that coming.

Runway: Wait

Rosetta: You liking the view of Jim's Auto Sales? What was that address again?

My private message bell rang.

Runway <private>: Don't do it. I'm serious.

Rosetta <private>: Oh, you are? So am I.

Runway <private>: C'mon man, I was just shitting you for the lulz.

Rosetta <private>: The lulz? I'm not laughing and you shouldn't be either.

Runway <private>: This is so uncool!

Rosetta <private>: I'm going to tell them your last name next, Olinsky.

Runway <private>: No! No! Don't!

Rosetta <private>: I want an apology.

Runway <private>: I'll do it. I'll do it now!

Rosetta <private>: Not now, not here. Live. On video. Tomorrow.

Runway <private>: OK! OK! Nine tomorrow, when my mom's at work.

Rosetta <private>: Good.

I didn't tell Peter aka Runway that, at that moment, I wanted to punch him right in the face. But I wouldn't. By tomorrow I'd have cooled down and he'd go back to being a kid—an unusually nasty kid, but a kid.

I went back to the chat room.

Rosetta: Show's over, folks.

Epomis: Peace.

I logged out, went to bed, hoping that the whiskey would help me sleep.

It didn't.

EIGHTEEN

THE WINDS HAD SHIFTED, and with them the approach paths at Logan. I got off the train at Wood Island and watched a plane descend toward Logan, bombing over the heads of people closer to the ocean.

You murdered your hot wife?

The chat session with Runway had reverberated in my head all night, driving insomnia interspersed with disorienting dreams. I had spent the early-morning hours reliving the attacks and disparaging how I had handled them.

I did NOT MURDER MY WIFE!

Great comeback, Tucker. Way to lose control.

I caught myself standing on the subway platform listening to another plane. It was almost nine, and time for the video apology that I had earned.

I headed off toward Peter Olinsky's house. I had decided to show Adriana the video after I'd gotten it rather than bring her along. The situation was delicate, and a guy like Peter would probably clam up rather than be humiliated in front of a girl. Also, I wanted to be in the role of the great hunter bringing home fresh meat.

Your wife got slashed, dude.

What was I supposed to have said to that? I knew I was being trolled, that Peter was saying whatever he could to get a rise out of me. It wasn't personal in any real sense. Peter didn't even know me. At that point I was just a target, a prop, a way for him to get that Tron idiot to type LOL.

Still, it didn't matter that it wasn't personal. A guy punches you in the gut, what do you care whether he did it because he didn't like you or just to make his buddy laugh?

A muscle near my eye twitched as I walked toward Swift Street. I'd hoped that a night's sleep would make me feel better, would let my maturity attenuate the rage. I'd hoped that when I saw Peter face-to-face that I'd simply tell him to make a short video: "I'm sorry for what I did, Maria." That was all it would take, all I would need.

Now I wasn't so sure.

My cell phone rang. I glanced at it, decided to answer.

Bobby Miller said, "Why didn't you pick up last night?"

"My phone was on mute," I said.

"I tried you about a hundred times."

"It was really only five."

"So you did see the calls."

"This morning. I was busy last night."

"Yeah, busy getting trolled by Runway."

"You were spying on me again?"

"I was not spying on *you*."

I stopped walking at Jim's Auto Sales. The Olinsky house stood across the street, its little window eyes no happier than they were yesterday.

I said, "Doesn't matter. It'll be over in a few minutes."

"What are you talking about?"

"I'm standing across the street from Peter Olinsky's house. I'm going to get a video of him apologizing to Maria, and then we'll be done."

"Jesus, Tucker. Just leave the guy alone."

"Yeah, sure. Right after I get this video."

"Goddammit! Motherfu—"

I ended the call. I'd need my phone anyway, for the video. Crossed the street and climbed the steps to Peter's front door. An aluminum storm door protected the paint-chipped wooden front door. I rang the bell, listened to it bing-bong its way through the house. Opened the screen door. Knocked. No answer. Tried the knob. Locked.

I turned, trotted down the steps. Maybe Peter was doing something in the backyard. Unlike the rest of the Capes in the neighborhood, Peter's stood alone on its block, as if ostracized. I walked down a strip of brown April grass, stepped into the brown back yard. Three daffodils squatted against the foundation forming a pathetic little garden.

No Peter.

Completing my circuit of the house, I walked back up the steps. Peered through the aluminum storm door, rang the bell. Nothing. Opened the storm door again. The wooden interior door was ajar. I was sure I had tried it, that it had been locked. I knocked on the door. No answer. Pushed the door open. No sounds.

"Hellooo!"

Silence.

"Peter, it's me, Tucker!"

Nothing.

The smell of bacon wafted through the house alongside the chemical-fraud stink of artificial maple syrup. I stepped into the kitchen, surveyed the dishes in the sink. Three dishes. One mother, two sons. Gustav off to school, Mrs. Olinsky off to Hertz to ask people how their rental had performed. Peter sitting upstairs?

I moved to the bottom of the stairs. Called up, "Peter!"

Climbed a couple of stairs, clomping to attract attention. Stopped walking. Listened hard. Heard nothing but the blood rushing in my ears and the creaks of the step where my weight pressed them.

"Peter?"

An old-time *Star Trek* communicator chirped, startling me and sending me scrabbling my smartphone out of my pocket.

A text from Bobby Miller: `Where are you?`

I climbed a couple of more steps. "Peter?"

Nothing.

Texted back: `Peter's house.`

I climbed the rest of the steps, found myself in a little hallway, started to turn the corner, and stopped.

Blood pooled across a thin carpet from around the corner. The carpet had absorbed what it could, been overwhelmed, and let the river continue until fresh carpet could stop it. The crimson pool nestled between green polyester fibers.

I stepped forward, careful to keep my foot out of the blood. Peeked around the corner into Peter's room.

The *Star Trek* communicator chirped again. Another text from Bobby. I ignored it, transfixed by what I saw in the bedroom.

Peter Olinsky's severed head lay sideways on the green polyester, red splashed across its cheeks where powerful jets of arterial blood must have spurted from his freshly slashed neck. His open eyes stared ahead, slightly parted blue lips appeared about to say something.

I looked at Bobby's text: `Run!`

NINETEEN

I TOOK ONE LAST glance at Peter's head, spun, ran down the steps, dashed through the living room, and burst out of the aluminum screen door. Ran right into Lt. Lee of the Boston Police Department, knocking him down the three steps leading to the entry.

"Shit—I'm sorry, Lee!"

I ran down the steps reached to help him up and heard a cop yell, "Freeze! Get on the ground! Get on the fucking ground!"

I looked up to see three police cruisers arrayed around Swift Street. The cruisers had delivered five cops, three of whom had guns drawn and pointed at me.

"Get on the ground!"

I lay down next to Lieutenant Lee. Whispered, "Sorry."

Lieutenant Lee, an Asian man with black hair splayed across his forehead, sat up and looked at me as if he'd just scraped me off his shoe. Lee and I had a lot of mutually annoying history, the most recent of which saw me solving one of his cases for him.

"Hello, Mr. Tucker."

I lay on my stomach, waved a little wave. "Can I get up?"

"That depends on what we'll find when we go inside."

"You'll find Peter Olinsky's head on his bedroom floor, next to his body."

"Then I think you should stay on the ground."

Rolled my eyes. "C'mon, Lee."

Lee stood, looked around. Waved at the cops. "Please put away your weapons."

One of the cops had run past me into the house. We heard a muffled "Holy shit!" from inside.

Lee said, "And naturally, you had nothing to do with this?"

Shook my head. "Left my broadsword at home."

"What were you doing here?"

I thought about explaining the whole thing to Lee, decided against it. "Long story."

Lee said, "Better told in an interview room?"

"Or a bar."

"Let's say that—"

Bobby Miller's Chevy Impala pulled up next to us. Bobby and Hunter climbed out.

Bobby said, "Goddammit, Tucker!"

I waved from the sidewalk. "Top of the morning to you."

"Why are you here?" Lee asked Bobby.

Hunter walked past us into the house.

Lee called after her, "That is a crime scene!"

Bobby said, "We know, Lee. To answer your question, that's why we're here."

"It is not your crime scene. It's a Boston Police Department crime scene."

"I guess we'll just have to share the crime scene."

"What does the FBI care about a Boston murder?"

"We care about all of God's children."

Lee narrowed his eyes at Bobby. "Are you mocking me?"

Bobby looked down at me. Nudged me with his shoe. "I told you to leave Peter alone."

Lee asked, "Peter?"

Bobby said, "The decapitated guy in the house is named Peter Olinsky."

"How do you know this?"

I said, "Peter Olinsky was an FBI person of interest."

Lee asked, "What are you talking about?"

"Can I get off the ground?"

"Fine." Lee pulled me to my feet. "What are you talking about?"

"A hacker named Runway stole something confidential and left a trail. Bobby and Hunter had linked the nickname to Peter."

Hunter joined us. "Jesus, Tucker, did you have to threaten to cut off his head?"

Bobby rolled his eyes. Put his finger to his lips. "Hey, rookie. Don't talk. Just listen."

Lee said to me, "You threatened the victim?"

"A little argument on the Internet."

"Did you threaten the victim?"

"Sort of."

"What do you mean sort of? You threatened him or you didn't."

"I only Internet threatened him."

"What's that mean?"

"People who make Internet threats never expect to meet the person they threaten. Nobody thinks they'll actually carry out the threat."

"Did you threaten to cut the victim's head off?"

"That was a metaphor."

"You metaphorically threatened to cut off his head?"

"I guess."

"And now his head is cut off."

"I can't explain that."

Lee asked Bobby, "Is there any reason I shouldn't arrest Tucker? You seem to like interfering with my doing my job, so I wanted to check."

Bobby said, "Beyond the fact that I need Tucker to help me now that Peter is dead, you don't have enough evidence."

"I have motive, apparently, and opportunity."

"Yeah, but you don't have means."

"Tucker owns a broadsword."

Bobby turned to me. "You own a broadsword?"

"I *don't* own a broadsword."

Lee said, "You just told me you did."

"It was a joke. I was breaking the I-just-saw-a-head-on-the-floor tension."

"I want you to come to the station for more questions."

"How did you know Peter's head was cut off?" I asked Bobby.

"Huh?"

"You knew Peter's head was cut off when you got here."

"Well . . ."

"And you texted me at least thirty seconds before Lee got here."

Lee asked, "Is this true?"

I showed him the text: Run!

Lee asked Bobby, "Why did you tell Tucker to run?"

"We didn't know if the killer was still in the house," said Bobby.

"Someone had been in the house," I said.

"How do you know?" asked Lee.

"The front door was locked when I got here. I walked around the house, and when I reached the front again, it was open."

Lee asked Bobby, "How did you know about the murder?"

"We saw a picture."

"Where would you see a picture like that?"

I said, "On 4chan.org."

Bobby said, "Yup."

"What is 4chan.org?"

I said, "If there's a hell, Lee—"

"There is."

"Okay. In hell, 4chan.org is the only thing on the Internet. Somebody must have posted Peter's picture there."

"Bingo," Bobby said. "It was posted with a Latin phrase."

"What phrase?" asked Lee.

"*Sic semper contumeliosis*," said Hunter.

"'Thus ever to the insolent,'" said Lee, looking at me.

"What did I do?" I asked.

"Wow, Lieutenant Lee," said Hunter. "You're up on your Latin."

"I am an alum of Boston Latin School. I took advanced-placement Latin to help with my Bible studies."

"That would do it," said Bobby.

Until now, I had been caught up in running away from a body, having guns drawn at me, and getting questioned by Lee. But the music had stopped, and images of what I had seen upstairs broke back into my consciousness.

Blood in a carpet.

Peter's parted lips.

Hunter said, "The picture popped up just before we called you."

The picture of Peter's head.

Stale adrenaline, combined with images of blood and carpet, settled in my stomach and—I ran to the curb. Threw up in the gutter. Stood there, hands on knees. Panted a bit. More images of Peter floated into my head. I fought them, pushing them down, down out of my field of view. Wrestling them into a little box, I felt a hand on my back.

"I'm sorry you saw that," said Hunter.

I retched a dry heave. Blew stale air out of my lungs. Stared at the splash in the gutter right next to a storm drain. *So close.* Spit some wet debris into the street. Hunter's hand appeared in my field of vision bearing two Altoids.

"Mints?" she asked.

I took the Altoids from Hunter's small hand.

"Thanks." I popped an Altoid in my mouth. Chewed. Swished it around. Popped the next one, let it dissolve.

A cop whose nameplate said *Hendricks* walked up to us. "Thanks, Agent Hunter."

"Special Agent Hunter," she said. "Thanks for what?"

"Thanks for giving him a breath mint. He would have stunk up my cruiser between here and the station."

TWENTY

IF ANYTHING'S WORSE THAN sitting in a police conference room, it's sitting in a police conference room while a hot red-headed lawyer in a black business suit gives you the stink eye.

"I told you to be quiet," said Caroline Quinn.

"I just said hello to Lieutenant Lee," I said, nodding in Lee's direction.

"That's enough out of you," said Caroline.

"Hello, Tucker," said Lee.

"And you," said Caroline, "can direct all your comments to me."

"I don't see why this has to be confrontational."

"You don't? Really. Okay then." Caroline rose. She had chosen a black-matte design on her left leg today, the prosthetic a memento of the day she stood in the wrong spot at the Boston Marathon. "Let's go, Tucker."

I stood, ever obedient.

Lee said, "You can't go yet."

Caroline asked, "Is Tucker under arrest?"

"No."

"Am I under arrest?" asked Caroline.

"No."

"Then we can go."

"I'd prefer you to stay."

"To what purpose? My client—"

"Your boyfriend."

"He is not my *boyfriend*," said Caroline.

"I'm sorry, I must be confused. Tucker, what is your relationship to Attorney Quinn?"

"I'm her—"

"You be quiet," said Caroline. "We're leaving."

"Do you realize that I've received over two hundred calls to our tip line identifying Tucker as Peter Olinsky's murderer?" asked Lee.

"Do you realize that random people calling a phone number is not an integral part of American jurisprudence?"

"It may not be evidence, but it is a reason for me to ask Tucker to answer some questions."

"Tucker is not answering questions. He's not here to do your work for you, Lee. He's here because you asked him to physically be here, and he won't be here for long."

"Tucker, you go by the hacker name Rosetta, yes?"

Caroline kicked me under the table. I said nothing.

"Let me read you this. Someone called Runway—"

"Runway is Peter," I said.

Another kick.

"Ow!"

"There's more where that came from," said Caroline.

Lee read. "It started with 'Your wife got slashed, dude.' Then there was some back and forth and then Rosetta said, 'I am going to'—um ... effing—'cut your head off.' Pardon my language."

I crossed my arms and stared at the table.

Lee continued. "And then Runway, who, as you say, was Peter Olinsky, got his head cut off."

Caroline said, "Yes. Yes. Are we done now?"

Somebody knocked on the door. Lee leaned back in his chair and pulled it open. Looked out, nodded. "Bring her in."

A cop pushed the door open and Mrs. Olinsky stood in the doorway, wearing her Hertz jacket.

"That's him," she said.

"What did he do?" Lee asked.

"He accused Peter of ruining Maria's life."

"Don't think I said that to you," I said.

"You said it online. The police told me."

I leaned forward. Caroline gripped my hand. Squeezed. I ignored her. "Mrs. Olinsky, I am sorry for your loss."

"Save it, you murderer."

"I didn't—"

"So he posted some dirty pictures on the Facebook, so what? You kill him for that?"

"I—"

"What? What are you going to say? You going to lie to me now?"

"No, I—"

Mrs. Olinsky didn't look fast. She looked short, and wide, and solid. Looks deceived. She shot from the doorway, leaned across the table and slapped me across the face. I saw stars as she reared back for another whack. The cop behind her caught her arm as it came forward.

"Murderer!" she screamed. "You fucking murderer!"

It took the other cop and Lee working together to get her out of the room.

"He murdered my boy!" echoed as her voice faded down the hallway.

Lee returned, glanced at me, did a double take, pulled his handkerchief from his pocket, and tossed it on the table.

"You're bleeding," he said.

"I've seen you blow your nose in that handkerchief," I said. "I'll pass on the blood poisoning, if you don't mind."

Caroline said, "That was a cheap stunt, Lee."

Warm blood slithered down my cheek. She must have caught my cheekbone with a ring.

Lee said, "I needed an identification."

"My client is bleeding. Why don't you go get him something sterile?"

Lee rose and left the room.

"You okay?" Caroline asked.

"Yeah, sure. She's not so tough."

"Your hands are bouncing."

I looked at my hands. Sure enough, they were doing their own little rat-a-tat-tat on the table. "Huh," I said.

Caroline covered my hands with hers. "You'll be okay."

The adrenaline stopped rattling my hands and settled in my stomach, making it feel as if I had eaten a jar of mayonnaise. "I think I'm going to be sick."

"If you do get sick, be sure to throw up all over this table. It would serve them right."

I focused on not getting sick. Caroline pushed my head forward, just as blood dropped on the table. "Let's keep the blood off your shirt."

"She's not wrong, you know."

"Who?"

"Mrs. Olinsky. She's right to blame me."

"You didn't kill him."

"No, I just unmasked—"

Lee returned with a wad of bandages. Tossed them on the table. "Here."

I used one to clean my cheek and another to apply pressure to the wound.

Caroline rose, pulled me up by the arm. "Any more baby games, Lee, or can we go now?"

Lee said, "I have means and opportunity."

"And Tucker has a need for an emergency room. Your boss is going to get the bill, Lee, and you guys had better pay it."

As we stepped into the hallway, Lee said behind us, "I just have to find the sword."

TWENTY-ONE

THE POLICE, WHILE WONDERFUL about giving me a ride to the police station, were not interested in giving me a ride to the emergency room. We stood over Caroline's new black two-door car.

"Nice," I said. "What is it?"

"It's a BMW 428i with a 2.0-liter engine."

"Pretty."

"You have no idea what I just said, do you?"

"The B stands for Bavarian."

"Very good. Do *not* get blood on it."

We climbed into the car. Caroline fiddled with a button. The roof lifted up and folded itself away. Pale April sun shone down upon us. It felt good to see the sky. I wondered how much sky one saw in prison.

Caroline worked the clutch, and we started off.

"You got a manual transmission?"

"Don't you start," she said.

"What do you mean?"

Caroline shifted into a valley-girl cadence. "Look at you! You lost a leg and you still drive a standard. You're so *inspirational.*"

"That seems nice."

"I don't want to be inspirational. I want to drive a clutch. It gives me something to do in bad traffic."

And that ended that conversation. Pretty much ended all of them as Caroline navigated her way through the city traffic in silence.

"Are you mad at me?" I asked.

"You literally threatened someone's life in writing?"

"Not literally."

"Yes. Yes. Literally. Writing something down is the definition of *literally*."

"He said that I must have sexually assaulted Carol before I killed her."

A beat of silence.

"You didn't kill her."

"Of course I didn't kill her."

"Why would he say that?"

"It's the Internet. He wanted to get a rise out of me."

"He succeeded in that."

"Succeeded?"

"You threatened to cut off his head."

I watched the city sidewalks slip by. The sun went behind a sky-scraper and April's chill settled into my bones. "He started it."

"And cutting off his head was simply the next step."

"Don't you start."

"I'm just pointing out the simple logic of the prosecutor's case."

"He got a rise out of somebody else too. There must be dozens of people he's pissed off."

Caroline turned onto Storrow Drive. The Charles River, now free of winter's ice, glittered blue in the springtime sunshine.

"Doesn't matter. He's dead now," Caroline said.

"Yes, he is."

"You don't sound sorry."

I remembered what Peter had said about Carol, and said nothing.

"Are you sorry?"

"I'm processing."

"So you're not sorry. I can see that. The jury will see it too."

"I didn't say that."

"Lee sees it now."

"Whose side are you on?"

"Just stating the case."

Caroline upshifted and downshifted her way through the Mass General parking garage. Then we sat around while the emergency room handled gunshot wounds, heart attacks, stabbings, and other more-serious-than-a-slap injuries. Though she sat with me, Caroline mostly worked her phone.

"What's really going on?" I asked. "You're mad at me for some whole other reason."

"I'm not mad at you. I'm worried about you."

"What? Because of one meeting?"

"It's not going to be one meeting, Tucker. It's going to be a big thing. Lee's going to arrest you."

"Not if I arrest him first."

Caroline didn't even crack a smile.

"Come on. That was a little funny," I said.

"Here comes the doctor," said Caroline rising and shrugging on her coat. "I'll call you later."

Three hours later, after various people prodded the cut, poured searing antiseptics into it, commented on its raggedness, and declared the need for a plastic surgeon, I left Mass General with eight tiny stitches holding my cheek together. They told me to expect a scar.

Sometime during the prodding, poking, sticking, and stitching sessions, Bobby Miller had sent me a text: Call me.

I called him.

He said, "Get your ass over here so that maybe we can keep you out of jail."

TWENTY-TWO

BOBBY AND HUNTER PEERED closely at my cheek, Bobby probing with the eraser end of a pencil.

"Does that hurt?" asked Bobby.

"Yes!"

"That's going to leave a scar," said Hunter.

"That's what they tell me. I am marred."

"It'll be dashing," Bobby said.

"Can't hurt," Hunter said.

Bobby had invited me down the street to his office in Center Plaza, where he said he would buy me lunch.

"And a drink," I had said.

"And a drink," he'd agreed.

Now Bobby and Hunter sat on either side of me at a curved bar in the Kinsale Irish Tavern, a warm, woody restaurant tucked improbably into the brutalist sweep of Center Plaza across the street from Government Center. Bobby and Hunter each sat behind a Guinness. I cradled a double Jameson's.

"That Hertz lady packed a wallop," Bobby said.

"She used a foreign object," I said. "I think it was a ring."

"Maybe you're just a bleeder," said Hunter.

"I don't blame her," I said. "She had just lost her kid."

"Actually, she thought you had killed her kid."

"Yeah, that too."

"Which raises a question."

I drank some whiskey. Let it settle in my stomach, tamp down some leftover stress from getting hit in my face. "Yes, Special Agent Hunter, what would that be?"

"How did you dox Peter?"

"Are you going to add this to the curriculum at Quantico?"

"Depends if it's clever enough."

I told her about Facebook.

Her face fell. "That's it?"

"This is why a magician never reveals his secrets. It's always disappointing."

Bobby said, "Have to admit, Tucker, you never fail to disappoint."

I toasted Bobby, drank more whiskey, ate a potato skin.

"The problem we have now," said Hunter, "is that Peter was our only link to PwnSec."

"What do you care about PwnSec?" I asked. "They're kids. They can't write software, they can only run scripts other people wrote."

"You're saying they're script kiddies?"

"They're not even script kiddies. They're just mean little shits."

"Our information tells us that they stole some important information."

"Confidential information?"

"Yes. We're supposed to find it before it gets out."

"What was it?"

"Confidential."

"Ah, well," I said, finishing my whiskey. "Good luck with that."

Bobby motioned the bartender to bring me another round.

I said, "It's a little early."

"You don't want it?"

"Make it a Guinness."

My beer arrived. I ate another potato skin. Blew out a big breath, suddenly exhausted. This thing with Maria had been jangling my nerves for days, a constant twisting of my guts. I'd been hoping for closure, but seeing the kid murdered wasn't closure.

You don't sound sorry.

I had said I was processing. Processing complete. I still wasn't sorry.

Bobby was talking. " … the same way."

"What?"

Hunter said, "Bobby wants you to help me find PwnSec the way you found Peter."

"Facebook would be happy to help. Look at Peter's account and do what I did."

"And if they're not on Facebook?"

"Then they're smarter than Peter."

I drank my Guinness. They know how to pull a Guinness here, of course. Probably should have started with Guinness. The whiskey had made me a little sleepy. Given the week I'd had, I deserved a nap.

"People are going to get hurt if you don't help me," said Hunter.

"People have already gotten hurt," I said, pointing to my cut. "Me least of all."

"Putting your head in the sand isn't going to help."

"Look, all I want to do is repa—"

I glanced out the pub's front window. Standing there, trying nonchalantly to peer through the glass, an impossible task, was the hook-nosed guy in a different suit. He'd gone from gray to brown.

"Don't look now, but who's that guy in the window?"

Hunter looked.

"I said don't look!"

"How am I supposed to see?"

Hook Nose realized that he'd been made, and took off.

"I don't see anyone," said Hunter.

"He's gone."

"Who's gone?"

I told them about the museum visit and about being followed.

"Guy in a suit with a big hooked nose?" asked Bobby.

"Yeah. You know him?"

"Never heard of him." Bobby went back to drinking his beer.

"What's he talking about?" I asked Hunter.

Bobby gave Hunter a glance, and she drank her beer instead of answering.

"This is bullshit, Bobby. If you know what's going on, you should tell me."

"Why? You said you don't want to help."

"I don't want to help."

"So go about your life."

"What about this guy?"

"He's harmless."

"Who is he?"

"Doesn't matter. I'm telling you he's harmless. I mean *you* scared him away."

"Hey, you know, I can get pretty ragey."

"Yeah, well, don't go all Hulk on us, okay?"

I pushed back from the bar. Stood.

"You didn't finish your beer," said Bobby.

"I'm done with this."

"C'mon, don't leave in a huff."

"Screw you, Bobby."

"Aw, jeesh."

"Bye, Special Agent Hunter. Thanks for the beer."

"Tucker, let's talk," Bobby said.

110

I turned from the two and stalked out of the pub, across the street, and down into Government Center station. It was time to put my life back together. I stood on the platform waiting for the train, pulled out my smartphone, and opened Twitter.

I had forty-five notifications. Forty-five people had mentioned me on Twitter.

That could not be good.

TWENTY-THREE

CLICK AND CLACK WERE unusually active, which for hermit crabs meant they were moving. I flipped open my laptop, opened the Twitter site. I was up to fifty-eight notifications. I clicked the notification number. Someone knocked on my door. Jael strode in.

Tall and lithe with black hair and gray eyes, Jael Navas was the only friend I had who carried a purse and a Glock 17. Bobby Miller had introduced her to me as a bodyguard back when I was going through a nasty bout of office politics in my previous company. We'd since become friends. Usually we were the kind of friends who'd have dinner a couple of times a month, but sometimes we were the kinds of friends where the one with the Glock 17 protected the one who couldn't shoot.

Jael said, "Have you seen the Internet?"

"You mean Twitter?"

"Yes."

"I just opened it."

We sat in front of my laptop, opened the notification screen. I now had more than a hundred messages mentioning me, @TuckerInBoston. All of them were discussing the notion that @TuckerInBoston had killed Peter Olinsky.

I recognized @PwnSec:

`@PwnSec: RIP our friend @Runway, killed by @TuckerInBoston #TuckerGate`

The tweet contained a link to the 4chan.org picture of Peter's murder scene.

"Jesus, they haven't taken that down?"

Jael said, "There are comments beneath the picture that say it is not real."

"It's real. I was there."

"You were there?"

"Yes. I found Peter."

"And you didn't call me before you went to his house?"

"I went there expecting his head to be attached."

The @PwnSec tweet had spawned a long conversation about whether I could have, or would have, cut off Peter's head. The damning bit of evidence was the same IRC post that Lieutenant Lee had latched on to, where I was speaking as Rosetta:

Rosetta: I'm going to fucking cut your head off.

Jael said, "A previous tweet says that you are Rosetta."

"The previous tweet was right."

"You threatened to cut his head off?"

"Don't you start."

"That is not like you."

Not like me.

It seemed to be more and more like me lately. My anger had emerged when I had entered into a strange parenting troika with Catherine and Adriana, a pair of women who had not figured out what to do with me. It had escalated when Peter had hacked Maria's Facebook page, spewing lesbian porn at her friends, and it had exploded when Peter opened the scab related to Carol.

"He accused me of killing Carol."

"That is ridiculous."

"After raping her."

Jael's lips tightened into a line. I'd seen that look a few times, and it had never boded well for those in her gunsights. But there was no one to shoot.

"He's dead," I said. "A twenty-year-old kid is dead, beheaded, and I can't even get myself to feel sorry."

"He hurt someone you love."

"Still, he didn't deserve this."

"And you never got the chance to forgive him."

More tweets appeared with my handle in them. They all had the #TuckerGate hashtag. I clicked on the hashtag to see all tweets related to #TuckerGate. There were more than five hundred.

The #TuckerGate controversy had exploded across Twitter. I scrolled through it, noting three strains of thought. The first was that I had killed Peter. The second was that I had killed Peter and the FBI was covering up for me, like with all the other people I had killed, including Carol. The third was that I was an innocent man. At least innocent until proven guilty.

@Eliza: .@TuckerInBoston has the FBI wrapped around his finger. #TuckerGate

@Epomis: Got any evidence of that? #TuckerGate

@Eliza: I got eyes. #TuckerGate

@Epomis: Oh well then, sure it's obvious. #TuckerGate

@CapnMerica: It's time for somebody to take @TuckerInBoston down. #TuckerGate

"This is just hot air," I said. "You didn't have to come over here."

Jael didn't answer. She stepped forward, traced her finger down the track pad, and brought up a tweet I would have missed.

@Eliza: #doxed @TuckerInBoston is Aloysius Tucker and he lives here:

The tweet went on to provide a Google Map link to my house.

"Oh," I said.

"Indeed," Jael said.

"Still, it's unlikely there'll be a physical attack. These guys don't do the real world."

"Then there is this."

@Tron: Hey, @TuckerInBoston, let us know when you plan to suicide…got to chill the champagne. #TuckerGate

I stared at the tweet. "These guys are nuts."

"All the more reason for me to be here."

"I don't want to put you out over guys like this. They're not going to do anything."

"You just said they were crazy."

"They are."

"You cannot predict what crazy people will do."

My phone rang. I put it on speaker.

"Tucker, you need to come over here for dinner," said Adriana.

"Need?"

"Yes. Are you on speaker? Do you mind if we talk privately?"

"I'm here with Jael. Say what you want."

"Just come over for dinner."

"With Jael?"

A pause, a covered mouthpiece, a faint, "He wants to bring a friend." Some murmuring, and Adriana was back.

"Yes. Fine. You'll want the support." She ended the call.

TWENTY-FOUR

JAEL PUT ON HER coat, grabbed her handbag of doom. I'd seen all sorts of things come out of that handbag: a pistol, zip ties, a lock-picking kit. Never a mint, never a tissue.

"You're armed for bear," I said as we descended my stairs.

"Yes," said Jael. "Unstable people know where you live."

I had to give her that. We emerged onto Follen Street, looked up and down through bare trees to see that there were no obvious threats. We headed toward Huntington Ave, where it would be easier to Uber to Government Center.

We turned the corner onto St. Botolph. A skinny kid in jeans and a Patriots pom-pom hat leaned against one of the bare trees planted along the brick sidewalk. He saw me, perked up, stepped forward.

"Aloysius Tucker," he said, brandishing a pair of handcuffs. "I'm placing you under citizen's arrest."

Jael stepped between us. Said nothing.

"You can't arrest me," I said.

The kid said, "I am making a legal citizen's arrest."

"You can't arrest me."

"Google it, asshole. *Commonwealth v. Lussier.*" He took another step forward.

Jael stiff-armed him back into the tree, if you can call applying pressure with one's fingertips a stiff-arm.

"That's assault!" the kid said.

"Actually, that's battery," I said. "Google it."

"I have a right to make a citizen's arrest if you can be shown to have committed a felony."

"I haven't committed a felony."

"There's a preponderance of evidence."

"Wow," I said. "I never thought I'd meet someone who, in fact, knew just enough to be dangerous."

"Other than yourself," Jael said.

"Thanks," I said.

He had rebounded from against the tree and seemed to be trying to figure out a way around Jael. He continued to brandish the handcuffs. "Also, there's a bounty."

"What bounty?"

"On bitcoinbountyhunter.com."

"For fuck's sake!" I was ready to strangle Al Gore and anyone else who had claimed to help invent the Internet.

"It's a full bitcoin bounty."

Jael asked, "How much is that in US dollars?"

"Who knows?" I said. "Still, it was enough to motivate Boba Fett here."

The kid made another lunge at me with the handcuffs.

It was clear that Jael had had enough of this. She took a step, tripping the kid with one foot while grabbing the wrist holding the handcuffs with the other. He squeaked a rat-like squeak and fell face down on the bricks.

Jael knelt over him, stuck a knee in his back, and snapped one handcuff over his wrist. Then she locked the other end to a wrought-iron fence against one of the houses.

"You can't do this!" he shouted. "You're violating my rights."

I said, "You have the right to remain silent. Have you ever considered exercising that right?"

"You're a crook, Tucker! Someone's going to bring you to justice!"

"Do you always talk like 1960s Batman?"

"You won't get away with this!"

"You do look a little like Adam West."

Jael had fished through the kid's pockets and pulled out his key ring.

"Hey, what are you doing with my keys?" The kid tried to free his wrist, locked to the bottom of the fence. "This is so illegal!"

Jael flipped through the ring, found the handcuff key, and removed it.

"You're not going to get away with this!" he said again.

"You need new writers."

Jael dropped the kid's keys onto his stomach. "We must keep moving," she said to me.

I followed her.

Behind us the kid yelled, "Hey! What are you going to do with the handcuff key?"

Jael dropped the handcuff key into the sewer. We walked away.

"You bitch!" the kid yelled after us. "Cunt!"

I turned away from Jael, back toward the kid.

Jael said, "No. Ignore him."

I ignored her instead, and squatted next to the kid handcuffed to the ground. "What did you call her?"

The kid flushed red.

I said, "You think this is Twitter? You think you get to say that stuff to a woman's face?"

"We must leave," Jael said.

I slapped the kid, open-fingered, across the cheek.

He screeched. "Stop it. Help!"

I pointed at him. "You don't get to say those things to women in real life. You do it again, I'll kick your ass. You'll be pissing blood."

The kid started to blubber, rattling at the handcuff that held him pinned to the ground.

Jael grabbed my arm and pulled. She got me going. We left the kid lying in the street sobbing. My vision narrowed to a little piece of sidewalk in front of me.

"That was foolish," Jael said.

I said, "It was necessary."

"It was *not* necessary."

"I'm sick of it."

"I know."

Breath hissed through my teeth. "Sons of bitches."

"I know."

"Fucking hiding behind their computers."

"I know. You must ignore them. There may be real dangers."

We reached Huntington. I pulled out my cell phone, tried to open the Uber app. My fingers banged at the screen, unable to hold still long enough to reach a button. Jael slipped the phone from my hand and worked the app. A station wagon with a glowing blue Uber logo pulled up. Jael guided me into the car. Told the driver to take us to Cleveland Place.

I stared out the window, watched the Colonnade slip by.

`Let us know when you plan to suicide…`

The phrase rattled around. *Let us know.* Let who know? The kid with a pom-pom and a dirty mouth? The denizens of Twitter? The self-selected group of assholes who decided to dispense justice because they were bored?

Who would I let know that I was going to suicide? I'd love to know, because I'd just as soon let them know that I was going to kill them.

TWENTY-FIVE

THE LASAGNA ADRIANA PLUNKED in front of us contained organic cottage cheese, gluten-free noodles, and cruelty-free spinach. But it was still lasagna, and I was starving.

"Aren't you and Catherine going to eat?"

"We ate," said Adriana.

"Is there meat in this sauce?" asked Jael.

"No," said Catherine, "it's vegetarian."

Jael picked up a fork and started in on the lasagna.

I hacked off a piece, shoveled it down. "Do you have extra gravy?"

Adriana took my plate out from under me, walked over to the stove, splashed some marinara sauce on the lasagna, deposited it back in front of me. "There you go, Captain Hacker." She sat next to Catherine across the table from us. Stared.

"What did I do?" I asked.

Catherine said, "We could have used a little bit of a heads-up."

"Yeah," said Adriana.

"I was a little busy."

"That's bullshit. Your phone doesn't have texting?"

"What was I supposed to text? `Hey. Peter's head's been cut off`. Maybe there's an emoji for that. I wanted to tell you myself, but I was busy being interro—"

Adriana's phone rang. She answered. "Hi, Katie. Yes, I called him. He's right here in front of me. We're having dinner. What?" Eye roll. "Of course I feel safe in my home. If you didn't think I could speak freely, why did you ask? ... Yes ... Yes ... It's fine. Thanks. Bye.

"That was my friend Katie," she said.

"I heard."

"She called earlier to warn us."

"About what?"

"That people on Twitter say you killed Peter."

"Did you tell her that's crazy?"

Catherine said, "So we looked on Twitter. Does the hashtag TuckerGate ring a bell?"

"Of course it rings a bell."

"So you weren't going to tell us about it?"

"That I was right about Peter having hacked Maria? Of course I was going to tell you."

"It really doesn't matter that Peter hacked Maria anymore."

"Now that it looks like you killed him."

"I didn't kill him. That's ridiculous."

Jael ate her lasagna, her eyes traveling around the triangle formed by Adriana, Catherine, and me.

"Aren't you going to say something?" I asked her.

"This is delicious," said Jael. "I would like the recipe."

"I'll e-mail it to you," said Adriana.

Catherine looked up from her laptop. Looked at Jael. "Are you Tucker's bodyguard?"

"I am his friend."

"But you also protect him."

"He has needed protection in the past."

"Does he need protection now?"

"No. I don't," I said.

"I didn't ask you. I asked Jael."

Jael said, "Why do you ask?"

"You might want to look at this," said Catherine, turning the laptop so we could see it.

@PitBull54: We're gonna get you @TuckerInBoston you fucking murderer. #TuckerGate

"Oh, that," I said. "That's nothing."

"That's a death threat," said Catherine.

"It's not a *real* death threat. It's an Internet death threat."

Catherine said, "You mean like this one?"

@BOS142409: .@TuckerInBoston, we're going to gut shoot you and fuck the hole. The FBI can't save you. #TuckerGate

"Oh my God. They published your address."

"I know."

"And look at this!"

@GR8AP3: If I ever see you I will literally kill you with my bare hands, @TuckerInBoston. #TuckerGate

"Doesn't that scare you?"

"No," I said. "Do you seriously think that fat load is going to crawl out of his parent's basement and kill me with his pudgy, Cheeto-stained fingers?"

Catherine turned to Jael, "I thought you weren't his bodyguard."

"I am not."

"Then what is this?"

@Metalhead: Watch Tucker beat up @CapnMerica.

The tweet featured a link to a YouTube video. A shaky camera showed the bounty hunter in his Patriots pom-pom hat trying to effect a citizen's arrest.

"You handcuffed him to the fence?" Catherine said.

"It was for his own safety," said Jael.

"What's this?"

The video showed me turning, walking back to the kid, slapping him in the head.

"You hit him!"

"He called Jael a name."

"Yeah? What name?"

I told them.

"That's no excuse for hitting him."

"It was just a little tap."

"Why is he crying then?"

"I might have threatened him." My lasagna had congealed into a gluten-free pile of mush. I didn't want it anymore. "Do you have any wine?" I asked Adriana.

"Wine?" said Catherine.

"You know, to go with dinner."

"No," Catherine said. "You can't stay here."

"What?" I said.

"What do you mean?" asked Adriana. "Why can't he stay here?"

"Don't you see?" said Catherine.

"See what?"

"We're in danger. Maria is in danger. I've been reading this thread. People are saying that Tucker killed Peter because of Maria."

"Has she been threatened?"

"*Yes!*"

@GR8AP3: I've heard that Maria is a twat. Instead of slapping @CapnMerica, @TuckerInBoston should slap her. I'll do it if I see her. #TuckerGate

"Jesus!" said Adriana.

"You can't be here," said Catherine. "You need to leave."

"C'mon," I said. "This is all talk."

Catherine pointed at the door. "Get out!"

123

Adriana looked at the tweet, then back to me. "Just for a while, Tucker. Just until things settle down."

Jael stood and headed for the front door. I followed. I grabbed my coat off the rack, started to knock on Maria's bedroom door to say good-bye, but Adriana caught my eye. Gave a little head shake. *No.*

I stood with my hand poised, ready to tell my cousin I wouldn't be seeing her for a while. I ran through the scenarios in my head. She'd ask me why, and I'd say … I'd say what? I'd say that the guy she didn't want me to go after was dead, that his head had been cut off? Would I tell her that people were threatening her?

Adriana was right.

I dropped my head. Let my hand fall to my side. Followed Jael out the apartment door, down the stairs, and out onto Cleveland Place. I looked back up at the apartment, my throat suddenly tightening. Jael patted my back.

Adriana, Catherine, and I had been engaged in a grand experiment of group parenting, helping each other find the way to take a shattered little girl and turn her into a strong woman. With no parents, no girlfriend, and a single guy's lifestyle, I realized that I'd come to think of these two women and that little girl as my real family, and of that apartment as my real home.

Now I was homeless.

TWENTY-SIX

JAEL WAS IN FULL-ON bodyguard mode as she walked me up to my apartment. It had been a quiet Uber home. Normally Jael plays the politely attentive listener to my blathering, but after being thrown out of Maria's life, I lacked the will to blather.

Parting with Jael is usually a mildly awkward affair. A handshake is ridiculous, a peck on the cheek is too mushy, a salute works sometimes along with "see ya." Today Jael broke with all of these approaches and pulled me close for a stiff hug.

"It will be better tomorrow," she said into my ear. "Stay in tonight."

"I will," I said, hugging her back. Then she left, moving down my spiral hallway staircase with her typical silence, and I was left sitting in my apartment with Click and Clack. The boys didn't seem in a talkative mood, so I left them alone, poured some of Clyde May's Alabama whiskey, and let its apples settle in my nose before taking a swig.

My phone chirped. I had a text message from Twitter: `328938 is your Twitter login code.`

I'd set up my Twitter account so that it would text me one of these codes every time I logged in from a new computer or phone.

But I hadn't logged in from a new computer or phone. That meant only one thing: somebody had guessed my Twitter password.

I shouldn't have been surprised. My password—*BiteMe!*—was pretty weak. It was short, numberless, and built of real words. Password-guessing processors that can make millions of guesses a second shouldn't have had too much trouble with it, and apparently didn't.

I sat for a moment, letting the Alabama whiskey wash away the instinctive gut punch of having been hacked. The irrational feeling of violation had me looking over my shoulder, listening intently to the apartment. Clack clomped across the sand, his scuttling filling my apartment with sound.

"Could you keep it down?" I asked him. He ignored me.

I opened my Twitter page, intending only to go to my settings and change the password. Online insults can only hurt you if you go looking for them, if your need to be noticed and your need to know that others are thinking about you overrides the good sense to avoid listening to an anonymous bully pillorying you as he stands in line at the unemployment office. I changed my password and then … peeked at the carnage on #TuckerGate.

`@Eliza: It's like Charles Stuart all over again. #TuckerGate`

Good God!

I decided to limit the damage to my psyche by avoiding #TuckerGate, and instead only viewing tweets that mentioned me, and only from people I followed. It still wasn't good.

`@Coffee4Hugh: You'd think Mr. MIT, @TuckerInBoston would be better at hiding a body. #TuckerGate #GoUMass`

That was just Hugh Graxton being a jerk, but others weren't so charitable.

Many people whom I'd followed because I thought they were smart and funny turned out to be stupid and inane when it came to talking about me. I unfollowed them all, except for Hugh.

It wasn't all bad. I had some defenders:

@Epomis: Sorry @CapnMerica, you want to be a hero, go do something heroic. What got you bitch-slapped? #TuckerGate

Idiot that he was, @CapnMerica told @Epomis what he had called Jael.

@Epomis: Serves you right. I wish @TuckerInBoston had kicked you too. #TuckerGate.

I sent Epomis a direct message.

@TuckerInBoston <private>: Thanks for the support!

Epomis replied immediately.

@Epomis <private>: It's not fair what they are doing.

Then:

@Epomis <private>: Want to get a drink?

@TuckerInBoston <private>: You're in Boston?

@Epomis <private>: I'll be at the Beehive at 10. Meet me there.

@TuckerInBoston <private>: What do you look like?

@Epomis <private>: I'm a girl.

@TuckerInBoston <private>: There are girls on the Internet?

@Epomis <private>: See you there?

I thought of my promise to Jael. The safest thing to do was just to stay here, chat on Twitter, find out a little more about Epomis from a distance.

I sipped my whiskey. I'd brought this whole thing on myself. Maria had told me to leave it alone, Huey had told me to leave it alone, Bobby had told me to leave it alone. So what did I do?

Peter's head stared back at me in my mind's eye.

Sitting here drinking alone wasn't the answer.

`@TuckerInBoston <private>: How will I find you?`

`@Epomis <private>: I'll find you.`

I grabbed my coat, headed for the door, ready to put the past in the past.

TWENTY-SEVEN

THE BEEHIVE FRONTED TREMONT Street in a part of the South End once famous for prostitutes, drugs, and muggings, but now known for theater, Ping-Pong tables, and trendy dining. I stepped through the front door and let my eyes adjust to the darkness. The main dining room, its red chairs arranged with exquisite haphazardness, held diners waiting for the jazz to start.

"Can I help you?" asked a guy wearing thin black glasses and a bolo tie.

"Heading downstairs," I said.

He made a by-all-means gesture toward the staircase, and I descended, stepping through heavy curtains into the Beehive downstairs bar. With its jazz music, exposed brick walls, duct-work ceiling, eclectic chandeliers, and heavy drapes, the Beehive looked like an Armageddon-proof bunker built by hipsters in hopes that future generations could enjoy our culture's irony.

Still, the place had a well-stocked bar (also a requirement for Armageddon), an intimate jazz stage, and little round tables where one could drink artisanal cocktails and listen to live music. Onstage now, a black woman crooned a jazz standard, backed up by three male musicians who might have been escaped high-school teachers. They made beautiful music together.

I sat at the bar, my back to the music, and ordered a Four Roses bourbon, double, neat. Given a moment of silence, my thoughts raced back to the Internet.

It's like Charles Stuart all over again.

What do you say to that? In the pantheon of Boston bad guys, few are worse than Charles Stuart. Whitey Bulger was a gangster, and Tsarnaev was the Marathon bomber, but Charles Stuart was a conniving son of a bitch who killed his wife and unborn infant right after a childbirth class.

That's it, honey. Breathe. It'll be over soon.

I flashed to a memory, long repressed, of my wife, Carol, lying in our kitchen, her throat cut, blood seeping along the floor tile's grout like red lines on graph paper. Imagined how Twitter saw me, standing there, holding the knife. Carol's image slipped away, replaced by Peter's head in the bedroom. Again the Twitter view, me standing there with a sword; apparently Twitter thought of me as a blade master. I drank half my whiskey. You're not doing shots if you don't drink it all.

I looked around the bar. Took a tally of their bourbon selection, let the jazz music slip back into my head. Thought about the Twitter app on my Droid. What was on there now? What else did the #TuckerGate hashtag and its legion of liars have to say?

The IRC chat that had started this seeped into my head.

Rosetta, did you do anything to her first?

That was it. The ignition point. The implication that I had raped my wife, then murdered her had sent me over the tipping point. The rage built again, narrowing my vision.

I'm going to fucking cut your head off.

I turned the phrase over in my mind, viewed it from all angles. Worth it? Worth having Lee breathing down my neck? Worth being

130

the center of some maelstrom of basement-dwelling, hashtag dweebs with nothing to do but opine and masturbate? Sons of bitches. Peter's head got cut off. Not the wor—

"What's that drink?"

I blinked, climbed back out of my head. An Asian girl sat next to me at the bar. Black hair, black eyeglasses, a cropped top that ended halfway down her midriff and floated above her flat stomach, supported by her breasts.

She pointed at my glass. "What are you drinking?"

I said, "It's Four Roses whiskey, neat."

"Neat?" she repeated.

"Yeah. They just pour it into the glass and give it to you."

"Seems pretty spartan."

"Stiffens the upper lip, for sure."

She held out her hand. "I'm E."

We shook. "I'm Tucker."

"I know."

"Wait—E? Epomis?"

E glanced left and right. "I never use that name in the real world."

"Really? What does Epomis mean?"

She motioned for the bartender. "Two more of these."

"You sure?" I asked. "It's pretty strong."

"You've had a tough day, and I'm always up for trying something new."

I drained my current drink to make room. "Twitter is a shit show."

"There's also the Internet Relay Chat. Of course 4chan makes Twitter look like a bunch of old ladies talking about knitting."

I thought of browsing over to 4chan.org. What would I see? What would they be saying? How much worse could it get?

" ... am I right?" asked E.

Refocused on her. *Pretty girl.*

"Huh?"

"My God, you *are* having a bad day."

Our drinks arrived. The bartender had doubled them like the first one. We clinked.

"*Salute*," I said.

"Yeah," said E.

The couple next to us cleared out. E hoisted herself into the bar seat next to me, her short skirt showing thighs with excellent muscle tone. She sat sideways in the seat, breasts forward.

I drank another slug of whiskey.

So one double plus one half of another double, makes three.

"So why contact me, E? What's up?" I asked.

"Rosetta is kind of a celebrity," said E.

"Only to hackers."

"Works for me." She sniffed at the whiskey.

"Are you a hacker?" I asked.

"I've got game."

"You sure don't look like a hacker. You're a beautiful woman, and you don't have Cheetos stains on your fingers."

"Wow. Cheetos? Does that make you a self-loathing hacker?"

"I think I've earned it."

"What about Runway?"

"You mean Peter?"

"Yeah."

"What about him?"

"Do you think he earned it?"

"What do you think?" I asked, playing it close.

"I think I asked first," said E, playing it closer. She cocked her head, waiting for my answer.

"I think he earned a mild beating," I said. "Tricking a little girl out of her password and humiliating her in front of her friends? Definitely worth a few slaps in the head."

"But not removal of said head?"

"No."

E took a tiny sip of her drink. "Wow, this is good."

"Really? I didn't take you for someone who would drink it straight."

"My father used to pour Johnny Walker Black Label at the dinner table with supper. So I'm used to drinking whiskey."

"Black Label's a good way to start."

"Kind of like training-wheel whiskey."

"Yup. Smooth."

E asked, "So who do you think killed Runway?"

"Clearly, you don't think it was me," I said.

"Ah … no. Picking up a murderer in a bar would be a little crazy."

"A step beyond daddy issues?"

"I don't need daddy issues to find you attractive."

"I don't know. I'm an older man who feeds you whiskey."

E put her hand on my leg, leaned closer. "I just like you. You have a nice vibe."

A pleasant warmth spread outward from my gut, triggered by having an attractive woman make eye contact and say something nice. Conventional wisdom has it that men are seduced from the crotch out; not true at all. That's just sex. The true engine of seduction is having an attractive woman pay attention to you. The feeling echoed kindergarten days when my teacher Ms. Potsdam would lean in close, her tropical-shampoo scent filling my nose, and ask, "What are you drawing, Tucker?"

"A dog."

"That's a great dog. Maybe add some whiskers?"

And she'd be gone to the next student, leaving me wishing for just a few more minutes to bask in her affectionate gaze.

E looked at me the same way, her hand tightening a bit on my leg, demonstrating that its position was no accident.

I coughed. "A vibe?"

"A nice vibe."

"Drink your bourbon."

E flashed a little smile, dutifully turned to her bourbon, took a tiny swallow.

I tried to break the mood. "The guy who killed Peter—"

"They know it's a guy?" asked E.

"Not for sure, but it kind of has to be."

"The FBI did a profile?"

"There are no women on the Internet. Present company excluded."

"And this killer has to be on the Internet?"

"This whole thing was started on the Internet."

"Don't you find that a little scary?"

"I find it annoying."

"I see."

The warm feelings of E's gaze had dissipated. I wanted them back. "Here's what I don't get," I said.

E's raised eyebrow peeked out from behind her eyeglasses. "What?"

"The whole Internet is telling you that I'm a depraved, sword-wielding killer. Why call me now?"

"You're famous now."

"More like infamous."

E leaned in, her hand returning to my leg, a little higher this time. "I have a confession to make."

Bourbon went down the wrong pipe. I coughed. "Confession?"

"I Googled you."

"You make it sound dirty."

"Read all about you. Every *Globe* article is still online."

"And yet here you sit."

"You're a good guy. Maybe a great guy."

"I wouldn't say gre—"

E leaned in, closed her eyes, parted her lips. But it seemed too soon, so instead of kissing E, I placed my hand on top of hers.

"Thanks," I said. "I needed to hear that."

E leaned back. "You left me hanging there. Kisses have the same rules as high fives, you know."

Her warmth, intelligence, and insistent grip on my thigh overwhelmed my vestigial chivalry. I moved my hand to E's bare lower back, slid it up her spine, and tipped her toward me. Brushed my lips against hers, let her tongue flutter along mine.

My other hand, freed of responsibilities, spilled my bourbon on the crooner's keyboardist, who had slipped up to the bar.

"Hey!" he said. "Get a room."

"Sorry."

His eyes tracked down E's body to her backside, and back to mine.

"No, seriously, dude," he said. "Get a room."

E laughed and leaned close. Breathed into my ear, "I live around the corner."

TWENTY-EIGHT

I woke to sunlight slipping around the edges of E's bedroom drapes. I lay on my back on a soft mattress in a cozy double bed. E lay on top of me, her leg thrown over my torso, her breasts tucked against my chest after an exhausting evening that had featured an unusual variant of jiujitsu. I wrapped my arm around her shoulders, my fingers resting on her toned arm.

The Internet intruded, grabbing my thoughts.

What were they writing? What had they said last night?

I slid my hand down E's flank, over her bottom, flashed on a memory of our lovemaking and hoped that it would happen again soon, then slipped out from under her. E slept on, as only the young seem able to do. Padding around the bedroom, I pulled on underwear and jeans, checked the pocket for my phone, and headed for the kitchen.

My phone had died in the night, my constant Internet checking having exhausted the poor thing. I looked around the unfamiliar kitchen for a charger. One of the advantages of a Droid is that it can use any Micro USB charger, and almost everyone has one lying around their kitchen. Not today; iPhone only.

There had to be some way to get a glimpse of the Internet. Perhaps the tide had turned; perhaps there was a new #TuckerIsInnocent hashtag. Perhaps there was no traffic at all and the heaving mob of trolls had discovered something new to be outraged about. Maybe somebody had managed to distract the trolls by stealing a bunch of naked celebrity photos.

I snooped around the tiny apartment. No computer in the kitchen, none in the television room; same for the bathroom and dining room table. Made sense; kids today didn't bother with desktops. Laptops are just as powerful, and could be—

E stood in the kitchen doorway wearing panties—just panties. She reached out for a hug, her breasts beckoning.

"Hey, you," I walked to her and placed my hands on the small of her back. E rose on tiptoes, making up the couple of inches between us, and kissed me. Ran her hand down my chest, then lower, appraising the situation.

"Seems you'd like to come back to bed," she said.

"Yes," I managed.

E took my hand and led me back to the bedroom, saying, "Then we get muffins!"

———

I hadn't paid much attention to where I was going the night before as E led me on a mad dash through the streets of the South End. As we emerged into the daylight, I realized that we stood on Hanson Street.

"Great location," I said.

"I know, right? Let's get breakfast."

She led me down Hanson on a quest for the most Wholy Grain. I chose a cheese, jelly, and butter-filled pile of breakfast goodness, while E went with a fruit cup. We found seats on a little patio out front. April had relented on its policy of acting like March and had decided that today it would act like June. Dusty warmth presented a disorienting contrast to the leafless trees lining the street. E reveled in the heat, wearing her crop top and tiny skirt from last night.

"My God," I said. "You're even prettier in the daytime."

E gave me a delighted smirk. "You look good too."

I drank some coffee. Took a bite of my pastry. I took out my phone to call Jael and tell her where I was, then remembered it was dead and put it back in my pocket.

E asked, "Do you have plans for today? Going to dox anybody?"

"I think my doxing days are over."

"Really?"

"You look disappointed."

"I figured after all PwnSec had done to you that you'd at least want to dox them back."

I ate some pastry. Thought about it. "I think it's time to polish my karma."

"If you change your mind, let me know. I want to help. I could be like Felicity Smoak."

"Who?"

"Seriously? You know, from *Green Arrow*."

"Green what?"

E adjusted her glasses and leaned in, causing her shirt to fall away from her breasts. "Okay. Let's go old school. I could be like Robin."

"Robin didn't look as good as you in a crop top."

"So, you get a modern, super-sexy female Robin."

I flashed back to yesterday, when I had a guy trying to arrest me. "No."

"No?"

"No. As much as I would like to have my own modern, super-sexy female Robin, I'm not going to have you following me around."

"Why?"

"Did you see how many death threats I got?"

"Yes. But they aren't serious."

138

"That CapnMerica guy assaulted me in the street yesterday. That's pretty serious."

"He's an idiot."

"Idiots can still be dangerous."

"I'm helping you and that's final."

This had to be nipped in the bud. I stood.

"Where are you going?" asked E.

"I need to get home."

"You're just dumping me? Last night was a one-night stand?"

I squatted in front of E. "It doesn't have to be. I like you." I leaned in and gave E a kiss, which she accepted in tight-lipped annoyance. "But don't forget, you still haven't told me your name, so this does kind of feel like a one-night stand."

I gathered my Danish and coffee. *Waste not, want not.*

E said, "Let me do something to help you."

I needed to give her something safe, something harmless. I pulled out my phone. It was dead. I told E my phone number.

"You're online more than me. Could you keep an eye on the mob for me? If it looks like something dangerous is brewing, give me a call."

"Like an early-warning system."

"Exactly."

E beamed at me. Stood. Pulled me in close for a longer and softer kiss.

"Does kissing me break some sort of hero-sidekick HR policy?" I asked.

"Oh, no," said E. "It's just giving the people what they want."

TWENTY-NINE

I HEADED OUT TO the sidewalk. Gave E a good-bye wave.

"Call me if you see something," I said.

"Yessir, Mr. Tucker, sir."

"Should it be Captain Tucker now that I have a sidekick?"

"Yes, but this can be your secret identity."

I grinned a goofy grin, turned, and headed down Shawmut Street toward home, taking a right on Waltham. I finished my Danish, drained my coffee, threw the remains in someone's forgotten trash can. It promised to be an amazingly warm day. The sun shone through leafless trees, baking me as I walked. Warm sunshine was something I hadn't felt since the fall.

The brick of the houses on the narrow street merged with the brick in the sidewalk, delivering the red palette that keeps residents of the South End sane during the long, gray winter months. I kicked at a small pile of snow clinging to a curbstone. "Die, snow, die!" Pulled out my phone to tweet the same, realized that my phone had not magically recharged in my pocket, and put it back. It was just as well. The Twitter app had become more of a portal to hell than a social-media tool.

A black car containing two guys in suits rolled down Waltham toward me and stopped. Hook Nose stepped out.

"Mr. Tucker," he called.

I kept a parked car between us.

"Um—who?" I said.

"We need you to get in the car, sir."

"Right," I said, and bolted up Waltham Street.

"Hey! Come back!"

"I don't do kidnapping!" I shouted over my shoulder.

Waltham Street was one-way in the wrong direction for the car to chase me. Hook Nose had the choice of chasing me on foot, or riding the car around the block to chase me. They adopted both strategies. Hook Nose started running. His partner drove the car.

I ran down Waltham in my sneakers. The guy chasing me wore a suit, so I suspected he had a matching belt and shoes. Those are great for impressing people, but not so good for running.

"Stop! That's an order! Stop!" he called from behind me.

Here is a crime-fighting tip from Captain Tucker: When someone chasing you yells "Stop!" *don't* stop.

His words and the slapping of his shoes on the uneven bricks receded behind me. Amazingly, I found myself winning a physical contest. I was giddy with the power of my own body, and there was no way I was giving that up.

I reached the end of Waltham and looked down Tremont to see that friggin' black car turning the corner from Milford. How the hell did that happen? Once a car gets stuck in the South End Amazing One-Way Maze, it almost never gets out.

I ran across Tremont, looking over my shoulder to see Hook Nose standing in the street, hands on knees, gasping for breath and waving for the black car to pick him up. I turned up Clarendon, running past another Do Not Enter sign that would keep the black car far behind.

I slowed to a jog. I wanted to be home more than anything. Then I could hole up and call for help, but I needed to get off the road. I pulled out my phone to check Uber or Zipcar. Still dead. *Dammit! Dammit! Dammit!* All those Luddites who ask, "What are you going to do if your phone dies?" would be laughing themselves silly.

I put my brain into spatial-relations mode, twisting and turning the map of the South End in my head, trying to remember the one-way streets and the way it all connected together. As I crossed Warren Street, I looked down to Dartmouth to see if the black car had figured things out. Didn't see it. It either had missed its chance to turn or had done the smart thing and continued down Dartmouth to my house. I didn't want to be on a two-way street, so I hustled past Warren, but now the roads worked against me. All the one-way roads allowed the car to get from Dartmouth to Clarendon. It was time to get off the street.

The South End is heaven for those of us who like food created in unique and quirky places. One of these places appeared in front of me, The Buttery. I entered, ordered a cup of coffee, and asked if I could use a charger.

"Sure!" said the kid behind the counter. He wore a nose ring and a black Red Sox cap. He gave me my coffee, produced an iPhone connector. "Here you go."

I pulled out my phone with its non-Apple connector. "Got a Droid charger?"

"We don't serve their kind here."

"Okay then, just the coffee—and a scone." I can never give up a chance at a scone.

"You got it." He put the scone in a bag and rang me up. "What can I get you gentlemen?" he said over my shoulder.

"We're good," a man said. "We got what we came for."

I turned. Hook Nose stood behind me with a stocky black guy, the one who had been driving the car.

Hook Nose said, "Mr. Tucker, would you come with us?"

"No," I said.

"What?"

"No. I'm not going with you. Do I look like an idiot?"

They stared at me.

"The answer is no. No, I do not look like an idiot." I pointed at the kid behind the counter. "What's your name, kid?"

"Um…"

"C'mon, what's your name?"

"Sanjay," said the white kid with red hair.

"Seriously? Did you just make up a name?"

The kid looked at his shoes. "No."

"You just made up a name."

The black guy touched my elbow, to guide me away.

I cocked my cup of coffee at him. "Don't touch me."

He pulled his hands back, held them up in a *wasn't-me-ref* gesture.

I said, "Sanjay, go dial 911."

Hook Nose said, "No, wait a second—Sanjay. There's no need."

"Looks like a big need to me," I said.

"We were sent to find you and take you to a meeting with our boss," said the other guy.

"Yeah? Who's your boss?"

"Kamela Jones."

"Never heard of her."

"You hear of Senator Endicott?"

"Of course I have."

"Kamela Jones is his chief of staff."

"And you are?"

"Other staff."

"I'll tell you what, 'other staff,' let's do this. You invite me to a meeting with Kamela Jones, and I go to the office where the meeting is being held at a certain time of day, and then we have a meeting, and then I leave. You think that would work?"

"We were going to do that, but nobody could find you," said the driver.

"You didn't answer your phone," said Hook Nose.

I waggled the dead phone at them. "Long night."

We set a time. At one o'clock I'd find out how I could be of service to a US senator.

THIRTY

FOR THE MOST PART, Boston dodged the stained-concrete bullet that was 1960s brutalist architecture. But, we took one straight to the chest when it came to Government Center. The broad brick plain, adorned with the imposing inverted pyramid that is City Hall, shows just how badly things could have gone.

The 1960s time warp extends to the John F. Kennedy Federal Building that sits just off of City Hall Plaza. The building looks like three eight-track tapes haphazardly thrown onto a shelf, two vertical, one on its side. Jael and I entered the base of the eight-tracks, walking past a statue named *Thermopylae* that looked as if the cast of the movie *300* had been the victims of a transporter accident on the *Enterprise*.

Hook Nose met us in the lobby. Stuck out his hand.

"Pat Turner," he said. He looked at Jael. "Who is this little lady?"

"My bodyguard," I said.

Pat laughed.

I didn't laugh. "Her name is Jael."

Pat shook her hand and we went through the metal detectors. Jael's handbag went through the X-ray machine without incident. I cocked an eyebrow at her.

"I planned ahead," she said.

"How did you plan ahead?" asked Pat.

"I left my handgun at home."

Pat laughed again, and again, he laughed alone.

"Jesus," Pat said to himself, pushing the elevator button. The rest of the ride was an exercise in awkward silence. We watched the elevator numbers change. The door opened and Pat led us to a conference room.

Mel Hunter sat in the room alongside a trim black woman with short gray hair wearing a black suit and sporting a gold Apple Watch. They stood as we entered.

"Kamela Jones," she said sticking out her hand. "You know Special Agent Hunter. I'm hoping you can help us."

"You might have found me more receptive if you hadn't sent Hook ... um ... Pat and his friend to chase me through the South End."

Kamela looked at Pat. "You *chased* him?"

"He ran."

"What are you, a beagle?"

"You said it was important."

Kamela shook her head and waved a hand in dismissal. Pat retreated, leaving the four of us in the room.

"I apologize," said Kamela.

"You're not the one that chased me."

"You know what I mean."

"Why am I here?"

"You're here because Mel said that you could be trusted to be discreet, and because you're somewhat involved in this situation."

I looked at Hunter. "She gets to call you Mel?"

"She works for a senator," said Hunter.

I asked Kamela, "What is this situation that I'm somewhat involved in?"

"Can you be trusted to be discreet?" Kamela looked me straight in the eyes.

"Sure," I said. "I can be trusted absolutely if you don't tell me anything and let me go about my business. Special Agent Hunter should be able to handle whatever this is."

"Are you saying you won't help?"

"I'm saying that I have no idea what's going on."

"Let's sit."

We arranged ourselves around the conference table: Jael and me on one side, Hunter on the other, Kamela at the head, iPad poised for note-taking. Kamela stared at me, tapping her Apple Pencil on the table. I relaxed and admired the handsome woman in her black suit and skirt. Intelligence worked behind her eyes as she looked from me to Jael.

"You are Jael?" she asked.

"Yes," Jael said.

"Mel said that you could also be trusted."

Jael said nothing. Waited.

"This is a hell of a thing," said Kamela, face in her hands.

"What is this thing, exactly?" I asked.

"I screen all of Senator Endicott's e-mail," said Kamela.

"He must get millions of e-mails."

"I mean his private e-mails."

"Ah."

"Recently the senator received an e-mail instructing him how to vote on an upcoming bill."

"Instructing?"

"They had attached a video to the e-mail," said Hunter.

"Aha."

"Exactly," said Kamela.

"Video of some hot young woman and the senator?"

"What?" Kamela radiated disgust. "No!"

"I just presumed."

"You presumed wrong."

"I'm sorry."

"That's ageist."

"I'm sorry."

"And sexist."

"Sexist? How can it be sexist?"

"You just assume that young women are throwing themselves at the senator."

"You mean it was a guy?"

"*No!* It was not a guy."

"Sorry."

"I find you insensitive."

"I'll cop to insensitive."

Jael offered, "And childish."

"And childish."

"And disgusting," said Kamela.

"Okay," I said. "But not sexist."

Hunter asked, "Why are you being a jerk?"

"I don't know," I said. "Just got a little peeved that Kamela sent goons—"

"Pat and Michael," said Kamela.

"Pat and Michael to chase me down to help the senator hush up a problem with keeping it in his pants."

"It's not so simple. The video—"

The conference-room door opened. A gray-haired man poked his head in: Senator Endicott in the flesh. I felt the momentary disorientation of having a face I'd only seen on TV and in the newspapers come to life before me. Endicott entered the room. Shook our hands. Sat down.

"Did you tell him?" he asked Kamela.

"We were just discussing it," said Kamela. "I'm trying to decide if he is the right man for the job."

"Special Agent Hunter spoke highly of him."

I gave Hunter a look. *You spoke highly of me?*

She rolled her eyes.

Kamela said, "Yes, Agent Hunter spoke highly of his skills."

"And of his discretion."

"Yes."

Endicott turned to me. "What did you think of the video?"

"I haven't seen the video," I said.

Endicott turned to Kamela. "What's up?"

"I was hoping not to have to show it," said Kamela.

"How is he supposed to know he's got the right video?" asked Endicott.

"It would be the only video with you in it."

"Still, he needs to know the stakes."

I interrupted. "Senator, Kamela tells me that you were instructed to make a certain vote?"

"Yes," said Endicott. "Regarding technology sales to China. I've been told to support China."

"Or else…"

"Dammit, Kamela, show him the video. I'm going to get some coffee." He stood and left the room.

"Is he embarrassed?" I asked.

Kamela pursed her lips, tapped a few times on her iPad, and positioned the screen so Jael and I could see it.

The video shook as someone propped what was probably a smartphone into place, then settled onto an ornate bed featuring a geometric metal headboard. A woman lay on the bed wearing a simple blue nightgown and fuzzy handcuffs. The handcuffs, one on each wrist, fastened her wrists to the headboard.

The woman said, "Landon, you're sure nobody will see this?"

Landon Endicott entered the frame wearing plaid boxers. "Nobody but me."

"Why do you want it?"

Endicott climbed into the bed and kissed the woman on the neck. "I get lonely in Washington."

"Why can't you just get porn off the Internet?"

"Because those women aren't as beautiful as you."

The woman smiled, tugged at her wrists. "I seem to be stuck here. There's nothing I can do to stop you, senator."

"Then it seems you're in luck, my dear."

The woman laughed. Endicott ran a hand up her thigh, sliding the nightgown higher.

"Wait. Before I forget," said the woman. "The man from the sprinkler company called. They need to turn on the system on the Cape house. Somebody has to let them in."

Endicott rolled away, reached for a pen, and made a note on a note pad. "Got it," he said, then rolled back to the woman and resumed his kissing.

I had seen enough. "Okay, I get it," I said. "You can turn it off."

Kamela stopped the video. "I've never made it past that point myself."

The door opened and Endicott stepped back into the room with a coffee. Sat. "So you've seen it?" he asked.

"Some of it," I said. "It's a movie of you and your wife."

"Yes," said Endicott. "Betty."

"Embarrassing."

"Sure."

"How are you going to vote?"

"I'm not going to let this video change my vote."

"I see."

"I refuse to let those bastards win."

"No, but the video—"

"The video shows that my wife, Betty, and I have a fun and active sex life after forty years of marriage—and that my wife is still beautiful. There's nothing to be embarrassed about."

"Then why are we here?"

"Because if that video comes out, Betty will kill me. I promised her that I'd never share it, and I never did."

"But it went into the cloud without you knowing it would," I said.

"Yes," Endicott said. "How did you know?"

"It's happened before. Somebody tricked you into giving them your password—through an e-mail, for example. Did you ever get an e-mail asking you to fix your account?"

"I don't read my e-mails."

Kamela said, "Oh, no—"

I nodded toward her. "Looks like you did."

"I'm so sorry, Senator. The e-mail said your phone would be cut off if I didn't confirm your information."

"That's the usual ruse," I said.

"I was so busy that day, a thousand things going on."

"They wait for that."

Endicott patted Kamela's hand. "I understand—"

Kamela pulled her hand away. Pounded the table. "I feel like an idiot!"

"It's easy to get tricked," I said.

"I should have been smarter."

Endicott said, "I need you to find that video in the next two days and destroy it."

"It may be impossible to destroy all the copies. There is probably a copy in your backup system right now, and there are probably backups online, and the person who took it probably has several copies."

"So what can we do? Betty will be mortified. She's very private. It embarrasses her to think that anyone believes we have sex, let alone—"

I said, "I think the only thing we can do is make sure that the person who has the video is as motivated as you to make sure it never gets out."

"How would you do that?" asked Endicott.

"We find the person who has the video and—"

Kamela said, "I think it's time you left the room, Senator."

Jael said, "Yes. That would be best."

"You need plausible deniability."

Endicott rose. Turned at the door. "Nobody gets hurt."

"Okay," I said.

The four of us sat in embarrassed silence.

Finally Kamela spoke. "Will you help us?"

I pointed my chin at Special Agent Hunter. "It depends on her."

"What does that mean?" asked Hunter.

I said to Hunter, "I'll help, on one condition."

"Really? A condition?"

"Only one."

She gave me an eye roll. I was starting to like it. "What is it?"

"I get to call you Mel."

THIRTY-ONE

Sitting at the head of the conference room table, Kamela Jones gave a start and looked at her Apple Watch. She tapped the watch, futzed with the crown, muttered, and stood.

"I have to go," she said.

"Pressing affairs of state?" I asked.

"My daughter threw up on her teacher."

"Or that."

"Keep the room," she said, hurrying out.

"So, Special Agent Hunter?"

"So what?"

"Do I get to call you Mel?"

"Fine. Whatever," said Mel, crossing her arms and rolling her eyes. She was cute when she was adolescent. Actually, she was cute regardless, a fact that had just started to worm its way into my consciousness.

"Bringing you into this was the senator's idea," said Mel. "I think it's stupid."

"How did the senator know about me?"

"Bobby had to explain why we were talking to you, a known hacker—"

"White-hat hacker."

"Right. White-hat."

"What, you don't believe that?"

"More like a dingy-gray hat, given what I read on Twitter."

I looked at Jael. "Can you believe this?"

Jael had been looking into her smartphone. "There is a lot on Twitter. More death threats."

"We told you to stay away from Peter," said Mel. "If you'd listened to us, none of this would be happening to you."

"Why did you tell me to stay away from Peter? Did you think he stole the senator's video?"

"We know he stole the senator's video. There was a clear trail from the link in Kamela Jones's e-mail to Peter's machine in East Boston. We had a warrant to watch his online activities to see what he did with the video. We told you to stay away from Peter because we didn't want him spooked. But you screwed that up, and now he's dead."

"So you've got his computer now?"

"Yes."

"And you found the video on it."

"No, they didn't," said Jael.

"How do you know?"

"Because if they had found the video, then we would not have been summoned."

"And you'd still be calling me Special Agent Hunter," said Mel.

"How could all the signs have pointed to Peter and then he doesn't have the video?"

"We think he handed it off to someone else in PwnSec."

"What is PwnSec?" asked Jael.

"The group of idiots who keep pushing #TuckerGate," I said.

"They were also Peter's online friends."

"With friends like that," I said.

"What do you mean?"

"I think we'll find that a guy named Earl Clary is in PwnSec."

"Why do you say that?"

"He's the guy whose Facebook comment linked Peter to his nickname, Runway. Earl accidentally doxed Peter."

"Why do you think he's in PwnSec?"

"I don't know. It's a hunch. It was a really familiar comment, something that a friend in both the online world and the real world would say."

Mel said, "And that's why you are in this meeting."

"I'm sorry, why was I in this meeting?"

"It took the cooperation of the FBI, Homeland Security, and a judge for us to dox Peter. You did it in an evening on Facebook. Clearly, you're good at this."

"I'm also outside legal authority."

"That too. You're a private citizen. You can do whatever you need to do to dox someone, no warrant necessary."

"And then I can report back to you."

"Exactly."

"So I'll be kind of a spy."

Mel looked at me, lips pursed, eyes narrowed. She stood, walked to the credenza, and poured herself a glass of water. She wore nicely-fitting black pants, a blue shirt, and a brown leather jacket. Her brown shoulder-length hair rested on her shoulders and down her back. But her shoulders were hunched. She was clearly angry, settling herself.

She sat down across from me. "What is your problem?"

"My problem is that I've got an Internet shitstorm accusing me of being in cahoots with the FBI, and you're asking me to be in cahoots with the FBI."

"You said they were all idiots."

"They are all idiots."

"Then what do you care what they think?"

"I don't care what they think."

"Then *what's your problem*? Why won't you help us?"

"Because I don't want to see the FBI screw anybody el—"

Jael, who had been sitting next to me the whole time listening, placed her hand on mine. I stopped, my train of thought interrupted by the rarity of the event. I looked from my hand and up to Jael's gray eyes.

"You should help them," said Jael.

"Help who?"

"The FBI. You should find these people with the video."

"But you saw what happened with Peter. You see what's happening online."

"Are you afraid?"

Was I afraid? Of a Twitter storm? "No."

"Then you should help this woman."

"Mel?"

"No. The senator's wife."

"Betty?"

"She allowed herself to be recorded in order to please her husband. She trusted him. He was ignorant and foolish, and her trust was broken. If the video becomes public, she will be shamed."

"Yes, but—"

"She is the innocent one here. She should be protected."

Landon, you're sure nobody will see this?

Jael's moral clarity stopped me cold. Who was I defending here? A bunch of kids who thought pranking people was fun, who would drive a girl to suicide for the lulz? Was the FBI so terrible for catching them before they hurt someone else?

I looked toward the glowering Mel, then back at Jael.

"You're right," I said to Jael.

"So what does that mean?" asked Mel.

"It means I'll help you dox PwnSec."

"Because of Betty?"

"Yeah," I said, "because of Betty."

Mel stood, walked around the table. Stuck out her hand. I looked at it.

"Partners?" she said.

"So you don't want to arrest me anymore?"

Mel left her hand out there. "No. I was wrong."

I ignored the hand. "Apology accepted."

"I haven't apologized." The hand stayed out. "Partners?"

"Sure, Mel, we're partners." I shook her hand.

"Good! What's our next step?"

"You said you had Peter's computer?"

"Yup."

"Let me know if you find anything funky on it. Any malware."

"Got it."

With that Mel left, apparently happy to have a specific assignment. The door clicked shut behind her.

"Thank you," I said to Jael.

"Thank you?"

"Thank you for helping me see the bigger picture," I said, "and for getting me to think about Betty."

Jael said nothing.

"What's next?" I asked.

Jael took out her smartphone, opened the Twitter app, and handed it to me. The invective continued to stream.

`@PwnSec: It's time to do something about Tucker. #TuckerGate`

`@Eliza: Got a plan coming together #TuckerGate`

I knew what I had to do next.

THIRTY-TWO

SOME PERSONAL PROBLEMS LEND themselves to long walks in the country, heart-to-heart soul barings, or howls at the moon. For everything else, there's beer.

The Bell in Hand Tavern juts into the corner of Union and Marshall Streets like the prow of a ship. I carried my Sam Adams and Jael's Lagavulin Scotch to the table at the prow of the building. I sat waiting for Jael, who had gone off to do something. I got bored and opened the Twitter app on my finally charged smartphone.

You can avoid an Internet fight simply by not participating. If you delete the Twitter app and go about your life, you can happily ignore the fact that countless trolls are dragging your name through the mud.

The problem is that you kind of want to know what the countless trolls are saying about you. Hence, I found myself searching for and reading tweets with the #TuckerGate tag. For example:

@PwnSec: Read the papers! @TuckerInBoston comes from a Mafia family. #TuckerGate

@NotAGirl: It's not the first time a connected guy had the FBI covering for him in Boston. #TuckerGate

Right. Now I was Whitey Bulger.

@PwnSec: It's time that we had some justice. You're a dead man, @TuckerInBoston. #TuckerGate.

@CapnMerica: #Doxed! Here is @TuckerInBoston's address for when the time comes.

And then he printed my Follen Street address again.

The wise thing to do was ignore all this, but I had had enough. I tweeted:

@TuckerInBoston: Hey @CapnMerica, my address is in the phone book, you dipshit. Why don't you publish yours? #TuckerGate

The effect was like taking a baseball bat to a log full of angry yellow jackets. The creatures swarmed, and it was a tribute to the IT skills of the folks at Twitter that their servers held up. Random trolls took up the tweets:

I'm going to cut out your fucking liver. #TuckerGate

You're what's wrong with the world. #TuckerGate

A white man gets away with murder, what a surprise. #TuckerGate

My cell phone rang. Caroline.

"What are you doing?" asked Caroline.

"I'm drinking a beer at the Bell in Hand with Jael. Want to join me?"

"What are you doing on Twitter?"

"Watching the mob."

"More like tweaking the mob."

"The mob is harmless."

"The mob tarred and feathered people right outside that window."

"Yeah, in the eighteenth century."

"You're going to see it in the twenty-first century if you don't stop tweeting, you idiot."

"I've got a right to tweet."

"No. You've got a right to remain silent, because anything you say can and will be used against you in a court of law. And that includes tweeting."

As Caroline continued her harangue, an Asian guy on the street caught my eye and made a motion that seemed to say *Stay there. I'll be right in.* I nodded and he set off toward the door.

"…because I'm not going to lose you to diarrhea of the thumbs," Caroline said.

"Jesus, could you be more graphic?"

"I'm serious. Stay off Twitter."

The Asian guy was standing next to me now.

"I'll stay off. I gotta go." I broke the connection.

The guy asked, "Mr. Tucker, may we talk?"

"Sure."

He looked out the window. "This is a nice view," he said.

I looked out the window. The ghostly smokestacks of the Holocaust Memorial exhaled steam into the afternoon gloom. "If you say so."

"It certainly lends perspective. It provides the big picture."

Creepy dude.

"You know my name, but I don't know yours."

"Exactly."

"Then I guess we're done talking."

"No," he said, "we're not." Leaning close, the guy snicked open a knife and touched it to my chest.

I backed away. He leaned in closer, hemming me against the window. The knife edged through the fabric of my shirt.

The guy said, "You need to stop your investigation."

"What investigation?"

"Do not toy with me."

"You can't believe everything you read on Twitter."

The knife slid along my torso, opening a tiny cut. "I'm not talking about Twitter."

"Then what are you talking about?"

"I'm talking about—"

Jael's voice broke in. "I will put my knife through your kidney."

She stood behind the guy, who had suddenly developed excellent posture. Still, his knife touched my skin.

He said, "Jael."

"No names."

"Of course."

"Put your knife away," said Jael. "Experience tells me that you will bleed to death three minutes after I puncture your kidney."

The guy pulled his knife away, folded it, dropped it into his pants pocket, and raised his hands.

"Yes," he said. "Three minutes is about right."

"Get out."

"Wait!" I said. I pulled out my phone, flipped open the camera app.

The guy started to move. Jael leaned closer, getting out of the picture, but also using her knife to straighten the guy up. I took the picture.

"Now, you can go," I said.

He said, "I will get your phone."

"Picture's already in the cloud. No getting it back now."

The guy stared hatred at me, turned, and walked out of the bar. Jael's eyes tracked him until he strode out the door, head high, making no eye contact. She placed a butter knife on the table.

"A butter knife?"

"I improvised."

"He knows you. How?"

Jael looked around at the bay window jutting into the street corner. "You have an instinct for finding the most insecure location in a room. We could be shot here from three sides." She picked up her drink and walked into the bar, selecting a table with a good view of the doors. I followed.

"How does that guy know you?"

Jael said, "Now is not the time. #TuckerGate on Twitter is getting worse."

"Do you know him?"

"You should look at Twitter."

I opened my app. The vitriol continued its sewer pipe flow. For every fifty tweets calling me a "cocksucking fbifag" or a "fucking snitchtwat," one promised to "cut off your balls and shove them down your throat," "feed your liver to the sea gulls," or "stick your severed head on the Public Garden fence." At least fifty death threats.

I drank my beer, but I'd given up on the idea that it would bring me any comfort.

THIRTY-THREE

AN AVALANCHE STARTS AS a tiny thing, a little bit of snow sliding down the mountain. Then it catches some more snow, gains some weight, catches more snow, gains more weight, then it really gets going and it's gone from a little thing to a big thing.

It's the same with meetings.

I had e-mailed the picture of the Asian guy to Mel, who showed it to Kamela Jones, who called the CIA, who contacted Lieutenant Lee, who harassed me, which caused me to call my lawyer, Caroline Quinn. I sat at one end of the table. Jael sat next to me. Caroline on the other side. Then Lee. Then Mel. Then the hook-nosed Pat from the senator's office, and finally some guy from the CIA.

"You know what this meeting needs?" I said. "More people. We don't have nearly enough people."

The CIA guy, Parks, blinked at me.

"Am I right?" I asked him.

"We'll see," he said.

A picture of my Chinese assailant flashed on the wall.

"Before we start," said Caroline, "Lieutenant Lee, are you planning to accuse Tucker of any more crimes today?"

"No," Lee said. "Not today."

"Then my work is done," said Caroline. She leaned back, began tapping on her phone.

"You want to leave?" I asked her.

"Are you leaving?" she asked.

"No."

"Then I'll stay here and make sure you don't reincriminate yourself."

Agent Parks of the CIA pointed at the picture. "His name is Xiong Shoushan and he owns Xiong Distribution."

"What does Xiong distribute?" asked Mel.

"They are Boston's leading supplier of plastic Jesus statues. The ones people stick on their dashboard."

"Dashboard Jesuses?"

I said, "The plural is dashboard Jesi."

Parks said, "No, I think it's Jesuses."

Caroline looked up from her phone, "Definitely Jesuses."

I asked, "Any reason plastic Jesus guys would want to keep me from working with the FBI?"

"He's not only a small business owner," said Parks. He flashed another picture up. A phalanx of Chinese guys in formal gray officer uniforms filled the screen.

"He's in this picture," said Parks.

"Where?"

Lee said, "You cannot find him in the picture?"

A mass of identical gray uniforms confronted me. All the guys wore the same black hat with golden seal, same gray jacket, white shirt, black tie, gold button. Same thousand-yard stare on all twenty faces.

"No."

"We all look alike to you."

"No, you don't," I said. Looked back at the picture. They all looked alike to me.

Jael said, "Second row, three from the left."

Lee said, "Yes. At least somebody is observant."

I said, "He's in the Chinese army?"

"He's a Chinese army officer assigned to the Ministry of State Security."

"What's that?"

"The Chinese CIA."

"Right. How do you know that?"

"Classified."

"And you found him with facial-recognition software?" I asked.

"Classified."

"Okay, then."

"Xiong Distribution is in Everett."

"They distribute dashboard Jesi from Everett?"

"It's next to the ships," said Parks.

"Right. The Shanghai dashboard Jesi haulers."

Parks ignored me. "We called them. They wouldn't talk to us, but they have a neighbor who runs constant video surveillance. We got this from him."

The next shot on the screen showed Xiong Shoushan getting out of a cab, walking toward the Xiong offices.

"I had better get out there," Mel said.

Lee said, "We'll get out there."

"Maybe it should be CIA," Parks said.

"No," Mel said. "It should be the FBI."

Lee said, "I think it should be the Boston Police Department."

Mel said, "But it's not in Boston."

Parks said, "I could head out there."

Mel said, "This is clearly my job."

Lee said, "It could be an unofficial visit."

It was time to change the dynamic. I tapped Jael on the elbow, motioned that we should go. We stood. Everyone looked at me.

I shook Caroline's hand. "Thanks, Counselor. I'm out of here."

Caroline asked, "Where are you going?"

"I'm going to check out Xiong Distribution with Mel."

Lee said, "We haven't decided who's going to Xiong."

Mel stood. "Yes, we have," she said. "When you all figure it out, you call us and we'll tell you what we found."

THIRTY-FOUR

THE WHITE CABLES OF the Zakim Bridge flashed overhead as Special Agent Mel Hunter drove toward Everett. Jael had wanted to go back to her Fortress of Solitude to re-arm, but Mel had insisted on moving.

"There's no telling when he'll run," she'd said.

"You are correct," said Jael.

"But you don't have your gun," I'd said.

"Special Agent Hunter is armed," said Jael. "That is enough."

We'd climbed into Hunter's Ford Escape, Jael and I engaging in a *no after you* dance that resulted in my riding shotgun and her sitting in the back seat. I looked out the window as the bridge's cables gave way to a view of Charlestown and the Bunker Hill Monument.

It's time for @Anonops to show we mean business and stop @TuckerInBoston #TuckerGate.

The remembered tweet launched the hamster wheel in my head, its repetitive clatter driven by endless and circular speculation. I hadn't had a chance to log on to the chat rooms under a fake nickname to monitor the proceedings, but the public nature of the tweet suggested that a small group of hacker leadership had decided upon a course of action and were now ready to rally their Anonymous minions.

What could they do? I didn't have a website to flood with spurious requests. I didn't own a fax machine that could be sent millions of pages. I supposed they could all send me e-mail, but I don't use e-mail for much. Maybe they'd just badger me on Twitter forever, but while I enjoy Twitter, I've always been meaning to take a break. I don't have a Facebook account, so there's no chance of a life ruin in that direction. They had to have a plan. The public nature of the tweet suggested that a small group of hackers … the hamster wheel spun again.

Mel let me brood in silence until she reached the long curving exit.

"Thanks," she said, disrupting the hamster wheel.

"Huh?" I said.

"Thank you."

"For what?"

"For backing me up in that meeting. They were all ignoring me."

"No thanks needed. You would have handled them."

"I've got the double whammy."

"What double whammy?"

"I'm young and I'm a woman."

"You forgot to mention that you're pretty. That makes it a triple whammy."

"Yeah," Mel said. "So thank you."

"My pleasure."

While Boston is no Pittsburgh, we do have three rivers converging on our city, and so we have our share of bridges. Mel swung off the Zakim Bridge and onto the Tobin Bridge. The Tobin towers above the Mystic River and connects Boston to Chelsea and other environs of the North. Mel angled the car down the first off-ramp over the river and turned left under the Tobin.

I looked out the window down Second Street and across Arlington at the low-rise industrial buildings, so different from the tightly packed triple-deckers in the rest of the city.

"It started right down this street," I said to the car.

"What started?" asked Mel.

"A few years before I was born, actually. Almost twenty before you."

"What started?"

"The Chelsea Fire. A perfect storm. High wind. Low water pressure." I waved my hand at a passing strip mall. "All this burned in an afternoon. They say you could see the smoke for miles."

"It looks like it came back okay."

I pointed at a city block consisting of nothing but brown April grass ringed by leafless April saplings. "Not everywhere."

"It's a park, right?"

"More like a vacant lot."

"It'll come back."

We drove on down Second.

"One spark. One flame. The right wind. The right conditions. The whole neighborhood was gone."

"This burned too?"

"Have you crossed the railroad tracks?"

A sign appeared warning of railroad tracks ahead. "No," said Mel.

"This burned too. All the way to the railroad tracks." We bumped over the tracks. "Welcome to Everett."

"You're in a cheery mood," said Mel.

Let us know when you plan to suicide…got to chill the champagne. #TuckerGate

The hamster wheel started squeaking again.

Sons of bitches. All of them.

Jael said from the back, "We need a plan."

"Plan?" I said.

Jael said, "I will watch the back door. Agent Hunter will go in the front."

"And what do I do?"

"You stay in the car," they both said.

I looked from one to the other. "I'm not staying in the car."

169

"It is safer for you in the car," said Jael.

"It is safer for you both with more people."

Mel said, "I can't watch out for you."

"I can take care of myself."

Jael snorted.

"What's that supposed to mean?"

"It means she doesn't think you can take care of yourself," said Mel.

"I *know* what it means."

"Then why did you ask?"

"I'm going in with you," I said.

Mel headed for the front door. "You are ridiculous"

"It's my funeral." *Maybe I should let Twitter know.*

THIRTY-FIVE

THE STENCILED-GLASS DOOR AT the top of the concrete walk read
XIONG DISTRIBUTION.

"This must be the place," I said.

"Thank you, Captain Obvious," Mel said.

We pushed through the glass door, stepped into The Room That
Time Forgot. Brown wood paneling covered the walls, the swirls and
patterns of its knotholes interrupted by parallel black notches simu-
lating planks. Two particularly sinister knotholes over a doorway
stared at us like the eyes of a sentry.

"Eyes," I said, pointing.

"Those are not eyes. They're simulated knotholes."

"They follow you around the room."

The room held a black steel desk with a linoleum top, an office
chair behind the desk with a torn seat cushion, a computer, and two
steel-and-black-vinyl armless guest chairs.

Mel inhaled sharply, about to shout.

I put my finger to my lips. "Let's keep the element of surprise."

"I don't have a warrant."

"Then don't search for anything or arrest anyone."

Two hollow wooden doors led from the room. I tried the lightweight doorknob on the first—lavatory. We moved past the desk. I imagined the wooden eyes of the paneling crossing as they followed us to the second doorway. The door was locked, but I jiggled the knob a bit and the lock shook loose.

"Not much of a security budget," I said.

"So far there's nothing to steal."

I opened the door, peeked through. A broad office space presented itself. Three desks, two phones, water cooler. The phones had the kind of Lucite buttons that light up when you push them. I took a step into the room.

Mel grabbed my arm. "You're trespassing."

"No, I'm not," I said. "There was no sign."

"That doesn't matter. The law says it's trespassing."

"Good thing I'm not a lawyer."

I stepped into the room, trying to be quiet on the threadbare carpets.

Mel followed me. "I'm not sure this place is even open for business," she said.

"The front door was unlocked. They must be expecting someone."

We moved through the empty office. So far there had been no place that Xiong Shoushan could hide. A metal door provided an exit from the room, or an entrance to something important. This door had some heft. I tried the knob. It turned.

I looked at Mel. She shrugged. "In for a penny."

I pushed the metal door open and we stepped into a large industrial space in which the floor switched to concrete. Dim fluorescent lights blinked over rows and rows of shelves. A warehouse.

I tiptoed into the nearest row. Xiong Distribution serviced more than the dashboard Jesus industry. This row featured a variety of crosses on beads, their boxes showing them hanging from rearview mirrors. Other boxes contained St. Anthony statues, mezuzahs intended to

172

adorn Jewish doorjambs, and commemorative plates featuring the Virgin Mary holding Jesus both as an infant and as a recently crucified adult.

The fluorescents flickered and sputtered overhead as we turned a corner, found a row of soccer paraphernalia. More commemorative plates, this time featuring a green, white, and red crest adorned with the word *Italia*. Another plate advised *Keep Calm and Call an Italian*.

Farther down the row we moved into the Irish neighborhood, featuring signs that warned *Irish Parking Only*; green-white-and-orange commemorative plates; and shirts that advised *Keep Calm and Kiss an Irishman*.

The international pattern continued as we moved down the aisles with Brazil, followed by Spain, Argentina, and Greece.

"Everybody but the Chinese," Mel said.

"The cobbler's kids get no shoes."

Xiong Shoushan turned the corner at the end of the row, raising a gun. I spun and pushed Mel to the ground, covering her as Xiong fired. The bullet ricocheted off a shelf next to my ear. Xiong fired again.

Mel shouted, "Get off me!"

I rolled off. Mel produced a gun, sat up, and aimed down the row, but Xiong was gone, his footsteps echoing down the warehouse.

Mel stood. "Stay here." She started off down the row.

I stood, followed.

"What are you doing?" she said.

"Following you," I said.

"I said to stay."

We had reached the end of the row. Mel peeked around. Gunshots rang out, echoing across the concrete flooring. The bullets hit a box of commemorative Bruins plates, showering us with black and gold shards of ceramic.

Mel squeezed off several shots and ran off to another row of tchotchkes, leaving me behind. More shots from Xiong and more

173

plate shattering convinced me to move to a safer spot. I ran back down the row, away from the gunfire. Heard more shots from Mel, a pause, more shots from Xiong. The back doors rattled, Jael trying to get in. The doors held.

I ran along the rows peeking down each one, looking for Mel. Saw her across the way, leaning out to fire at something. I continued to run down the warehouse, peeking into the rows. Saw what I had hoped to see: Xiong standing at the end of the row, looking toward Mel, firing his gun. I'd have only one chance.

I looked around for a weapon. I'd moved from the international portion of the warehouse to the Boston Sports section, and had landed right in Red Sox Land. I saw the box I needed, slipped my hand inside, and pulled out my weapon of choice: a Red Sox baseball bat the size of a police baton.

Xiong started firing another volley at Mel. I took the opportunity to attack while he was distracted by aiming his shots, came up behind him, and brought my tiny baseball bat down on his head.

Turns out that physics matters. A tiny wooden baseball bat, no matter how fiercely wielded, is not going to knock a guy out. It pissed him off instead. The wood clacked off Xiong's head, then bounced off his shoulder. He swore in Chinese, turned, and hit me across the face with his gun.

Right in my stitches.

Metal gun, one; wooden stick, zero.

I reeled, saw him turning to shoot. The gun fired, but missed. I decided poking people with a wooden stick would be more effective than hitting them, so I poked at Xiong's face. He dodged, grabbed the bat out of my hand, raised his gun, and crashed to the floor as Mel landed on his back.

I sat on his head while Mel applied the handcuffs.

THIRTY-SIX

DESPITE BEING A VISITOR to our country, Xiong Shoushan had shown a firm grasp of our laws and customs.

"Lawyer," he had said as Mel hauled him to his feet, and then he spoke no more.

Now, Mel, Jael, and I sat in an FBI conference room, the whiteboard a scribble of box-containing ideas and multicolored connections.

Bobby walked in on us, looked at the whiteboard, and said, "No luck, eh?"

"Why would you say that?"

Bobby pointed at one box labeled *Xiong* and the other box labeled *Senator Video* and then the whiteboard between them. "I don't see any lines connecting these two."

Mel crossed her arms. "We're working on that."

"There is one connection," I said. I stood, picked up a purple marker, checked that it was actually erasable, and started drawing in the white space between the boxes.

Bobby said, "Is that supposed to be you?"

Mel said, "It looks like a constipated monkey."

Jael said, "No, it is definitely him. A monkey does not wear a Red Sox hat."

"Yes, it's me!"

"It's always about you," said Bobby.

"I visit the senator and I immediately have Xiong threatening me? That's the link."

"How did he know you were working for the senator?"

"Surveillance," said Jael. "It makes sense to be watching the lobby."

"And Pat greeted us in the lobby," I said.

"Exactly."

"What about Peter?" said Bobby. "He's the one who stole the video."

Mel said, "We're not so sure about that."

"What are you talking about? We traced the hack to his computer."

"Now that we've got access to Peter's computer, we scanned it and—"

"It didn't have the video."

"If you would let me finish," said Mel. "It had some pretty nasty malware on it."

"Nasty how?"

"Nasty enough to turn it into a zombie."

"Zombie?" asked Bobby.

"Yes," said Mel.

"What are you talking about?"

"Somebody else was controlling Peter's computer," I said.

"When he hacked your niece's Facebook account?" asked Bobby.

"Cousin," I said. "And no, he did that on his own."

"Then when?"

Mel got up and walked to the whiteboard. Drew a passable desktop computer, then a lightning bolt to another computer. Then she drew an angry-faced stick figure sitting at the other computer. "Somebody could have used Peter's computer to hack the senator."

"Could have used?" asked Bobby.

"There's no way to tell," I said. "It would look exactly as if Peter were typing."

"Wouldn't Peter have seen that happening?"

"Not necessarily. He could have been sleeping, or their system might have created another KVM set and used that."

"Exactly," said Mel.

"KVM?" asked Bobby.

"Keyboard, video, mouse," I answered.

"You couldn't just say that?"

"Who's got the time?"

Bobby walked to the whiteboard, drew a remarkable likeness of Peter between the senator and Xiong.

"Wow, you can draw," I said. "Who knew?"

"I dabbled in cartooning."

"Look at you with the layers," I said. "You're like a huge onion."

"I think Peter may be the real link between Xiong and the senator." He drew a dotted line from me to Peter. "You just stuck your nose in here and got entangled."

"I stuck my nose in because Peter hacked my cousin."

"Yeah, well, whatever reason you had, you became part of Xiong's problem."

"What problem?"

Jael said, "He needs to protect the video to keep the pressure on the senator."

"There you go," said Bobby. "Jael understands it."

Not a surprise. Jael's previous job was with Mossad.

I said to Jael, "That makes no sense."

"Why?"

"There was no way for Xiong to know I was after Peter."

"Unless somebody told him," said Jael.

Silence settled across the conference room as each of us wrestled with the implications.

Mel stood, walked over to Bobby's drawing of Peter, added a squiggly line at the neck in red marker, and a single drop of blood.

"Eww," I said.

"None of this explains Peter's murder. If Xiong wanted to keep Peter quiet, he'd just shoot him. Why cut off his head, and why put it on 4chan?"

I sat back and looked at the whiteboard. I imagined sliding around the boxes, the lines, and the remarkably accurate drawing of Peter, mentally reconnecting them, grouping them, ungrouping them. There was still something missing. I stood and added something to the board: @PwnSec

"I had forgotten about them," said Mel.

"They're the loose end," I said.

"How do you mean?"

"Peter's dead. Xiong's not talking. The senator doesn't know anything. All we've got is that PwnSec is clearly upset at me about Peter. Peter was one of theirs. They give us a place to start."

"Some more doxing?"

"Yeah," I said. "I've got a plan. Got to do a little coding."

"Can I help?" said Mel.

"You mean like team coding?"

"Yeah, I can help catch your typos."

Did I want a pretty woman watch me do what I did best? It turned out that yes, yes, I did want a pretty woman to watch me do what I did best. Also, I remembered one of Jael's rules.

"Isn't this Shabbat?" I asked her.

"Yes. It started a half an hour ago."

"Shabbat?" asked Mel.

"Jael doesn't work Saturdays."

Mel's eyes widened. "Oh … "

"So it's just you and me."

Bobby said, "You two need to get a room."

I said, "And a computer. And maybe even some pizza."

THIRTY-SEVEN

THE UBER DRIVER DROPPED Mel and me off at the head of Follen Street. It turned out that my wish for pizza had been answered by the pizza gods. A pizza truck sat in front of my condo, the driver standing on my front steps staring up at the building.

I called out, "Can I help you?"

"I'm looking for this guy named Aloysius Tucker."

"What for?"

"He ordered pizza."

"No, I didn't."

"So you *are* him. Help me with these."

The pizza guy waddled around to the back of his SUV, raised the lift gate, and looked up at me. "C'mon, they're getting cold."

"What's getting cold?" I asked.

"Your pizzas."

I peered into the SUV. Pizza boxes filled every available spot. The pizza guy said, "There you go, twenty-five, assorted."

"Twenty-five pizzas?"

"Yeah. Just like you ordered."

"I didn't order twenty-five pizzas. I wasn't even home."

The pizza guy cocked an eyebrow. "Don't even."

"What do you mean, 'Don't even'? I didn't order these."

"You know I could have you arrested."

"For what?"

"Wire crime."

"Wire fraud," said Mel.

"Yeah, that one."

"I didn't order these pizzas," I said.

"We got your name. We got your phone number."

"So does everybody. I'm in the book. Do you have a credit card number?"

"No. You're supposed to pay now."

"I'm sorry, dude, you've been punked."

"What?" said the pizza guy.

"It was a joke," I said.

"I'm not laughing."

"Neither am I, but I guarantee the guy who ordered the pizza is. He's having a good time telling his buddies about how he found a pizza place that would take an order for twenty-five pizzas without even asking for a credit card. They must have looked for days."

The pizza guy slammed his hand on the side of the SUV.

"So what? I'm out the fucking money?" Then to Mel. "Can he do that?"

"Technically—" said Mel.

I said. "I didn't order the pizzas. Why would I order twenty-five pizzas? They don't even fit in my condo."

The pizza guy said, "Goddamn it! Goddamn it! Goddamn it!"

"I'm sorry."

"That's twenty-five bucks down the fucking drain!"

"What twenty-five bucks?"

"Ingredients."

"You only put a buck's worth of ingredients in a whole pizza?"
The pizzameister crossed his arms. "We buy in volume."
"What do you buy in volume? How much volume can that be?"
"Plenty of volume."
"Oh my God. How much was this order?"
The guy consulted a long slip of paper. "It's $317.25."
"Hell of a profit."
"There's overhead."
"I'll bet."
The pizza guy flipped me off, lowered the SUV gate, waddled back to the driver's side, and hoisted himself in. "Where's the police when you need them?" he said to Mel.

Mel said, "Right here. I could arrest him if you want, but it won't get you paid."

Pizza guy started his engine. "Motherfucker, shit," he said, and started to roll the SUV down the street.

I ran after the van. "Hey, wait!"

He stopped, glared at me. "Yeah?"

"You know the homeless shelter on Columbia Ave?"

"Yeah?"

I pulled out my credit card. "I'll buy them. You deliver them there."

"You got it!"

I opened the SUV back, grabbed a pizza, and let the SUV head off.

Mel said, "That was really nice."

"Seemed a shame to waste twenty-five dollars' worth of ingredients."

As Mel and I climbed the steps to my condo, I did a mental sweep of my housekeeping. Dishes in the sink? No. I cleaned those. Underwear on the floor? Maybe. Keep her out of the bedroom. General clutter and the like? No. I don't allow general clutter and the like.

I opened the door to my apartment and glanced around. All was as I had hoped, ready for company. I tossed the pizza on the kitchen nook counter, grabbed out a couple of plates, and placed 12 cents of ingredients on each plate. Needed something to wash it down.

"Coffee, tea, wine, whiskey, beer?" I asked.

"Do you have water?"

"Water?"

"You know, to drink."

"Blech ... I guess."

I ran the tap, let it get cold, filled a glass for Mel and one for myself.

"You don't have to drink water," said Mel.

"Better than letting you drink alone," I said. "Plus, I can also have a beer. Either way, we have some coding to do."

I sat next to Mel, opened the laptop, and opened Twitter.

I searched Twitter for #TuckerGate, and scrolled through the results. Each insult felt like a little punch in the gut.

`...murder...`

`...rapist...`

`...mastermind...`

`...criminal...`

`...mafia kingpin...`

The last one made me laugh.

"What?" asked Mel.

"Kingpin? Who even says that anymore?"

I did a search for *pizza* and found this:

`@PwnSec: Pizza Party at @TuckerInBoston's house.` Then my address.

"You should tell them what you did with the pizza," said Mel.

"Can't."

"Can't?"

"I promised my lawyer I wouldn't tweet. Besides, it would only encourage them."

The doorbell rang. I went to the intercom and pressed the button.

"Pizza! Pizza!" someone yelled into it, then snickered.

I ran to the front window, saw two figures bolting down the street. *Idiots.*

"Pizza, pizza, my ass," I said. "Let's dox these bastards."

THIRTY-EIGHT

THE GREAT HALL OF Geek Fantasies has many rooms. There is the "I am Actually a Wizard" Pavilion, the "I Wrote a Million-Dollar App" Gallery, and the "I Won the Video-Game Tournament" Alcove. But place of pride, largely because it is the only one that could really happen, goes to the "I'm Eating Pizza and Coding While a Sexy Person Watches" Rotunda.

Sitting in my kitchen with an open laptop, a box of pizza, and Mel by my side should have been a high point in my life. The incarnation of my fondest fantasies.

It wasn't working out that way.

"You misspelled *tweet*," said Mel.

"Thanks." I fixed it and tried to remember what I was doing.

Mel and I had scoured Twitter and had seen that PwnSec tweeted a lot. The tweets all had a similar ring to them, telling me that they were being written by one person. While many people liked the tweets, there was definitely a recurring set of names who almost always had something to say about them. This gave me a plan.

Most people are under the impression that Twitter, Facebook, and other social-media companies consider users to be their customers,

185

and that these companies provide wonderful means of sharing pictures of one's lunch in order to better the world, or at least in order to better the lives of their users.

I imagine that pigs on a farm see it the same way. They lounge about all day, comparing the quality of today's slop to yesterday's slop, complaining that the barn was pretty drafty last night, and generally acting as if they are the farmer's customers. But of course, they are not. They are the product. And so are we.

Social media allows those with the right tools access to information that could only be guessed at by the Mad Men of the 1960s. Whereas those guys were forced to hold focus groups, send out surveys, and rely upon the genius of guys like Don Draper to suss out the great trends in the market, today's Mad Men can go to Facebook or Twitter and extract a detailed and extensive web of information about who influences whom, who talks together, and how they feel.

Doing all this requires that programmers be able to access the data on a social-media site, and it was that data that I was going to access tonight. My plan was simple. Gather up the @PwnSec announcements, see who liked them the most, and work from there.

But Mel was getting in the way.

The first problem was not her fault. It was mine. I was unaccustomed to having a pretty woman in my condominium, and I'd never had one there who could understand the code I was writing. The caveman part of my brain grunted in approval.

Tucker write program. Tucker get woman.

The problem with the lower part of your brain is that even though you know it's an idiot, you can't keep it from coloring the way you see the world. In my case, an insistent hum of sexual distraction caused the typos that Mel caught.

The second problem was, perhaps, Mel's fault. She had an uncanny ability to ask me a question just as I was getting a clear picture of what I needed to do next in my program. I'd get the picture, then

Mel would ask "What if we did it this way?" and then my plan would be gone.

"You know," I said. "I'm not making much progress. I'm pretty beat. It's bedtime."

"I knew this would happen," said Mel. "I just knew it."

"Just knew what?"

"This always happens. Typical guy."

"Don't flatter yourself. I wasn't inviting you to bed with me."

"Inviting me to bed? I didn't think you were inviting me to bed. Eww."

"Eww? What were you talking about, then?"

Mel pointed at the two empty beer bottles. "You're too drunk to code."

"That's what always happens?"

Mel stood, grabbing her jacket. "That's what always happens when guys drink and code. They get sleepy, then sloppy, then they poop out."

She headed for the front door and turned. "Give me a call tomorrow after you've gotten some sleep." The door clicked shut behind her.

The caveman in my brain was not pleased, not one little bit.

Write code! Show her!

And so I did. Unencumbered by "teamwork," I was able to crank out a program that catalogued all the PwnSec tweets, the tweets of those who liked those tweets, and the network of followers that surrounded the whole thing. It became clear that there were four people who really cared about PwnSec: @Runway aka Peter aka the headless hacker, @Eliza, @Tron, and @NotAGirl.

All four aliases followed @PwnSec and followed each other. They liked or commented on almost every PwnSec thread, except for @Eliza, whose own tweets read remarkably like PwnSec tweets, making it pretty clear that @Eliza was the author.

Now to do some doxing.

Having a nickname on the Internet forces one to choose between fame and privacy. If you want identity, then the best thing to do is to use the same nickname on Twitter, Facebook, and the Internet Relay Chat. That way, people who meet you in one place can find you in other places. If you want privacy, however, you use different nicknames in different places, and never engage in cross-channel communication.

The PwnSec nicknames broke all these rules. These kids were definitely in it for the fame. Some Googling showed their names all over the place, and as Peter had learned, it's almost impossible to have that much cross-communication without having someone make a mistake. I doxed them all. They all lived in and around Boston.

Tomorrow, they'd be getting a visit.

THIRTY-NINE

IN THE 1880s HENRY Whitney, owner of all the land along Beacon Street, had a dream: a dream of a day when trollies would carry commuters to his land and jack up his property values.

He also owned a trolley company.

The West End Railway ran tracks and horse-drawn trollies out to Cleveland Circle, making Beacon Street one of the nineteenth century's hottest properties.

Today, Henry Whitney's goldmine is named the C branch of the Green Line. I sat in an electric trolley, watching workers put up barricades in preparation for the Boston Marathon. For the most part, the Marathon runs down Commonwealth Ave, but at Cleveland Circle it shifts to Beacon Street, bisecting the city into those who are on this side of the Marathon and those who are on that side of the Marathon. Bostonians choose their side carefully, because they're stuck there for several hours.

The trolley stopped, let some people on, started again. I thought back to last night when I had completely doxed PwnSec through a combination of Twitter programming, Googling, and a little social engineering (trickery) on the IRC.

There had been four people in PwnSec: Peter Olinsky (Runway), Russell Nguyen (Eliza), Earl Clary (Tron), and Dorothy Flores (NotAGirl). So NotAGirl was, in fact, a girl, a counterexample to the Internet adage "There are no girls on the Internet." And I was on my way to visit her.

The trolley rattled its way to the end of the line, Cleveland Circle. I hopped off the train and looked around for Dorothy's house. There is, in fact, no circle at Cleveland Circle. There are ball fields, a trolley depot, a CVS, and a strip mall consisting of a series of single-story restaurants, hair salons, banks, and hardware stores, but no circle.

The single-story nature of the strip mall ended at the corner where somebody had built a convenience store in front of a three-story brownstone. The now-entombed brownstone loomed over the convenience store's shoulder like an older brother ready to take on a bully. My doxing efforts told me that Dorothy "NotAGirl" Flores lived in the looming brownstone.

I ducked down in a gap next to the convenience store, ran up the steps, and tried the door. Locked. I rang the first-floor bell, and got a buzzing in return. The hallway had the utilitarian, painted-over look of housing for young people—kids who have yet to be convinced that a tastefully appointed entryway is the essence of happiness. I headed up the steps. Dorothy lived on the third floor. Someone opened their apartment to see who had buzzed.

"Sorry," I called down. "Wrong button."

Dorothy's apartment door stood at the top of the steps. I knocked. Waited. No answer. Knocked again. Heard a woman: "Just a minute!"

The door opened and a petite girl wearing jeans and an apparently ironic Styx T-shirt stood before me: straight black hair, olive skin, almond eyes, and a silver septum ring whose barbells stuck out of her nostrils like two mercury snots. The sparkling nostrils caught my eye.

"Can I help you?" she asked.

"Are you Dorothy Flores?"

"Yes."

I took a step in, stuck out my hand. "Hi. I'm Aloysius Tucker."

Dorothy screamed an ear-shattering scream, reached down next to the door, grabbed a wooden baseball bat and took a swing at me. She had excellent form. The bat smacked into my ribs, shooting pain through my side and dropping me to one knee.

"Stay away from me!" she yelled, and raised the bat over her head in what would definitely be the coup de grâce.

I decided to reason with her. "What the fuck?" I said, raising my hand to block the bat if it came down.

"You stay away from me!" Dorothy repeated.

"Stay away from me, you psycho!" I said, the pain in my ribs destroying any shreds of diplomacy.

Dorothy lowered the bat, kept it ready. "I'm not a psycho."

I pressed my hand into my side, winced. "My ribs say you are."

"You killed Peter! Now you've come for me!"

A frail voice called out from the back room. "Dorothy? Dorothy, what's the matter?"

Dorothy said nothing.

"Should I call the police?"

Dorothy looked at me. I said, "I don't care. Call them. You're the one with the bat."

"You're the killer."

"Dorothy?" the voice called. "I want to get into my chair."

I made an *it's your call* gesture. "I was going to warn you, but now I'm not so interested."

Dorothy looked from me to the voice in the back and back. "I'll help you in a minute, Auntie," she called. Then to me she said, "You need to leave."

I got to my feet. "Fine. Don't blame me when the FBI surprises you and I'm not there to help."

Dorothy said, "After today, you're not going to be helping anybody."

"What's that supposed to mean?"

"Just get out."

I got out. Reached the street, gingerly touched my ribs. Just a bruise. Still hurt. Went across the street to the CVS next to Mary Ann's Bar, bought some Advil, and stood in the street.

I had kept my PwnSec doxing to myself in hopes that I could use its secrecy as leverage with Dorothy. That didn't work out. Dorothy had drunk all the Internet Kool-Aid when it came to me. So the next step was to share what I knew and see where that got me.

I called Mel. Told her what I had.

"Meet me for coffee," said Mel.

"Sure. Where?"

"The 7 Pond Coffee Bar."

"Where is that?"

"Um ... 7 Pond Street?"

"Smart-ass."

"Smarter, anyway."

I closed the call and put in a request for an Uber. It was time to stop messing around with PwnSec and get some help. Dorothy said that something was supposed to happen today. I didn't like the sound of that.

FORTY

A TESLA SPORTING AN Uber windshield ornament glided to the curb with battery-powered silence. I pulled open the passenger door. Checked out the driver. Fat face, fat stomach, fat legs, and fat stubby arms. The guy filled the seat the way pudding fills a bowl.

"Mind if I sit in the front seat?"

"What is your name, sir?"

"Aloysius Tucker."

"Then come on in."

I climbed in. The Tesla slid off down Beacon Street, took a right at Dean, and lost itself in a warren of residential housing.

I said, "You don't see many Teslas doing Uber."

"Are you *the* Aloysius Tucker?" the driver asked.

Uh-oh.

"You mean *the* as in 'the famous Aloysius Tucker' or as in 'the infamous Aloysius Tucker'? Because if it's the second one then no, I'm not me."

"You're the guy they're talking about on the #TuckerGate hash, right?"

"And you are?"

"Derrick James. On Twitter I'm @BosUberTesla."

I treaded carefully. "And how are things on Twitter?"

"Did you really slap that guy on the head?"

"Yes." I opened my Twitter app, searched for @BosUberTesla.

"I don't think it's right to slap people."

"I don't think it's right to insult women. Ah, here you are," I read from the app: "'Tucker is just a dumb asshole.'"

Derrick's fat face flushed red.

"I'm a dumb asshole?"

"I didn't mean it that way."

"Really? How else does one mean 'Tucker is just a dumb asshole'?"

"I was defending you."

"You were defending me? Let's see. What else did you have to say in my defense? Oh, here's one. 'If that dumb fuck tried to slap me I'd beat the shit out of him.'"

Derrick's blush started to fog the windows. "I was angry because—"

"You were angry? Why? Did you have some dick try to handcuff you?"

"No, but—"

"Did he call your friend the C-word?"

"No, but—"

"Should I keep reading? Did you have other things to say about me?"

Derrick kept his eyes on the road.

I flipped through Derrick's comments. Found a good one. "You called me a 'motherless son of a bitch.' That doesn't even make sense. I should give you a one-star rating for slaughtering logic."

Derrick whispered a comment.

"What? I couldn't hear you. But, you know, I'm just a dumb asshole. Probably deaf too."

"I'm sorry," Derrick said, barely audible above the nearly silent electric motor.

"You're sorry? You're sorry for what?"

"I'm sorry I called you those things. But—"

"Everything before the *but* is bullshit, Derrick."

"I mean, I said those things but I was defending you. Can't you see that?"

"You mean when you wrote, 'You guys should take it easy on Tucker, the poor motherless son of a bitch.'"

"Yeah. I mean, they're not being fair."

"I'll give you that."

"So I was defending you up and down, and then you slapped that guy and I looked like an idiot."

"Why are you even defending me at all?"

Derrick negotiated a rotary at Chestnut and drove between stone walls separating the road from a park. The brown grass and leafless trees of the Emerald Necklace in April did nothing to suggest that spring was on its way. The Tesla's tires made the only noise in the car.

"I don't understand," said Derrick.

"What don't you understand?"

"Why wouldn't I defend you? People are being stupid."

"How is this your problem?"

"I don't know. I just like Twitter."

"So I'm just an online character to you?"

Derrick tightened his lips and tapped the giant Tesla touchpad with fat fingers. Soft jazz slipped from the speakers. Apparently, we were done talking. As Derrick popped out onto the Jamaicaway, I realized what a disappointment I'd been. Derrick had been excited to meet his Internet hero, the guy he'd been defending against hoards of misinformed trolls, and that hero had just turned out to be a gigantic douche bag.

"Thank you," I said.

Derrick flicked his thumb. The music got a little louder.

"Thank you for defending me," I said. "I'm sorry I was a jerk to you."

"You should have read the whole thread."

"I know."

"Instead of just taking things out of context and looking for the bad stuff."

"I know," I said. "I'm sorry."

"Don't worry about it."

More jazz. I tried a different tactic. "Do you mind if I ask what you do for a living?"

"You mean so that I can afford a Tesla?"

"Yeah."

"I wrote an app."

"Which one?"

"Dumpster."

"The one that finds the nearest public bathroom?"

"Yeah."

"That's a pretty cool app."

"Yeah, I made a ton in royalties to start, then I sold the whole thing to Google."

"So then why are you doing Uber?"

"I like to drive."

"That's cool."

Traffic clogged at a light.

"So what are they saying?" I asked.

"Who?"

"The Twitter people on #TuckerGate."

"There are three camps. First, there are the people like me and Epomis who say that you're innocent."

"Epomis? That's sweet."

"You know her?"

Whoops. "Just online."

"Yeah, so she's one of the folks defending you. Then there's the people who say that you killed Runway. They say you're the HackMaster."

"Who's the HackMaster?"

"Some guys on Reddit did analysis of the pictures of Runway. They had a long, technical reason for why it had to have been done with a samurai sword. So they called the killer the Samurai."

"Why not the Ninja? They're assassins too."

"Right? That's what I said. There was another group arguing for the Shinobi, because that's Japanese for *ninja*, and it was disrespectful not to use the Japanese word. Then someone accused everyone of cultural appropriation, so they dropped the whole samurai thing and—"

"By the power of the collective intelligence settled on the Hack-Master."

"Yeah."

"Why does the collective intelligence think that I'm the Hack-Master? There's no connection to me."

"That's what I said! No one has ever shown that you can use a sword."

"That's because I can't."

"Right."

"You said there were three groups."

"The third group says that you're not the HackMaster, but that you did kill your wife."

"Why would I do that?"

"For the money. I guess you got a lot of money from your old company?"

"They say that I killed my wife for a severance package?"

"Yeah, and the FBI helped."

"Why would the FBI help?"

"It was a lot of money."

"So now I'm paying off the FBI?"

"You have to admit that you have friends in the FBI."

I didn't mention that I was heading to coffee with my friend from the FBI. "This is ridiculous," I said.

197

"When you spin it all together, it creates a pretty good case."

"So you're on their side?"

"No! No! I never would have picked you up otherwise. Are you kidding me?"

Derrick parked on Pond, across the street from a little coffee bar. Mel sat in the front window at a counter. She waved.

I opened the door to get out. "So what do you think?"

"I think she's cute."

"No, I mean about #TuckerGate."

"I think you're innocent, but—"

"But?"

"I also think you're screwed."

FORTY-ONE

THE CHOICE OF A favorite coffee shop may not be one of life's most significant decisions. Still, it should not be taken lightly. Whether you go for the Old World ambiance of a Caffe Vittoria, the subterranean coolness of Wired Puppy, or the Boylston Street bustle of the Thinking Cup, you're choosing a place that becomes both your refuge and your office, your kitchen and your den. It's a place to meet friends, read a book, cruise the Internet, and, sometimes, drink some coffee.

I admired Mel's choice of 7 Pond Coffee Bar as her coffee shop. Like Caffe Vittoria, it sported big glass windows that made you part of the street scene while letting you watch it from climate-conditioned comfort. While Caffe Vittoria looked out onto the tight, bustling confines of Hanover Street, Mel's seat in 7 Pond let her look out upon the quiet residential foot traffic associated with two stately triple-deckers, plus a glimpse of the action on Centre Street. Nicely done!

I got myself a double espresso and made myself comfortable on the stool Mel had saved for me.

"So, Mr. Doxer," said Mel, "you have news?"

"News and a bruise."

"A bruise?"

I pulled up my shirt. "Baseball bat."

"Who did that?"

"Dorothy Flores, but you know her as NotAGirl."

"NotAGirl is a girl?"

"Pretty clever."

"When did she hit you with a baseball bat?"

"Right after I introduced myself at her front door."

Mel gave me a twisted frown and drank some cappuccino, the heart shape in the foam getting distorted by her lips. "You introduced yourself at her front door?"

"Yup."

"Why didn't you call me first?"

"The idea was that I'd threaten to contact you if she didn't talk to me."

"You could have done that after talking to me."

"Not with a straight face."

"So she beat you with a bat, and now you're talking to me."

"I think I would have gotten beaten even if I had talked to you first. She was terrified. I think they really believe what they're writing."

"Who?"

"The PwnSec trio. There's Dorothy, then Russell Nguyen who goes by the name Eliza, and Earl Clary, who is Tron."

"Good work."

"I'm not sure how this helps us find the senator's video."

We drank our coffee and looked out upon the quiet pedestrian traffic. Mel started to say something, stopped, started again, stopped.

"Sox won," I said, trying to break the ice. "We're nine and three."

"Is that good?"

"Pennant fever grips Hub."

"Huh." Mel was miles away.

"You might as well tell me."

"I'm not supposed to."

"I'll find out anyway. I'm Master Doxer, remember."

"Mr. Doxer, not Master Doxer."

"I can't be both?"

"We've found something on Peter's computer."

"The senator's video?"

"No. A selfie of a topless Asian girl with a shoe on her head."

"Why is that important? Peter was twenty-two years old. That computer must have been choked with porn."

"Less than you'd think. This was the only picture."

"What was special about it? Other than it was evidence of a life hack."

"Yeah, I got that. Peter must have been tormenting the girl and forced her to take the shoe-on-her-head picture to get him to back off."

"A classic hacker move. Was there anything special about it?"

"Two things. First, it was not in our database of porn. That means it was a one-off, a picture someone took themselves."

"That makes sense. Selfies wouldn't be in the database."

"And it contained the malware."

"The zombie malware?"

"Right."

My espresso was empty. I got up from our nook and bought another. Looked back at Mel, who was sitting on her stool and scrolling through her phone, looking concerned. She was objectively a pretty girl who knew how to wear a pair of jeans. I pushed down thoughts of dating a twentysomething, then realized that E was probably a twentysomething. It didn't matter, anyway. Mel and I were working together. No sense complicating that.

I climbed back onto the stool next to Mel. My phone rang. It was E.

"Have you seen Anonops?" she asked.

"No."

"They're planning something at your house."

Mel interrupted. "Have you seen this?" she asked, pointing at her phone.

"Who's there?" asked E.

"Just a friend."

Mel gave me a look that said *just a friend? Where did that come from? She's not just a friend?*

I said into the phone, "Thanks for the heads-up. I see it now."

"Be careful," said E.

"I will." Ended the call.

Mel said, "Is she also just a friend?"

"We only met yesterday."

"And?"

A gentleman never tells.

"She says something's up with Anonymous."

"Something is up with Anonymous. They're staging a big protest in Boston today."

"Let me guess. Going to the Federal Reserve to protest their student loans?"

"Those student loans are no joke."

"Okay, fine."

"I'm up to my butt in student loans."

I resisted the urge to look at Mel's butt. Resisted the urge to make a smart comment about student loans. Apparently one gets wily in his thirties, and becomes the master of tact.

"So what are they protesting?"

"They say they have a hundred people."

"A hundred people protesting what?"

"You."

FORTY-TWO

THERE IS SOMETHING PARADOXICAL about walking the streets of Boston wearing a good coat of face paint. On the one hand, you get a lot of attention. People look at you as their lizard brains note that something is amiss, and they swivel their heads at you. On the other hand, you get ignored. People immediately avert their eyes and not one of them could give an accurate description of what you look like.

What did he look like?

He looked like a guy with face paint.

I had left Mel and headed up Newbury Street to a little shop I'd never expected to visit, Back Bay Body Painting and Tattoo. You know that a trend has gone upscale when it reaches Newbury Street.

I stepped through the door, greeted the owner. "I need a face painting."

He pushed a catalog toward me. "Anything in particular?"

I flipped a page or two, found what I wanted, pointed.

"That's cool. Good choice!"

I left, walking down Newbury, and had gotten almost to St. Botolph before I saw my first Guy Fawkes. Or he would soon be a Guy Fawkes, because he had his mask lifted onto his forehead as he

walked. Like everyone else, he glanced my way, but instead of averting his eyes he broke into a big smile.

"Dude, that is awesome!" he said, giving me the thumbs-up.

"Thanks," I said.

He fell into step next to me and we continued down Ring Road,
entering the South End. "I wish I'd thought of getting Guy Fawkes
face paint."

"Masks get sweaty."

"You got that right."

"Any idea how many anons will be there?" I asked.

"Naw, man. No telling. I mean, I think it's a lot. It's like an all handser."

"All handser?"

"All hands on deck. We're going to bring Tucker down."

"Finally!"

Guy stuck out his hand. "I'm Joe."

"Call me T."

"T like Tucker?"

"Unfortunate, right?"

"Man, that guy pisses me off. He's what's wrong with the world
today."

We turned onto St. Botolph and I could see trouble brewing two
blocks down, where a milling mob stood at the corner of my street.

"You better put on your mask."

"Yeah, let's do this thing," said Joe, sliding his mask into place.

The Guy Fawkes mask is the perfect tool for public protest.
Fawkes's curly mustache, plumb-line soul patch, and knowing eyebrows presented the face of a man who knew your secrets and found
them pathetic. Unlike the more traditional towel-over-the-face
mask worn by many protesters, a Guy Fawkes protester was clearly
identified as someone bent on justice with a side order of mischief.

There had to be over a hundred of them. The dead-end Follen Street turned into a protesters' courtyard as they spilled off the sidewalks and onto the road. I glanced nervously at handmade signs that shouted *JUSTICE FOR ALL, TUCKER KILLS*, and *WHY DO WE LET THIS MAN WALK AMONG US, THIS KILLER AND COR-RUPTOR?* This last sign had started in a large font, but eventually shrunk, finally crunching the word *corruptor* up against the lower right-hand corner. The messages on the signs didn't worry me as much as the wooden handles.

My Guy Fawkes face paint continued to get thumbs-up and rave reviews, except for one guy. A short guy in an emo-black outfit said, "You're supposed to wear a mask."

"Nobody can tell who I am."

"I can."

"Really?" I slipped around him, looking to get a straight shot run to my front door.

"Yeah, you're a douche bag."

"Hey, c'mon now."

"You look different from us."

"I look just like you."

"No, you definitely look different. The masks give us solidarity."

"Really. I thought we were Anonymous, not Solidarity."

"What?"

"I mean you took History of Protest in college, right? The cool kids all took it."

"There's no such class."

"Not cool enough, huh?"

"Fuck off, man."

I left him and milled around the protest. It was kind of like going to your own funeral and discovering that everybody hated you. Snatches of conversation had nothing good to say. Two Guy Fawkeses engaged in mask-muffled conversation.

"He's rich, you know."

"Yeah?"

"A one-percenter."

"I guess he made his money in tech, like with Uber or something?"

"Naw man, he extorted it from the place he worked."

"That's kind of cool."

"Cool? He killed his wife and blamed them."

"Holy shit!"

"He's a bad dude."

I thought about breaking in with a defense, but it would have been unwise.

Another Fawkes approached me. "Love the face paint," a female voice said from behind a mask.

"Thanks."

"This mask is hot."

I made a show of looking her up and down. "That's not the only thing."

"Don't be a pig."

"Little late for that advice."

She looked up at the houses. "I wonder which one is his."

"That one," I said, pointing. *Mr. Know-it-all, showing off for the ladies.*

"How do you know?" she asked.

"Um—I just know."

"Really."

"I'm going to go take a closer look." I left her behind, sauntered over to where anons had clustered in front of my door. Found the Guy Fawkes mask whose owner had the most leader-like bearing. Sporting a purple-tipped Mohawk, he stood shoulders back, arms akimbo, staring up at my windows.

"So what's the plan?" I asked.

"Plan?" Mohawk replied in a reedy voice.

"Yeah. You all came out here. What did you plan to do?"

"What do *we* plan to do?"

"Yeah."

"*We* plan to protest."

"What do you do if he comes out?"

"You keep doing that."

"What?"

"You keep saying *you*."

"Um."

"Like you're not part of all this."

"You all have masks. I forgot I had the face paint."

"So the face paint makes you different?"

"No, what I mean is—"

"Huh. Do you know what Tucker looks like?"

"Never seen him with my own eyes." *Mirrors don't count.*

"I do."

"Really."

"Yeah, guy around your height, your build, your hair color. Looks a lot like you."

"Lucky devil."

A commotion started up over the guy's shoulder. The woman had gathered a small crowd.

"That's him," she said, pointing.

The accusatory sound caused more heads to turn, then some bodies.

Mohawk asked, "Who?"

Like a fight in the grandstands, the commotion caused a ripple of attention. Heads turning, bodies moving, a tight circle of Guy Fawkes masks forming around the two of us.

Mohawk called out, "Hey, CapnMerica!"

The circle closed ranks. There would be no way to get to my front door without going through twenty anons. One of the Guy Fawkes protestors broke through into the circle.

Mohawk asked, "You recognize this guy?"

The Guy Fawkes protestor called CapnMerica peered at me, his mask jutting forward. "That's him! That's Tucker!"

Despite the mask, I could hear that CapnMerica was the guy who had tried to perform a citizen's arrest but instead got slapped for his potty mouth.

"I thought so," said Mohawk.

The circle around me tightened as the masks closed in. Voices rose.

"Suck my cock, Tucker!"

"Killer!"

A group launched into the Darryl Strawberry chant, "Tuuuck-errr, Tuuuck-errr, Tuuuck-errr." Another had a call and response going. "What do we want?" "Justice!" "When do we want it?" "Now!"

I called out to CapnMerica, "You going try your citizen's arrest again?"

He said, "Naw, man. You'd be right back on the streets."

"You are on my street."

The cacophony of individual taunts, chanting, and rehearsed rhyming grew in volume. But I had realized something. None of these people was going to break the circle. None of them was going to fight me. They were all signs and screaming, but I'd lived through worse. A lot worse.

I walked to the edge of the circle, up to a knot of masks. Stood erect, leaned forward a bit, looked into their eyes through their masks, said, "Excuse me." The group looked at each other, parted. I heard Mohawk over my shoulder.

"Hey, Tucker, you fucking pussy," he said.

I ignored him, stepped to the next group. "Excuse me." They too realized that they didn't want anything physical, stepped back. Mohawk was right behind me, keeping up a litany of insults: "pussy," "killer," "cocksucker," "rapist." I continued through the crowd, ignoring him, staring down group after group. I reached the front step, climbed it. Turned to look at the mob of angry-sounding masks. The "Tuuuck-errr" chant continued. Then another group picked up with "Jail! Jail! Jail! Jail!"

Mohawk stood on the sidewalk in front of me, raised his arms for silence. Got it. The crowd waited to see what would happen next.

Are you not entertained?

Mohawk called out, "Aloysius Tucker, you killed Runway!"

I figured I had nothing to lose. "I didn't kill anyone."

Someone in the crowd yelled, "Prove it! Prove you didn't kill them!"

The crowd picked up with "Prove it! Prove it! Prove it!"

I raised my arms. "I don't have to prove it. I'm telling you all I didn't do it!"

Mohawk pointed. "You did!"

I stepped away from my front door, stood behind Mohawk. The silence returned. Looked straight at Mohawk. Spoke quietly, so the crowd had to lean in.

"Are you calling me a liar?"

"Yeah," he said. "You're a fucking liar."

"That's enough!" I yelled and launched into Mohawk, driving my shoulder through his chest. He fell back, his head hitting the concrete with a thud with me on top of him. I grabbed the chin of his mask, ripped it off. Mohawk had an Asian face and frightened eyes. I slapped him and he started to cry.

Oh, a tough guy.

The mob was of three minds: fleeing, watching, or wading in. A group of five anons waded in, grabbing my arms and pulling me off Mohawk. I couldn't free my arms, so I kicked him in the leg. He cowered.

They dragged me back. One guy said, "That's enough! That's enough!"

A small anon in a skirt ran in front of me, pushed her hands onto my chest, and lifted her mask. E wrapped her arms around me, sobbing wet tears onto my chest. "Tucker! Tucker, stop."

Two anons knelt next to Mohawk and helped him up. They lifted their masks. One was Dorothy Flores.

"See?" said Dorothy. "This is why nobody likes you."

FORTY-THREE

SIRENS SOUNDED IN THE distance, causing anons to scatter like kids who'd broken a window. E released me, kissed my cheek.

I felt like a shit.

E tugged me toward my front door. "We should get off the street."

We single-filed up the steps to my apartment door. I unlocked the door, paused. The guy who had helped Mohawk up still wore his Guy Fawkes mask.

"Masks off in my house," I said.

"You have a mask," New Guy complained.

"I have face paint."

He pulled off the mask to reveal a thin, craggy face and buzz cut.

I opened the door, waved the procession into the condo. New Guy, E, Dorothy, and Mohawk clustered in the hallway, looking uncomfortable.

I stuck out my hand to Mohawk. "I'm sorry."

Mohawk sniffled, rubbed his nose, shook my hand.

I wiped my hand on my pants. "You need a tissue?"

He nodded.

I got a box of tissues, gave it to him. "By the way, I'm Tucker."

Mohawk looked at his shoes. "I know."

"Now you tell me your name," I said.

"Eliza."

"Your real name."

"You'll dox me."

"Already did. Your real name is Russell Nguyen."

"Hey..."

"You live on Clinton Street, near Dorothy."

"You suck!"

I turned to New Guy. "I'll bet you're Tron, and your real name is—"

"No, man, don't do it."

"Earl Clary."

"Dammit!"

"You live on Lambert Street in Cambridge."

Earl stamped his little foot. "What did you do that for?"

"You pissed me off."

Earl pointed at E. "Who's she?"

"She's E."

"Why didn't you dox her?"

"She didn't piss me off."

Blue and red lights flashed in the street as the police came to check out what had once been a public protest. The lights flashed through my front windows as the cops considered their next steps. If Lee was with them, their next step was likely to be to harass me.

"Think we'll get swatted?" asked Earl.

"Not with one police car," I said. "You want a beer?"

Nods all around.

I pulled out several bottles of Green Monsta IPA from a case I had bought on Opening Day. Handed beers around. "One for Dorothy, one for Russell, one for Earl, one for E."

Mostly doxed, we stood around my kitchenette drinking beers. The police lights disappeared. Despite my hospitality, I still felt like an asshole. A ragey asshole.

"I am sorry, Russell," I said. "I'm sorry I lost my shit."

"You can't go around hitting people," said Russell.

"You called me a liar."

Russell pouted.

"You stood right in front of me and called me a liar."

"But I thought—"

"Whatever you thought, you thought wrong."

"But you killed Peter!"

"I did *not* kill Peter. When are you going to get that into your head?"

So much for apologizing without reservation. The Internet was worming its way into my soul, turning me into as big a jerk as the rest of them. More silence. More beer drinking. I drained mine, opened another.

E said, "Russell, you need to learn to fight better if you're going to insult people in real life."

"Oh, you can fight?"

"I don't insult people in real life, but I could teach you some jiujitsu."

Dorothy asked, "What does E stand for?"

E tapped at her Samsung, didn't answer.

I said, "Epomis."

E gave me a dirty look.

"Hey, at least you're not doxed."

Dorothy said, "Epomis? I know you. You've been defending Tucker all over the place."

"I like Tucker."

"If you like him so much, why were you at the protest?"

"I thought he might need someone to dial 911. I was right."

I asked, "Who had the bright idea for this public protest?"

Earl said, "I don't know, man. The idea just came up in the Anon-ops chat room."

Russell said, "Everyone thought it was a great idea."

E said, "Ahem."

"Except for Epomis."

Dorothy said to me, "You needed to be stopped."

I lifted my shirt, showed her the bruise. "You almost did that with your baseball bat."

"That's what happens when a killer knocks on my door."

I said, "Stop. This whole #TuckerGate thing is bullshit that you guys made up before you started breathing your own air and thinking you had heard it somewhere else. I didn't kill my wife. I didn't kill Peter. And I'm not the HackMaster. I can't even use a sword."

Dorothy said, "We didn't make it up."

Russell said, "The evidence—"

"There is no evidence. There's a narrative. You made up a story and jammed in selected facts to fit. Where they didn't fit, you used coincidence and innuendo as mortar."

Silence from Russell.

"If anyone is owed an apology, it's me."

Silence from everyone.

"Can I get another beer, man?" asked Earl.

"Sure." I got him a beer, popped the top. Handed it to him. "You know, you guys are victims here as much as anyone."

"What do you mean?" asked Dorothy.

"Somebody framed you guys for a felony."

"What felony?"

"Phishing a US senator and stealing information from him." I wasn't going to tell them what kind of information.

"We didn't do that."

"The FBI thinks you did. They're closing in on you."

"How would you know?" asked Russell.

I gave him a significant look.

"You *are* in their pocket."

"I'm not in their pocket."

"They're in yours."

"Maybe we just work together sometimes."

"Like right now, you're setting us up."

"No, Russell, if I were setting you up you'd be in jail by now."

"So what do you want?" asked Dorothy.

What I wanted was to find the HackMaster. What I wanted was to clear my name. What I wanted was to get my life with Maria back to normal. What I wanted didn't seem to matter.

Still, I could use some help with all of that. I looked around at my ragtag group of hackers. Could I get four kids who lacked an instinct for teamwork and basic trust to help me catch a killer? Maybe, but what a shitty plan.

"We work together," I said. "We catch a killer."

FORTY-FOUR

RUSSELL LAUGHED, A HIGH-PITCHED braying that made me want to slap him again. Instead, I asked, "What's so funny?"

"That's fucking stupid!" he said.

"Thank you for sharing."

Dorothy said, "What do you mean we help you catch a killer? How would we know how to catch a killer?"

"This all started with Peter phishing the senator."

"I keep telling you that we had nothing to do with it."

"And I keep telling you—"

My phone rang. Mel. I told the group, "This is Special Agent Hunter from the FBI." I put her on speaker. "Special Agent Hunter, I'm here with PwnSec."

Mel said, "You mean Dorothy Flores, Russell Nguyen, and Earl Clary?"

Dorothy looked at me, wide-eyed with alarm. "You doxed us to the FBI!"

"You hit me with a baseball bat," I said.

"I'm glad I hit you with a baseball bat, you son of a bitch!"

"As you can hear, Agent Hunter, PwnSec and I are bonding."

"People just love you."

"It's a gift, really."

"Did you tell them about the malware?"

"What malware?" asked Earl.

I said, "The malware that somebody used to take over Peter's computer and phish the senator."

Mel said, "It came in a photo on Peter's computer. A photo of the Asian girl with the shoe on her head."

Earl had been one of several anons carrying a backpack. He dropped the backpack to the floor now and started rooting around in it.

"What picture of a girl with a shoe on her head?" asked Dorothy.

I said, "We don't know who she is. She's just topless with a shoe on her head."

"We think Peter got the picture doing a life ruin," said Mel.

Earl had opened his laptop. He tapped his fingers waiting for it to come up. "What does the malware do?"

"That's what Mel is going to tell us."

Mel said, "It took a while. The thing was pretty well hidden."

"What does it do?" Dorothy repeated.

"Like Tucker said, it takes over the computer," Mel said.

"You mean it makes it a zombie?"

"Not really," said Mel. "A zombie usually just runs some command that the zombie master sends. In this case the screen, keyboard, and mouse control all go to the computer running the malware."

"So they can control your computer?"

Earl had his laptop running and had pulled up a picture of a topless Asian girl with a shoe on her head.

"Earl's got the picture of the shoe-head girl," I told Mel.

"Where did you get that?" Dorothy asked him.

"Um," he said pointing at the phone. "The FBI's on the phone."

"Don't screw with me, Earl," said Mel. "You were doing a life ruin, weren't you?"

"Um."

"Dammit, Earl," said Dorothy. "We talked about this."

"Peter was doing it too. And Russell."

"None of you should have been doing it."

Earl sulked. "It was just for lulz."

"So Russell writes these manifestos about fighting the Patriarchy."

"That was your idea," said Russell.

"You went along, *Eliza*," said Dorothy. "And after all that bullshit you jokers go out and torment women."

"To be fair, this one's a bitch," said Earl.

"Yeah?" asked Dorothy. "How do you know?"

Earl said nothing.

"Let me guess. Some troll on 4chan told you that she wouldn't sleep with him."

"She led him on!" said Earl. "He had the e-mails."

Dorothy went over and looked at the picture. "Oh, and that's not creepy."

"C'mon—"

"Stalker!"

"Earl," said Mel through the phone.

"Yeah?"

"She isn't a real girl."

"Yeah she is!"

"Then why did Peter have the same picture?"

"We both life ruined her?"

"When you e-mailed with her, did she sound like someone else was life ruining her?"

"No, but—"

"Exactly," said Mel. "One other question. Do you have a camera on your computer?"

"Yeah," said Earl.

"Is the little green light next to the camera turned on?"

We all looked. The little green light glowed green.

I peered at the light, pointed. "Earl, look here."

Earl looked closely at the green LED. "What am I looking for?"

"Tucker, that was mean," said Mel.

"I think Earl deserved it."

"What am I looking for?"

"You're not looking for anything, Earl," said Mel. "The person who took over your computer is using the camera."

Earl slammed the laptop shut. "He can see me?"

"Yup," I said.

"And you got me to look into the camera!"

"You had been sitting in front of that camera for a while. I just provided a close-up."

"What about me?" asked Dorothy. "I looked at the picture."

"I think he's pretty much seen all of us," I said.

Earl shoved the laptop into his backpack. "It's the HackMaster. He's going to kill us!"

I said, "That's why you need to work with me to catch him."

"We can't do that," said Russell. "It will ruin our brand."

"Your brand?"

"People will say we're FBI stooges," said Dorothy.

Mel said, "It might be a little late for that."

"What do you mean?"

"Have you seen Twitter?"

I pulled up Twitter on my phone. #TuckerGate had exploded. The first tweets were links to multiple videos of me in my Guy Fawkes face paint beating up on Russell in his Guy Fawkes mask. I smacked Russell across his face, he screamed a whiny scream and beat his hands on my chest.

E said, "You've got pretty good form there, Russell. Ever consider a career in MMA?"

"Shut up," said Russell.

"What's that move? Screeching Fist of Death?"

"Ha!" said Earl. "You fight like a girl."

"Shut up!"

We moved on from the fight videos to videos showing the PwnSec trio entering my apartment with an associated tweet.

`@BruinFan3324: I knew @PwnSec was working with @TuckerInBoston! #TuckerGate`

"Shit," said Russell. "We're screwed."

Russell was right. The conspiracy theorists got themselves into full throat, explaining how PwnSec had been the perfect undercover operation.

"We've got to get out of here," said Dorothy.

"You've got to explain to them," said Earl to Russell.

"Explain what?"

E smirked, "Explain how you pwned yourselves."

The PwnSec trio grabbed up their stuff, headed for my front door with E in tow.

Dorothy said, "We are not helping you!"

"We're going to get you, man!" said Earl.

Earl opened the door, and the four of them left with E pausing to give me a wink before she shut the door behind her.

Mel said from the speakerphone, "What just happened?"

I picked up the phone, put it to my ear. "You cleared the room."

"I'm watching the YouTube videos of your fight again, and I have some advice for you."

"Yeah?"

"Wash the face paint off before you leave the house. You look like hacker Braveheart."

FORTY-FIVE

I SAT IN MY apartment, rubbing at my face paint and watching Twitter and the IRC.

It was a disaster.

Russell had already jumped back into the fray as Eliza, swearing up and down that PwnSec had been coerced into my apartment as part of an FBI plot to discredit them. Meanwhile Earl was on the IRC as Tron claiming the same thing. It was clearly a hastily conceived cover story, and the conspiracy theorists on Twitter and IRC recognized it as such immediately.

Still, I had to admit that they had some success. People who had been watching the tirade against PwnSec came to their defense right after Eliza and Tron gave them something to say. Each side was now proceeding to hammer home their talking points in a crescendo of ire. They could both agree on only one thing: that I was a menace, that I needed to be stopped, and that the Anonymous collective was just the collective to do it.

Of course, that raised the question about what "stopped" meant. I'd known people—Xiong Shoushan, for example—who equated "stopped" with "killed." I was pretty sure that Anonymous had never killed anybody, despite the constant death threats. Still, we lived in a time where boundaries were being broken every day.

I looked at my phone, considered calling Jael. Decided to respect her Sabbath. I should be able to go one day without someone killing me. I could just stay in the house, let things calm down, and think things through.

I went to the fridge, grabbed another beer. Sat at my kitchen counter. Looked at Click and Clack.

"Well, boys, this is another fine mess you've gotten me into."

Click and Clack disavowed all responsibility by scuttling onto their sponge. *We're going to eat our dinner and ignore you.*

"Question is, how are you guys going to get me out of it?"

I grabbed my laptop, watched the #TuckerGate Twitter feed splash vitriol for a bit, then closed the laptop. Time to think. Peter's computer had been taken over by someone else, probably someone else who used it when Peter wasn't looking to set up a phishing attack on the senator. It was perfect. You take over someone else's computer, run the attack as if you were that person, and intentionally leave breadcrumbs for the FBI to follow. While the FBI thinks they are cleverly outsmarting a hacker, they're really heading down a blind alley.

The video had downloaded onto Peter's laptop, but then the person must have moved it somewhere else, probably using anonymizing routers to block any pursuit. So Peter was a dead end, but another end had opened up.

Someone with Chinese interests at heart had threatened the senator and tried to influence his vote, and Xiong Shoushan and his dashboard Jesi company had surely been at the center of some sort of work in that direction. The right thing to do now was to pick up the trail with Xiong Distribution and Xiong himself and find out if he had the video and what it would take to keep it secret.

I yawned. The fight with Russell, the arguments in my house, the realization that we were being watched had all kept my adrenal glands pumping their magic juice into my bloodstream. Now it was just me, Click and Clack, and a beer. The adrenaline flow had stopped and the crash had begun.

I rubbed my face. Felt face paint. Needed a shower.

I stood in my bathroom, staring at my Guy Fawkes face paint in the mirror. I had to admit that it must have been terrifying for Russell to have this coming at him. Mel was right: I did look like hacker Braveheart.

The shower steamed as I stripped. I climbed in and washed my face until paint stopped running down the drain, then I washed the rest of me. Finally I stopped moving and just stood under the water, realizing that I—

The bathroom door jiggled. Somebody had bumped it.

"Hello?"

The door's simple push-button lock rattled. It wasn't a real lock; it was only meant to protect from an *oh Jesus I'm sorry* moment. The lock clicked as something scratched at its mechanism. Steam filled the tub, sliding down my lungs, producing a cough. I looked down at my pale postwinter skin, glanced around for a weapon. A bar of soap maybe. No. A plastic bottle of shampoo?

"Hello?"

The clacking at the door stopped. The knob creaked. The door swung open, steam swirled as a shadow appeared at the curtain, arm raised, the shower curtain flung back. I flinched and cowered.

"REET! REET! REET!" said a naked E, pantomiming a stabbing motion.

"Jesus, E! How did you get into my apartment?"

"I picked the lock. It's not very good."

"I've been told."

E laughed and hopped into the shower.

I said, "You scared the crap out of me."

E wrapped her arms around me and pulled herself close, rubbing her breasts against my wet belly. "You should have seen your face."

I placed my hands on her slick skin, slid them down to the small of her back. "That was mean."

E kissed me on the nipple, slipped down, water splashing her hair. Kissed me again next to my navel. Lower.

"I'm sorry," she said. "Let me make it up to you."

FORTY-SIX

E DISAPPEARED LATER AS mysteriously as she had arrived, giving me a peck on the cheek and promising to call. I sat at my kitchenette counter as the door snicked shut and the silence closed in. Clack ate from his sponge, his carapace scratching the sand, creating a racket in my quiet apartment. I breathed in, breathed out, relaxed in my solitude.

The relaxation fled as the hamster wheel in my head started up, revolving around thoughts of Twitter. I reviewed the things that had already been said about me online, and wondered what was being said right now. I glanced at my closed laptop, battling the need to know how I was being maligned.

After a brief struggle, I lost the battle. I flipped open my laptop, started to click on my browser icon and stopped, looking at the little camera lens at the top of the screen. The light next to the lens was off, but it got me wondering. What had Earl's computer shown? What had Peter's?

Taking over Peter's computer was genius, and using the lens to see when it was safe to type commands was double genius. Whoever had done that had almost unlimited ways to dox Peter Olinsky. It hadn't been my fault. Peter would have been killed regardless of whether I got into a shouting match with him on the IRC.

At least that's what I chose to believe.

It was possible that the hacking and the murder weren't connected, that the hacker and killer were separate people. The hacker had inhabited Peter's computer only to use it as a front for phishing the senator and the killer had gotten Peter's information from my infantile flaming. That was the worst of all worlds: no connection, no way to pull on one thread to find the other.

Of course, this brought up the question of Earl. Peter's computer had been taken over so the hacker could phish the senator and get Peter blamed for it. If Earl had been hacked the same way, one had to wonder what plan the hacker had for his computer. For Earl's sake, I hoped that there was no connection between the hacking and—

My phone dinged with a message, a photo of a Guy Fawkes mask that had been modified to create a meme. Text in Impact font shouted from the bottom center of the photo:

`Fuck you Tucker.`

An unpleasant jolt of violation rippled through my stomach. The doxing was complete. Someone had my cell phone number. I grabbed the phone, opened the message app, and swiped to delete the pic—

Another ding.

Another Guy Fawkes:

`Fuck you Tucker.`

You missed a comma there, Meme Master.

This was not good. I waited a moment before trying to delete this picture. Sure enough, another ding, another picture.

`Fuck you Tucker.`

Someone was running a program sending the same message to my phone over and over. This could go on forever.

Another ding.

I silenced the message app on my phone. I wouldn't be getting any text messages until I got a new phone number. Someone had initiated a denial-of-service attack on my texting.

The phone rang, an unknown caller. I silenced it.

Phone rang again, unknown caller.

Silenced it.

Rang again.

I opened the call and listened. Cesar Romero as the 1960s Joker laughed at me.

Hung up.

It rang again.

My phone was useless. I silenced it. Left it to fend for itself.

Rage tickled my gut. *These fuckers would pay.*

Time to go to the mall. I grabbed my coat, ran down the stairs, out the front door, and almost into the arms of the senator's hook-nosed lackey, Pat Turner, who had been about to ring the bell.

"Hey! Whoa!" said Pat.

I stepped around Pat.

"Where are you going in such a hurry?" he asked.

I turned. "How is that any of your business?"

"Look, we got off on the wrong foot."

"You think?"

"I'm sorry I scared you."

"You didn't scare me."

"And that's why you ran?"

Touché.

Pat continued, "I'm just here to get a status report on the video."

"No status."

"What about Dorothy Flores?"

I started walking. "I need to go buy a new phone."

Pat followed. "Why?"

"Anonymous."

"What's that supposed to mean?"

"Don't worry about it."

"What about Dorothy Flores?"

"How do you know about Dorothy Flores?"

"The FBI told us."

"Great."

"You going to get some information out of her?"

"There is no information to be got out of her."

"Yeah. Sure. You fucking her?"

"Jesus! What?"

"I mean, that's the only reason I could see for you protecting her."

We had reached Huntington Avenue. There was a Sox game today, and the traffic showed it. Overcome by a fit of common sense, I pushed the walk button and waited.

"I'm not protecting her," I told Pat. "I don't think she knows where the video is."

"She was friends with that Peter guy."

"Yeah."

"The guy who got his head cut off."

"Yeah."

"Could happen again."

The walk signal lit up. I walked. Pat didn't. Just as well. I didn't need him screwing up an already screwed-up situation. The entrance to the Prudential Mall stood before me like a portal to shopping nirvana, but next to it was the entrance to the Cheesecake Factory, a portal to cheesecake nirvana. Cheesecake would be good.

Soon, my Precious.

FORTY-SEVEN

LEAVING YOUR PHONE TURNED on while attending a hacking convention is like hanging salmon out of your pockets and hiking in grizzly country. The problem is even worse when you throw in all the Internet functionality of a smartphone.

Having Anonymous after me was pretty much as bad as going to a hacker convention. That was why I bought a flip phone, technology so antiquated that I might have been accused of hipster-grade irony. Still, it was the safe bet, because trying to hack a flip phone is like trying to pickpocket the James Michael Curley statue.

My new little burner phone resting in my pocket, I descended the escalator and turned into the Cheesecake Factory. Normally, I avoid restaurant chains. Boston has so many homegrown restaurants that it seems a sin to waste them.

But … cheesecake.

I got seated on a long couch, alone at a table for two. The server arrived: young, short hair, white shirt, and red striped tie.

"I'll have the Blackout cake. It's been a long week."

"Whipped cream?"

"Hell yeah, I'm on a bender. Coffee too."

While I waited for my cheesecake, I called people to give them my new phone number. Called Mel. Called Bobby. Called Jael. Called Caroline. Nobody answered, I left them all messages and my new number. Called Maria. Got Adriana.

"Who's this?"

"It's Tucker."

"Why do you have a new number?"

"It's a long story. Could I talk to Maria?"

"You need to come to dinner tonight."

"Okay."

"Six thirty."

"Okay."

"Be there."

"Can I talk to Maria?"

"Sure, tonight." She hung up.

No wonder cousins aren't allowed to marry.

"Aloysius Tucker."

I looked up. The potty-mouthed vigilante known as CapnMerica stood before me, apparently trying to look menacing.

"Tucker is fine," I said. "Preferable, really."

CapnMerica said, "Aloysius Tucker, I—"

The server arrived. "Excuse me, sir."

CapnMerica stepped aside. The server deposited my cheesecake.

"Thanks!" I said.

"Would you like anything else?"

I said to CapnMerica, "You want cheesecake?"

He shook his head, made a waving motion. "I'm good."

The server left.

I forked a piece of cheesecake. "You were saying?"

"Aloysius Tucker, I am makin—"

"Mmmm … this is really good."

"I'm arresting you, dude."

"Sure you are."

"You assaulted Eliza and kidnapped PwnSec."

"Yeah, I apologized to 'Eliza.'" I air quoted. "I think we're good."

"There's still abduction."

"Where's your videographer?"

"What?"

"No, never mind, I see him." Earl Clary sat at the bar, pointing an iPhone at us. I called over, "Earl, you want cheesecake?"

Earl looked panicked. Shook his head.

"You should kind of wave the phone back and forth so the audience will know you're shaking your head."

Earl frowned but kept recording.

I turned back to CapnMerica. "You sure you don't want cheesecake, Billy?"

"No, I—wait. You doxed me?"

"Yeah—sorry. You pissed me off."

"You bastard!"

"I get that a lot. Probably deserve it."

A server veered around Billy carrying a tray.

"Why don't you get out of the aisle, Billy? Sit down. Have cheesecake. You look thin."

Billy sat. "You're not my mom, dude."

"I'm sorry. I interrupted you. You were arresting me. What are the charges?"

"You killed Peter, you beat up Eliza—"

"Russell."

"Um, yeah. Russell. And you kidnapped Earl and the rest of Pwn-Sec."

"Kidnapped."

"Yeah!"

"So that's what they're saying. That's their excuse."

"Tell it to the judge!"

I ate more chocolatey goodness, drank coffee. "So you think I killed someone, beat up Russ—"

"You beat me up too!"

"Sure, okay. And kidnapped people."

"Yeah!"

"Wouldn't that all make me a pretty dangerous man?"

"Exactly. That's exactly what #TuckerGate is all about. Keeping a dangerous man off the streets."

"Yeah, and Gamergate was about ethics in video-game reporting."

"It was! It totally was!"

"Let's not get distracted. So I'm dangerous."

"Right."

"Fine. Where is your gun?"

"I don't have a gun!"

"Really? You mean you followed me, a dangerous fugitive, from my house to the Cheesecake Factory and you didn't even bring a gun?"

Billy's face took on the hue of the decadent whipped cream that adorned my cheesecake. Which reminded me to take another bite and drink more coffee.

"You should have brought a gun," I said.

Billy asked, "Do you have a gun?"

I looked him straight in the eye. "No. I don't," I deadpanned.

"My God! You *do* have a gun!"

I ate cheesecake.

Billy stood, knocking his chair over backwards. Pointed. "Gun! Gun!"

People turned. One woman screamed and ran into the street, shrieking, "Gun!"

"For fuck's sake, Billy, you're causing a panic."

Two cops, a man and a woman, burst in from the street.

Billy pointed at me. "He has a gun!"

The two cops put their hands on their weapons, walked over to Billy and me. Earl continued to record, a flushed *This is going to be great!* grin spreading over his face.

The woman cop asked, "Sir, do you have a gun?"

"No," I said. "I don't have a gun."

"Would you step outside with us?"

"But I have cheesecake."

"Step away from the cheesecake."

The four of us walked out of the Cheesecake Factory into a blustery April wind blowing down Huntington Ave. Earl followed, recording.

"Sir, I'm going to ask you to consent to a search."

I assumed the position against a column. The male cop patted me down. He said to his partner, "He doesn't have a gun."

"He told me he did," said Billy.

I said, "Actually, shithead—"

"Sir!" the male cop said.

"Sorry. Actually, *Billy*, I specifically told you that I did not have a gun."

The woman cop said, "Can I ask how the topic of a gun came up?"

"Billy was planning to kidnap me. He's carrying handcuffs."

The cop put out her hand, pointed at it. Billy placed the handcuffs in it.

"It's not kidnapping," he said. "I was making a citizen's arrest."

"Billy learned about this on the Internet."

The male cop said, "The Internet! Well, it must be true."

"You should still arrest him," Billy said. "He killed a guy."

The cops looked at me. I shrugged. "Internet."

"Right," said the woman. "Okay, Billy, that's enough vigilantism for today."

"Can I go?" I asked.

"Yes."

I went back into the restaurant. They had thrown away my cheese-cake.

FORTY-EIGHT

HERE IS ANOTHER TUCKER Tip. If you're going to follow someone, figure out a way to hide your ridiculous purple-tipped Mohawk.

I left the now cheesecake-less factory using the mall entrance, apparently surprising Russell, whose purple-tipped Mohawk flashed in the April sun as he pushed through the revolving doors. So, two out of three PwnSec kids were following me. Where was the third?

Rather than follow Russell, I took the escalator up and ducked into the bookstore. Hustled to the back wall, which featured a set of windows to the street. I watched as Russell, standing in front of the Colonnade, met Earl, clasped upturned hands, hugged it out, and fist-bumped. Apparently the two thought they had come through a harrowing adventure and were reveling in their survival.

I waited. Sure enough, Dorothy "NotAGirl" Flores crossed the street and joined the other two, though to much less fanfare. And finally, there was Billy "CapnMerica" Janks, hailed by the other two men as a conquering hero. They gathered around Earl's smartphone, watched something—presumably Billy's death-defying assault on my cheesecake snack—high-fived all round, and broke up. Billy,

Russell, and Earl entered the T stop at Prudential while Dorothy walked back to the light, waited, and crossed back toward me.

I started to turn from the window, intent upon running down the staircase and intercepting her, when something caught my eye as Dorothy crossed the street. Pat Turner emerged from the Prudential stop exit and fell into step behind Dorothy.

This is not good.

I ran to the top of the escalator and watched through the giant glass windows as Dorothy walked past on up Belvidere Street. Headed back down the escalator, reached the bottom as Pat followed. Dorothy had never seen Pat before. She'd have no idea that she was being followed. Then again, Pat would be focused on keeping her in view, so he'd also have no idea that he was being followed.

I pushed through the revolving doors, saw Pat's back as he walked past a giant concrete horse in front of P. F. Chang's, and got into step behind him. We continued up Belvidere—past the concrete I. M. Pei building that lay on its side at the Christian Science Plaza, as opposed to the identical one that stands erect—and on up past the Sheraton.

It turns out that following someone is not nearly as interesting as I had imagined. Pat simply walked straight ahead, looking neither left nor right. Ahead of him I could see Dorothy doing the same thing.

Bored, I dialed my new flip phone.

Mel answered. "New phone number?"

"Doesn't anyone listen to voicemail anymore?"

"No. Why the new number?"

"Anonymous has launched a denial-of-service attack against my smartphone."

"Meanies."

"Yeah. Guess what I'm doing?"

"Drinking?"

"No. Why does everyone guess that?"

"What are you doing?"

"I'm following Senator Endicott's muscle man Pat, who's following Dorothy."

"An espionage train."

"Sort of."

"What do you expect to get out of this?"

"No idea. Just want to see what will happen."

Ahead of me, Dorothy had reached Mass Ave and had turned towards Back Bay. I had a suspicion of where she was heading. Pat followed her.

Mel said, "I'm getting pressure from the senator on finding that video."

"I think Pat's feeling it too."

"Want to do some brainstorming tonight?"

I needed to catch up so as not to lose them on the busier street.

"I'll call you back."

As Pat turned the corner onto Mass Ave, I broke into a run, reached the corner, slowed down, peeked. Nothing had changed. Dorothy walked, Pat followed. He reached the Berkeley Performance Center. I fell in behind. Things got a little clogged as we reached the corner. Dorothy waited for the light, Pat stood next to her, confident that she had no idea who this hook-nosed guy in the gray suit really was. Pat knew me, so I hung at the edge of the waiting crowd, bending over to "pick something up" as he turned and scanned his surroundings.

The light changed, and the crowd crossed. I waited until the walk signal turned into a blinking don't-walk signal and ran across behind the crowd. Dorothy, Pat, and I walked over the Pike, past the love locks clamped onto the chain-link fence.

I express my love for you by throwing this key onto highway traffic.

And I was right. Dorothy turned into the Hynes Convention Center T stop. Here Pat almost lost her. Dorothy, who obviously owned a Charlie Card, went right through the turnstile. I had a Charlie Card. Pat had to buy a ticket.

Moron.

While Pat stood in frustration behind a woman whose purse dog got in the way of her actually using her purse, I slipped past him and down to the outgoing train platform. I saw Dorothy. She didn't see me, as I had cleverly moved behind a green concrete column at the end of the station.

Pat was in real danger of losing Dorothy now. She could take any train from this station if she was willing to walk five minutes.

A train rattled into the station. Pat still hadn't navigated the turnstiles. Dorothy looked from her phone up to the train, noting the letter sign in the front of it. A B line train. She looked back down at her phone. Apparently she had walked far enough for one day.

The train unloaded, started to load. Pat ran into the station, saw the train loading, and ran up to climb aboard. The guy didn't have a Charlie Card, so he probably didn't know his train letters. Must live in the suburbs.

As Pat climbed aboard the train he glanced down the station, saw Dorothy, and jumped off the train just as the doors closed, catching his suit jacket.

Smooth move, buddy.

Dorothy, obliviously engaged in something on her phone, missed the whole thing. So much for our nation's campaign for people to be aware of their surroundings.

The next trolley was a C train, the one that stopped in front of Dorothy's house. She and Pat got on one car. I climbed in several cars down. I knew she was staying on until the end of the line.

I had a bad feeling about Pat.

FORTY-NINE

THE TRAIN LURCHED TO a stop at the end of the C line: Cleveland Circle. I exited the train surrounded by a crowd of students. Dorothy stepped off the train, her eyes glued to her phone screen. Pat stepped off, eyes glued to Dorothy. Both oblivious.

Is this how I look to Jael?

Dorothy crossed the street, entered the Tedeschi's. Pat stood around waiting for her to come out. I hid behind a tree. Dorothy emerged from the Tedeschi's swinging a jug of milk and turned into the alley next to the store. Pat waited, then followed. I ran to a spot where I could see the front door, but Pat had already done the doorbell trick and was gone. I followed, also rang the first floor doorbell, got buzzed.

A woman in a housecoat came out of the first-floor apartment. "Why did you buzz twice?" she asked, clearly peeved.

"I didn't buzz twice, I—"

Dorothy's scream echoed down the stairwell, followed by a man's rumbling voice and a door slamming. I bolted up the staircase, thankful for my cardio regime. I took the steps two at a time, navigating the turns as the staircase reached up to the second floor. Ran past the second floor door, turned a corner, launched myself up another pair of steps, grabbing the railing and centering myself as I took the turn. Almost there, another few sets of double steps, took the final turn. Stopped.

A closed door barred my way.

Inside I heard Dorothy: "Stay away from me!"

Tried the door. It opened.

I stepped through. Dorothy had retreated to a far wall of the living room. Pat stood in front of her, baseball bat in hand. "Where's the video?"

I pulled the phone from my pocket, raised it. "Hey, Pat! Say cheese!"

Pat turned and I realized that I was holding a flip phone, a relic from the days before cameras. Maybe I could bluff.

"Think the senator's going to like seeing a picture of you threatening a young woman?"

Pat said, "That phone doesn't even have a camera."

"Sure it does!"

"Bullshit."

Dorothy picked up on the idea. "Doesn't matter. I've already got a movie of this guy breaking into my place."

Pat turned back to her. "No, you don't."

Dorothy pointed at the fireplace where a Cyclops X-Men figurine stood. "He's a camera."

Pat turned, raised the bat.

I moved, getting between the figurine and Pat. "Don't bother, Pat. The video goes right to the cloud."

"Yeah!" said Dorothy.

Pat looked from Dorothy to me to Cyclops, who threatened to raise his tiny visor and deliver a tiny optic blast.

"Fuck me," said Pat.

"Yes, Pat. Fuck you," I said. "Now why don't you leave, and maybe I can convince Dorothy not to release what would be an extremely damaging video. Even more damaging than the senator's sex tape."

"Senator's sex tape?" asked Dorothy. "Which senator?"

"Should I tell her, Pat?"

"No!"

"Let Kamela know that you spilled the beans?"

"No."

"Get out."

Pat got out, leaving the baseball bat by the front door.

I said, "Dorothy, that baseball bat is not working for you."

"Maybe I should get a gun."

"Maybe start with a Taser. That would be much—"

"Dorothy!" a voice called from the back of the apartment.

"Coming, Auntie!" Dorothy stepped around, heading deeper into the apartment. I could either stand in a strange living room by myself or follow. I followed. Dorothy stood at a bedroom door.

"I can't lift you, Auntie," she said.

"I want to use the bathroom," came a voice from within the bedroom.

"Marla will be here in a little while. Can you hold it?"

"No."

Dorothy looked resigned. "I'll find the bedpan."

I said, "Can I help?"

Dorothy started. "What are you doing here?"

"I just followed."

"What could you do to help?"

"I can pick things up and put them down."

"My aunt Ruby is not a thing."

"I can pick aunts up too."

"Who are you talking to?" asked Ruby from the bedroom.

I poked my head around the corner. Aunt Ruby pulled the blankets to her chin. I averted my eyes, waved a little wave. "I'm Tucker. Dorothy's friend."

"Did you make her scream?"

"No, Auntie. Tucker helped me."

"I need to get out of this bed."

"Show me what to do."

Dorothy had Ruby sit up, then cinched a wide belt around her waist. "You hold the belt, help her stand, turn a step, and help her sit."

"Okay," I said.

"Make sure you hold it tight."

"Right."

"And don't take any steps; just turn."

"Right."

"And check that the wheelchair's brakes are on."

"Right." I kicked at the wheelchair. It didn't move. "Ready, Ruby?" I asked.

"Yes."

"One two three, stand!"

I grasped the belt around Ruby's waist, lifting as Ruby stood. She was heavier than I expected. The belt slipped, scraping up her body, lodging on her boob.

"Ouch!" said Ruby.

"Sorry." I grabbed for the belt. Got boob.

"Young man!"

"Sorry! Sorry! Sorry!"

Ruby lost her balance, landed back on the bed.

Dorothy said, "I'm sorry, Auntie. Maybe we should wait for Marla."

"I need to use the bathroom."

Dorothy worked the belt buckle, tightened it. We tried again. This time Ruby came right up, we turned, and she sat right down. Perfect! We wheeled her into the bathroom, executed the same maneuver at the toilet in reverse.

"Thank you," said Ruby.

"You're welcome."

"Dorothy, is this nice young man your boyfriend?"

"No, Auntie. He's too old for me."

Way to hurt a guy.

A knock reverberated down the hallway. We left Ruby in privacy. Dorothy placed one hand on the baseball bat, opened the front door with the other. A strong-looking middle-aged woman stood in the doorway.

"She's in the bathroom, Marla," said Dorothy.

Marla headed down the hall to attend to Ruby.

"Want a beer?" asked Dorothy.

"Sure."

We moved to the kitchen. Dorothy opened a couple of Miller Genuine Drafts. Not a bad choice. The best industrially brewed beer on the market. The food engineers must have been very proud.

Dorothy sat at the kitchen table and asked, "How did you know that guy was going to be here?"

"I didn't," I said. "I saw Pat following you, so I followed him."

"Why?"

"He's kind of threatened me as well."

"What's this about Endicott's sex video?"

"Who said anything about Endicott?"

"Senator Blair is a woman," said Dorothy. "Women don't get caught on sex tapes."

Unless they're married to Senator Endicott.

"That's sexist," I said.

Dorothy rolled her eyes. "Why would anybody think I have the video?"

"Because PwnSec phished the senator."

"No, we didn't!"

"Peter's computer did."

"But you said that Peter didn't do it."

"Dorothy."

"Yeah?"

"Do you think Pat understands any of that?"

"No."

We drank our beers in silence. Marla's voice drifted from the bathroom as she helped Ruby from there back to bed.

"Just you and your aunt?" I asked.

"Yeah," said Dorothy.

"Must be lonely."

"I have my online friends."

"I guess you do."

More silence.

"I forgot to thank you," said Dorothy.

"For what?"

"For helping me with that Pat guy."

"*De nada.*"

"Thanks anyway."

I stood, drained my beer. "You know what you could do to make it up to me?"

Wariness crept into Dorothy's voice. "What?"

I headed for the front door. "You could start trusting me."

FIFTY

ADRIANA OPENED HER FRONT door, appraised me. "You brought wine?"

"Yeah," I said.

"We've got wine."

"I know. I'm just being nice. Can I come in?"

"Yeah, of course."

Adriana stepped back, I entered, and she kissed me on the cheek in perfunctory greeting.

Maria's door flew open and she ran to me. "Hi, Tucker!"

I picked her up and she kissed me on the cheek, we being a family that saves lip kissing for other things.

I carried Maria down the hall to the kitchen where Catherine was cooking what looked like tacos, put down Maria, and raised my arms for a hug. Catherine looked up at me, said hi, and looked back at her cooking.

"So," I said. "Tacos. Yum!"

"What's wrong with tacos?" asked Catherine.

"Nothing's wrong with tacos. I like tacos."

"You sounded sarcastic."

I shook my head slowly. "No. I was just saying 'yum.'"

"Exactly. Very sarcastic."

I asked Adriana, "Should I open the wine?"

"Sure."

"I think it's red wine with tacos."

"I want white wine," said Catherine. "I've got some in the fridge."

"Okay, then," I said. I opened the red wine, poured a generous helping for Adriana and me, opened the fridge, unscrewed Catherine's white wine, poured her the same amount. I raised my glass to the ladies.

"*Salute*," I said.

"*Salute*," Adriana responded.

"Are you trying to get me drunk?" Catherine asked, looking at the glass.

"Look, should I just go back out and knock on the door again?"

"Why?" asked Maria.

"It just seems that we should start over."

"Why do you have a new phone number?"

"I was getting a lot of phone calls I didn't want," I said.

"You mean like selling you stuff?"

"No, like people being mean and calling me—"

"You don't have to tell her about that," said Catherine. "She doesn't need to know *everything*."

Silence hung between the four of us. Maria walked out of the kitchen, down the hall to her room. Catherine stirred ground meat in a pan. Adriana sipped her wine. I sat at the kitchen table. Beginnings of conversations formed in my mind and were vetoed just as quickly by a superego that played them out and showed me how they would fail.

Catherine pulled warm taco shells out of the oven, dumped them in a bowl, and scooped the meat into another bowl. Bowls of lettuce, tomato, and shredded cheese sat on a counter, ready for the table. Still the silence hung in the air. I moved from deciding that I should break it to deciding that I should let it play out to deciding to just try to be normal.

"Could you call Maria?" Catherine said to Adriana.

Adriana walked to the door. "Maria, supper!"

I pointed to the bowls of food. "Should I put those on the table?"

"I've got them," said Catherine. "Just sit."

I sat in my usual spot. Maria returned, sat in hers. Catherine placed the bowls on the table. Adriana sat. We stared at the bowls.

"So," said Catherine. "Eat."

I took a shell, scooped some meat, lettuce, and cheese into it, started to spoon salsa onto it.

"She doesn't like salsa," said Catherine.

"You don't?" I asked Maria.

She shook her head.

I served Maria the taco. Then gestured to Catherine. "Ladies first."

"For crying out loud," said Catherine. She grabbed a shell, splatted some meat into it, tossed on some toppings, dropped it on her plate. Adriana made a taco, and I followed.

Despite the mental warning bells, I started a conversation.

"You going back to school Monday?" I asked Maria.

"No, she's not going back to school, Tucker," said Catherine. "Monday is Patriots' Day, then there's school vacation."

"Right," I said. "I forgot."

"Of course you did."

I bit into my taco. The shell had burned a little in the oven. Carbon bitterness filled my mouth and nose, overpowering the taste of the filling. I chewed, swallowed, put the taco on my plate, drank some wine.

Catherine said, "What's wrong with it?"

"Nothing," I said.

"You don't like it?"

"What's going on here?" I asked Adriana.

Adriana had not touched her taco. She drank her wine and said, "Maria got in a fight today."

"You did?" I asked her.

Maria nodded.

"Me too."

"We *know* you too, Tucker," said Catherine. "We saw the video of you beating up that poor kid. Maria showed it to us."

I pushed my plate away. Drank more wine.

"Is that why you got in a fight?" I asked Maria.

"Olivia Incaviglia said you were a crook," said Maria. "She said that all the Rizzos were crooks. So I pushed her down like you did in the video."

My lizard brain smiled, but I blocked the expression before it could reach my lips.

"That was the wrong thing to do," I said.

"I see how it is," said Catherine. "Do as I say, not as I do."

I ignored Catherine and said to Maria, "I apologized to Russell—"

"Who's Russell?" asked Maria.

"The guy I pushed."

"You did more than push him," said Catherine. "You have a serious anger-management problem."

"I apologized," I repeated to Maria, "because it was wrong to hit him."

"What did he say?"

"It doesn't matter. Did you apologize to Olivia?"

"No. She said my father was a crook even after I hit her."

But he was a crook.

I looked at Adriana. She shrugged.

"You should apologize," I said.

We crunched our tacos. I hit a burned spot, but decided to chew and swallow the bitter piece of carbonized corn rather than spit it out and start a fight. More crunching, more chewing, more swallowing, no talking.

Finally, I said, "What's going on?"

Adriana and Catherine exchanged a glance, with Adriana giving Catherine a pointed look, then inclining her head toward me.

"He's your cousin," Catherine said.

"It's your idea," Adriana said.

"You said you'd support me."

"I am supporting you, but you tell him."

"Tell me what?" I asked.

"Fine!" Catherine said. She looked me in the eye. "We don't want you to be part of our family anymore."

"Who's we?" I asked. "Don't you mean *you*?"

"We think that you're a bad influence on all of us."

"You all think that? Does Maria think that?"

Maria said, "No!"

"Don't bring her into this," said Catherine. "She's a child."

"I *want* Tucker in our family!"

"Maria, go to your room."

"No! I'm staying with Tucker."

"You see what I mean?" said Catherine to Adriana.

"Maria, you know what?" I said. "Why don't you go to your room and let us talk about this."

"I don't want you to leave!"

"It will be fine."

Maria hopped off her stool and looked daggers at Catherine. She yelled, "I hate you!" and stormed out of the kitchen.

"So you support this?" I asked Adriana.

Adriana shrunk inward, picked up her taco, put it down, looked up. "There are safety concerns."

"What safety concerns? You're afraid of those dweebs at Anonymous?"

Catherine said, "No."

"No? Then what safety concerns?"

"I'm afraid of you."

"Me? What did I do?"

"Twitter says you killed a man."

"I did *not* kill Peter."

"Not Peter."

My mind jumped to a kick in the nose, bone driven into brain. Nobody knew about that.

"What are you talking about?"

"Have you killed a man?"

I swallowed.

"You have?"

Adriana said, "Oh my God, Tucker!"

Lying seems like a simple proposition. You just say words that don't reflect what really happened. We do it all the time. We tell people that their clothes don't make them look fat, that we were late because of traffic, that they weren't invited to the wedding because we ran out of space. We tell ourselves that we're going to quit drinking or smoking or snarking. We go online and tell the world that we're having a great day, that we actually like the photo of someone's dog wearing a party hat, that we give a shit about how delicious their lunch was. Lying seems simple.

But it's not. At least not for me, not when it matters, not when I'm talking to people I love.

"Who did you kill?" Adriana asked.

Where should I start?

"That settles it," said Catherine. "You have to go, get out of our family, don't come back."

I looked deep into Catherine's eyes. "No."

"No?"

"No. I refuse."

"You can't refuse! It's my right to tell you to stay out of our lives."

I stood. "I'm leaving now."

"And don't come back."

I looked at Adriana, who sniffled back tears. "I'm disappointed in you," I said.

The dam burst. Tears splashed down her cheeks. "It's for Maria!"

"Sure it is," I said, and to Catherine: "This isn't over."

"I'll get a restraining order!"

I said to Adriana, "You need to fix this."

I left the table, walked down the hall, past Maria's room, and out into the night.

FIFTY-ONE

RAGE, LIKE NUCLEAR-WASTE HEAT, has to vent. It churns and boils in your gut, leaking out at every door slammed open then slammed closed, every chuck of melting snow kicked across a street, every shot glass drained then slammed back onto the bar. The rage stretches the seams of whatever system you've built to control it so that you can remain a conforming member of society, someone who doesn't haul off and punch a guy in the face, someone who doesn't kick a pigeon that gets too close, or shake a fist at a baby. There's no place in the world for rage.

Which is why we invented the Internet.

I took my rage-addled self to the Corner Cafe, a little bit of South Boston tucked into the North End. The neighborhood bar sits solidly in a residential building under an apartment. I had stormed out of Adriana's house, walked around the corner, plunked myself onto a barstool, and ordered a double Jack Daniel's. Reached for my phone to vent some rage on the Internet.

And I still had the fucking flip phone!

I cocked my arm, ready to throw the useless thing into the trash. The bartender caught my eye, shook his head. I shoved it back into my pocket. Knocked back my drink. Asked for another, this time with a beer chaser.

"What kind of beer?"

"Draft. I don't care."

The bartender chose the Stella Artois—sure, Tennessee whiskey and Belgian beer: let's travel the world.

I played the expulsion back through my mind. Recounted Catherine's clear leadership in cutting ties with the Internet monster who had ruined her marriage. I'd like to think that she was wrong, that her fears were unfounded and her actions uncalled for. But she wasn't.

In the course of a week, the dweebs of Anonymous had ruined my reputation, disrupted my phone service, and fomented a mob in front of my house. They had taken the dark impulses normally tamped down in my psyche and drawn them into the light. Slapping CapnMerica for calling Jael names, beating up Russell, even mass doxing the whole PwnSec contingent had not been the products of my better nature.

See? This is why nobody likes you.

I shot back my whiskey, drank some beer. Let the alcohol derail my brain, lurching it off of the self-pity track. Brought it back around to the question of hooked-nose Pat and his threats. I had doxed Dorothy and told only one person. I flipped open my phone, clicked through recent calls, found Mel's number—

"Mr. Tucker." A presence loomed over my shoulder. I turned, watched Xiong Shoushan take the barstool next to me. He ordered a Johnny Walker Black neat.

There had been a time when a Chinese man sitting in a North End bar was at best an oddity and at worst a provocation. But those days were gone, the tribal barriers of Boston's neighborhoods having been eroded and washed away by tides of young professionals. It was an improvement, certainly, but then again it would have been nice to know that a Chinese spy was at least a little bit unwelcome in a bar around the corner from my now ex-family.

"Neat?" I asked. "Most people get Johnny Walker on the rocks."

"Rocks are for babies," said Xiong. "I don't like ice."

I leaned close, hoping my Jack Daniel's breath would stun him. "And how did you get out of prison?"

"America is a wonderful country. Defending your property is still allowed, even from the FBI."

"Property? Are you heir to a commemorative plate fortune?"

"I own the building."

"And so why aren't you in it? What are you doing here? Where's your knife?"

"I don't need my knife."

I drank my beer. Turns out that Belgian beer isn't a great chaser for Tennessee whiskey. So much for internationalism.

Xiong continued, "I have something simple to tell you."

"Good. Maybe I'll remember it."

"I'm going to release the senator's video on Monday."

I finished my beer. Made a writing motion in the air. *Check please.*

"Didn't you hear me?"

I turned to Xiong. "What are you doing here?"

"I told you."

"No, I mean here. In this bar. How did you know to find me here?" I pulled out my flip phone. "This piece of shit has no GPS."

"You have family here."

"Yeah?"

"I waited."

"How long have you been sitting outside my cousin's house?"

"Only a day."

Catherine was right. I was a danger to them. I stood.

"Didn't you hear me?" Xiong asked.

"Stay away from them," I said.

"I only wanted to find you."

"Stay away from them!" I slammed my hand down on the bar, the slapping crack turning all three heads in the place toward us. The bartender turned toward me, started to talk. I threw a twenty on the bar and left Xiong. Stormed out the front door, headed down Prince Street. Heard Xiong's footsteps behind me as he ran to catch up.

"You're drunk!" he said as he pulled alongside.

"Great. I get the world's only judgy spy."

"What?"

"I didn't ask you to comment on my coping mechanisms."

"Did you not hear me?"

"Yeah. Yeah. You're going to release the senator's video Monday. So why tell me?"

"Because you seemed to be under the impression that those Pwn-Sec children had stolen the video."

"Where did you hear that?"

"On Twitter."

"Figures."

"If you thought they had the video, then you would not believe it would be used."

I strode down the street, turned the corner at Salem, kept striding. "So you want me to believe that you have the video?"

"I have the video."

"How did you get it?"

"Hacking."

"Specifically."

Xiong said nothing.

I stopped walking. "You didn't get it yourself."

"I have it."

"You have people who got it. You don't even know how it was done."

"Does it matter?"

I regarded him. "No."

"I will post the video."

"What am I supposed to do with that information?"

"Tell the senator that if I am bothered again I will post it, and that if he votes wrong I will post it."

I crossed my arms. "Are you finished with the pointless threats? I have things to do, places to be."

Xiong looked at me, disgust tugging at the corners of his mouth. "You are a drunk."

I pointed back up Salem Street. "Everett is that way."

He headed off in the direction I had pointed. I digested the simple fact that I had brought a dangerous guy to Maria's door. What was next?

I pulled out my phone. Started to call E. Stopped. Called Mel instead.

"You've got to hear this," I said.

FIFTY-TWO

MEL AND I HAD gone through a brief negotiation of "your place or mine" involving whether it was better for her to come to the South End or me to head to Jamaica Plain. I settled the issue using geography.

"I'm in the North End right now," I said.

"Okay?"

"And you're in JP."

"Right."

"So the South End is halfway between us."

"Wait, that's not fair. It's right near your house."

"One cannot argue with geometry."

"I thought we were using geography."

"Both. I simply bisected a line segment on a map."

Mel said to someone off-phone, "Why am I talking about having a drink with someone who would bisect a line segment?"

"Two reasons," I said.

"Yeah?"

"First, a guy who can bisect a line segment is undeniably hot."

"Swing and a miss. What's the second?"

"Xiong told me to give you a message."

We now sat at the end of the bar at Cleary's in the South End, a ten-minute walk from my house. I had stuck with my whiskey plan—Jameson's now—while Mel drank white wine.

"What did Xiong say?" asked Mel.

"Wait a minute. Butter a guy up first. Ask me how to bisect a line."

"Really? You're going to mansplain geometry?"

I drank my whiskey. "I got kicked out of my family today."

"Because if you're just—what?"

"And they're right to do it, because Xiong was waiting for me right by their front door."

Mel put her hand over mine. "Let's start over."

I did, telling Mel about how Catherine had dumped me out of our quasi family and how Xiong had caught up with me at the bar and delivered his message.

Mel asked, "How do you feel about Catherine's point?"

I drained my Jameson's, motioned the bartender for another.

"I see," said Mel. "It's upsetting you."

"Probably won't be as upsetting after this one."

"Drinking's not the answer."

"You don't know that."

"We should just focus on Xiong before you're too blotto to make sense."

My drink arrived. "Also, you have to stop sharing information with the senator."

"What? Why?"

"The senator's guy Pat is not the lovable goofball he appears to be. He broke into Dorothy's apartment and threatened her with a baseball bat."

"What are you talking about?"

I told Mel about what happened with Pat and Dorothy, and how I caught Pat in the act of assaulting Dorothy and demanding the video.

"He thought she had it," I said. "Where would he get that idea?"

"I told Kamela that we'd made progress and told her who we were following."

"You shared the names I doxed?"

"It was the only progress we'd made."

"You have to stop doing that."

"I can't. This is my first investigation. I have to show something."

"Look," I said. "I understand the need for positive feedback."

"What?"

"You wanted the pat on the head."

"That's insulting!"

"Am I wrong?"

Mel crossed her arms, looked at a TV playing the seventh inning of a Sox game.

"All I'm saying is that once you let information out of the bottle there's no getting it back in."

"You should know about the bottle."

"Har har. I'm serious."

"And so am I. I can't stonewall a senator."

"Yes, you can. And in this case you shared bad information."

"It's what we had."

"Xiong seemed positively insulted by the idea that we would suspect, what did he call them? Oh yeah, 'those PwnSec children.'"

My drink was empty. *How did that happen?* I raised my hand to order.

Mel pulled my hand down. "Stop."

I grimaced at her. "I think I know what I'm doing."

"Oh, you know what you're doing. I just don't think it's a good idea."

The bartender approached. "Can I help you?"

"Club soda for both of us," said Mel. "And the check."

I considered asking for whiskey in mine, but didn't. Mel had broken the spell, causing more-healthful thoughts to intrude. The club sodas arrived. I paid the bill.

"So, what do you think?" I asked.

"I think we should get you home."

"I mean about Xiong."

"I'm more worried about your problem with Adriana. You're a mess."

"Xiong's a spy."

"Yes, and we'll get to him. But you're still a mess."

I pulled out my flip phone. "I've been reduced to this."

"That is pretty low."

"It doesn't even have a camera."

"Let's go. Lead the way."

I stepped off the stool, took another couple of steps to catch my balance. "Where to?"

"Your place, Drinky McDrinksalot."

"Ha! Drinky."

"Yeah."

We left Cleary's, headed down Columbus Ave toward my house. The sun had set hours before, and April's chill bore into me, knocking aside some of the whiskey's effects. I didn't have a coat. Being cold was worse than being depressed, so I focused on being cold.

"It's cold," I said.

"Do you want my coat?"

"What kind of gentleman would take a lady's coat on a cold night?"

"You're just loving that patriarchy."

I shook my head. "I'm a shitty patriarch."

"What do you mean?"

I told Mel about Maria, about her behavior. "She's acting out or something."

"And you think a father figure would help?"

"I think another adult would help, another perspective."

"You provide that, right?"

"Yeah. If what she needed was a fun cousin." We reached West Canton. "Turn here."

"She probably does need a fun cousin."

Clearly taking West Canton had been a tactical error. Trees vied with bricks for control of the sidewalk. The trees had been surrounded by granite slabs and cobblestones in an attempt to give them some growing space, but the greedy bastards weren't satisfied. They heaved the granite slabs up, turning them into big tripping hazards, and deformed the brick sidewalks the way muscles deform the Incredible Hulk's pants.

I tripped almost immediately. Mel grabbed my arm, but there was no saving me. I went down in a heap, a root-heaved granite slab poking me in the back.

I looked up at Mel. "Some father figure."

"C'mon, big guy," said Mel, giving me a lift to my feet. "Let's get you home."

Mel wrapped her arm in mine. I thought it was for support, but then she wrapped her fingers within mine and squeezed tight. "Tomorrow will be better."

FIFTY-THREE

WE STOOD IN FRONT of the steps leading to my condo. I sat on the curved railing, fumbling through my keys, trying to decide whether this was a date. Was there a kiss involved now? I found the key.

"Thanks for the walk home," I said to Mel, and leaned in, aiming to plant a kiss on her cheek.

Mel ducked. "Not so fast."

"Huh?"

"I need to use your bathroom."

"Sorry, I should have offered. Come on up."

I led her up the steps, had a better time with the key to my condo door, unlocked it, and swung it open. The apartment lay dark and silent before us. A straight line from my living room in the front, past my kitchenette, to the bedroom in the back.

I swiped at the hall light switch, entered and pointed toward the bedroom. "Bathroom is that way."

"Thanks." Mel hustled past me and on to the bathroom.

I turned on more lights, checked on Click and Clack. "How are you doing, boys?"

The hermit crabs had been sleeping, were still sleeping, were still enjoying the Zen-like state of living in the moment inherent to the brain of a crustacean. I envied them. Sprinkled some flakes on their sponge. They ignored that too, knowing in their crabby wisdom that the flakes would be there when they decided to eat.

Mel returned from the bathroom. "This really is a nice little place."

"Thanks." Remembered my manners. "Want a nightcap?"

"Really?"

"I don't have to walk anymore."

"Got beer?"

I pulled out a couple of Harpoon Winter Warmers, the last of my winter-beer stash. Poured them into glasses, making nice heads on each, and handed one to Mel.

"Want to come into my parlor?" I said, moving toward the couch.

"Sure."

We sat next to each other on the couch, clicked glasses, drank some spiced ale.

"Thanks for the walk home," I said.

"My plea—"

"Did you hear that?" I asked, putting my beer on the coffee table.

Mel put her beer down as well. Reached for her purse. "What?"

Murmurs slipped through the door.

"Somebody's in the hallway," I said.

"Yup," said Mel, sliding her hand into her purse.

A fist pounded my front door. "Police! Search Warrant! Police!"

I said, "What the—"

The door blasted off its hinges as a battering ram swung through. Somebody tossed something in. The thing exploded, filling my head with light, ringing my ears. Mel swore.

Men in black uniforms poured through the smoke. "Police! Police! Get on the ground!"

A guy in black shoved Mel to the ground.

"Hey—"

Another guy grabbed me, threw me next to her. Pushed my neck to the floor. I turned my head and saw Mel next to me, lying with her face in the rug as a cop cuffed her. The guy on my back grabbed my wrists, cuffed them. They dragged Mel and me to our feet, pushed us down on the couch.

"What the hell is going on?" Mel asked the guy, then me. "What the hell is going on?"

More guys in black swarmed in. They went through my rooms and into my office, came out with my computer.

"Sons of bitches," I said.

"What?"

"They swatted me."

"Who?"

I looked up to see Lieutenant Lee step through my blasted front door. He walked over to Mel and me. He pointed at Mel and told the officer, "Release Special Agent Hunter. She is with the FBI."

The cop said, "Jesus, sorry," and unlocked Mel's handcuffs.

Then Lee turned to me and said, "Aloysius Tucker, you are under arrest for threatening the Boston Police Department and for the murder of Earl Clary."

FIFTY-FOUR

THERE'S A LOT TO love about Caroline Quinn. She's beautiful, with red hair and a yoga-toned body. She's smart, the top criminal-defense lawyer in the city. She's tough, lost a leg to the Marathon bombing, yet drives a stick. But the thing I loved most about Caroline Quinn at this moment was that she was on my side.

As for me, I was having an out-of-body experience. They say that beer on whiskey is mighty risky, but it's not half as risky as jail on whiskey. I'd spent the night in a holding cell with an open toilet bowl and a cot. Nothing that happened in that room could be counted as sleep. My beard scuffed at my collar, my mouth tasted like dog crap, and my eyes could only approximate looking in the same direction. Dizziness and crankiness vied for my soul.

"Gentlemen," Caroline said to Lieutenant Lee and his boss, Captain Black, "do you think a five-million-dollar settlement would do it, or should I go for twenty?"

Black and Lee, sitting next to each other in the conference room, glanced at each other. Lee shrugged. Black, using his steel-gray crew cut to look menacing, decided to out tough Caroline.

"You'll never get a dime, Quinn. We were protecting the city and our own," he said.

"Really? Not a dime?" Caroline turned to me. "Tucker, don't you have Jerry Rittenhauser from the *Globe* on speed dial?"

"Yes, I—"

Caroline cut me off. "I'm thinking of a headline: *Keystone Cops of the Internet Age*."

Lee said, "We had evidence that Tucker was dangerous."

"Lee—"

"Lieutenant Lee."

"Right. Lee, it's so sad that you're losing your mind. How long have you known Tucker?"

Lee crossed his arms.

"A couple of years, at least," said Caroline.

"We had a threatening Twitter."

"It's a tweet," I said. "You had a threatening tweet."

"Yes, a tweet."

"Let's see it," said Caroline.

Lee glanced at Black.

Caroline said, "C'mon, you'll need to hand it over anyway before I take your jobs."

Black nodded. Lee pushed a sheet of paper toward us, a screen shot of a tweet.

`@TuckerInB0ston: I killed Earl and next Ima kill me some cops. #TuckerGate`

Black said, "That's your Twitter account, Tucker."

"No, it isn't," I said.

"You're TuckerInBoston."

"Yes, but I'm not TuckerInB-zero-ston."

"Huh?"

"The second letter in *Boston*. That's supposed to be an oh."

Black said, "Oh?"

266

Caroline pointed at it. "Oh!"

Lee and Black looked at each other. "Oh …"

"Yeah, it's a zero," I said. "That didn't come from me."

Caroline read from the tweet, intoning an accent. "*Ima kill me some cops.*"

"Seriously?" I said.

"Lee actually thought you wrote that."

"We grew up hard in Wellesley."

Lee looked ill.

"We had a murderer to catch, and a tip that it was you," said Black.

"Right. Did you ask me for an alibi?"

"What alibi?"

"Was Earl killed like the other one?"

"What do you mean?"

"Head cut off, picture on 4chan?"

Black said, "What's 4chan?"

"Are you shitting me? You don't even know the MO?"

Lee said, "Yes. Same MO."

"What time did the picture go up?"

"Half past seven, yesterday evening."

"You think maybe you should ask where I was at half past seven yesterday?"

"Okay. Where were you at half past seven yesterday?"

"I was visiting my cousin in the North End."

"Anyone see you?"

"Besides my cousin in the North End?"

"Yeah."

"A Chinese spy named Xiong. You'd recognize him."

Lee narrowed his eyes. "Are you mocking me?"

"No. I would never mock you."

"I need to talk to Xiong."

"Take it up with the FBI. I have a friend."

Lee said, "So the FBI is covering for you again?"

Black said, "Let's not go down that path. I'm not accusing the FBI of anything."

Caroline said, "To be clear, you sent a SWAT team to my client's house when you could have made one phone call to find out where he was. Got anything else in your magic folder of evidence to justify destroying his apartment?"

"We got a phone call," said Black.

"Yeah, what did it say?"

"It said that Tucker had taken a woman hostage and there was screaming."

"Any screaming when your SWAT goons arrived?"

"We haven't analyzed the body-camera feeds."

"I'm going to need those feeds, by the way. All the better to nail you with."

"How do you know what they'll show?"

"They'll show Tucker and FBI Special Agent Mel Hunter sharing a beer on the couch. As far as I know, that's a rare posture for a hostage situation. And I'll bet you there is no screaming."

"It was good beer," I said. "There would have been no screaming."

Lee and Black sat, eyes downcast, Lee fiddling with his folder.

Caroline asked again, "So do I go for the five million or twenty?"

"The city will fight you."

"The city will cut you two losers off at the knees as soon as they figure out how much money you wasted. Tricked by a hacker? Do you think that story will fly?"

"We're not letting Tucker go," said Black.

"He'll need to post bail," said Lee.

"Are you two going to represent the city in court?"

"Our assistant district attorney will."

"Dan? Dan won't touch it with a ten-foot pole. He's too smart."

"He's got our backs."

The conference room door opened, a sandy-haired guy with two days' growth poked his head in.

"Hi, Dan," said Caroline.

"Hey, Caroline!" Dan's surprised smile stirred something in me. Jealousy? "Are you still here?"

"We were just talking about whether you're going to arraign Tucker."

Dan glanced at me, grimaced. "I think not. I was just coming by to tell Lee that the Commissioner needs a rundown of this fiasco so he can write a detailed apology." Dan reached out a hand to me. "And I too am sorry, Mr. Tucker. We made a terrible mistake."

"Thanks, Dan," I said.

Dan closed the door behind him.

Caroline slid her view to Lee and Black. "What's it going to be?"

Black said to Lee, "Get his stuff and get him out of here."

I didn't move, said, "Aren't you forgetting something?"

Black and Lee looked at each other. "What?"

"C'mon, out with it."

Lee said, "What are you talking about?"

"The Commissioner's sending me an apology, but it's not really his fault, is it?"

"You want an apology?"

"Yes, I want an apology. I also want a restraining order."

"There is no such thing."

"Then restrain yourselves."

"What's that supposed to mean?"

I pointed at Lee and Black. "I want you two and the Boston Police Department to stay out of my hair."

Black said, "Mr. Tucker, you have counsel here who can speak for you."

Caroline said, "I think he's doing fine."

"If I'm brought down here again for any reason, if I'm followed or investigated, if I hear anything about that video of me slapping a guy—"

269

"What video?"

"Google it," I said. "If I even get a notion that you guys are following me, investigating me, or intending me any inconvenience whatsoever, I will tell the Commissioner to tear his apology in half and shove a piece up each of your asses."

Black said, "Listen, you're luck—"

"Shut up. I'm talking now," I said. "Do you understand what I'm telling you?"

Caroline said, "I'm thinking twenty million is the right way to go."

Lee crossed his arms. "Fine."

"Fine? What does that mean?"

"I'm sorry."

Black looked at Lee as if he'd lost his mind. "You *apologized?*"

"'Fools mock at reparation, but among the upright there is favor.'"

"What?"

"Proverbs 14:9."

"For Christ's sake!"

"Please don't swear."

Black crossed his arms, sulking. "Fuck this shit."

"And another thing," I said. "I'm going to find out who murdered Peter and who murdered Earl, because it's the only way I'm going to get you morons and the Twitter mob off my ass."

"And you want our help?"

"No. I want you to stay out of my way."

"Fine."

"And one other thing."

"What?"

"I want a new door on my condo by noon."

As we left the conference room, my phone chirped a text message from Adriana: We need to talk.

FIFTY-FIVE

I SAW ADRIANA BEFORE she saw me. She sat alone in Caffe Vittoria's front window, looking down Hanover Street past the cannoli line at Mike's Pastry and on down toward St. Stephens. I tapped on the glass as I walked by, eliciting a jump, a little smile, then a scowl. I walked up the stairs and saw that Adriana had already ordered biscotti. I nodded to Nick, ordered a double espresso, and sat in the window with Adriana. My brain sloshed slightly in its pan as the hangover spun it.

"Hey," I said.

"Hey."

"Are these biscotti for both of us?"

"I think I'm getting a divorce," Adriana said.

"Oh."

"Yeah."

I leaned back, absorbing the news, parsing the words. Nick brought me my espresso. I thanked him, took a sip. Bit a biscotti. It was the first decent thing I'd eaten all morning. I chewed, waited to see if the sugar helped my brain. It didn't. The biscotti tasted like wheat, chocolate, and sugar instead of a cookie.

Adriana said. "Catherine is such a bitch."

"You guys fighting?"

"So fucking tired of it all."

"Is this over me?"

Adriana shrugged. "I told her she was out of line telling you to stay away."

"Because you guys shouldn't break up over me."

"You're family. She should stick by family."

"She's scared."

"It's no excuse."

I drank my espresso.

Adriana looked me over as if for the first time. "You look like shit."

"Thanks."

"Rough night in jail?"

"You know about that?"

"It's all over Twitter."

"Of course it is."

"Catherine was reading the #TuckerGate stuff to me. I told her to stop."

"Why?"

"She was lording it over me, saying she told me so."

"Told you so what?"

"That you were a killer. That you had killed that guy."

"Earl Clary."

"Yeah."

"Ha! You two are my alibi, you know."

"Really?"

"She was busy throwing me out of the house when someone cut off Earl's head."

"Then why did they arrest you?"

"Prank phone call."

"Bastards."

"Who?"

"All of them."

I nibbled the biscotti. No better. The my stomach rocked. I looked out the window, watched people walking on Hanover Street, living in the real world. A world where destroying someone took more work than typing or making a phone call.

"I can see why Sal used to like it here," I said.

"Why?"

"People walking. Different people, same directions. You never see the same thing twice. Kind of like watching a lava lamp."

Adriana looked out across the crowd. "God, I miss him."

"Yeah. Me too. Can't imagine what it's like for Maria."

"Poor kid. I don't know what to do for her."

"I think you're doing what you should be doing."

"Fighting in front of her?"

"No, not that."

"Because we've been doing a lot of that."

"I meant loving her. Giving her a home."

"Sure, when I'm not telling Catherine to go fuck herself."

"What are you fighting about?"

"I want you to stay in our life. Be whatever kind of dad you can."

"You told me that I was a shitty dad."

"Better than nothing."

I raised my espresso. "Here's to being better than nothing."

Adriana punched my arm. "You know what I mean."

"Yeah, but"—I shook my head—"not a good time for me to be any kind of dad."

"Seriously. You going to say you're too busy?"

"Imagine if that SWAT team broke down your door."

"Why would they?"

"Same reason they did it to me. Someone called them."

"They'd do that to us?"

"Yeah. If I were there."

"So Catherine is right."

"She's wrong about me being a killer, but right about me staying away."

Adriana bit a cookie. Put her face in her hand. When she looked up, tears wet her cheeks.

"So they win."

I shrugged. "For today."

"I don't know what to do about Catherine."

"Are you asking for advice?"

"Marriage advice from you?"

"I was married."

"You two fought like badgers."

"Yeah, but we stayed married to the end."

"Do you think you would have made it if Carol hadn't been murdered?"

I ate a little more biscotti. Still tasted like ingredients instead of a cookie. My sloshing brain told me that I didn't need a cookie. I suggested to my brain that it didn't know what it was talking about. My stomach sided with my brain. I pushed the cookies away.

"I think we would have made it. We loved each other."

"Really?"

"We didn't like each other some days, but that's the deal. That's how marriages work. Is Catherine talking divorce?"

"No."

"Then don't you start it. That's my advice. You can go back and fight with her about whether I'm welcome in the house, but don't threaten the marriage."

"So you *are* giving marriage advice."

"'Stay married' is pretty basic marriage advice."

Adriana stood, I followed. We stepped out of the coffee shop and into the chill. Spring had decided to toggle back to March rather than test out May. The marathon runners would be happy.

Adriana wrapped her arms around herself. "So what now?"

"Now I figure out who killed Peter and Earl."

"Why you? Why not the cops?"

"It's better if it's me. It would put the whole #TuckerGate thing to bed."

Adriana opened her arms. We hugged.

"Love you, cousin," she said.

"Love you too."

"Don't stay away long."

We broke the hug. Adriana set off down Hanover. I imagined going home, lying down in a dark room. Sweet idea. My flip phone chirped. A text from Mel.

`Need your help.`

FIFTY-SIX

It was a short walk from the North End to Government Center. Mel waited for me next to the transporter-accident sculpture. She saw me, waited for me to reach her. Took a step back.

"You stink," she said, crinkling her nose.

"Prison changes a man."

"You know, when you invite a girl up to your apartment, handcuffs are supposed to include consent and a safe word."

"What does the senator want?"

Mel had looked up at the building and said, "He's pissed off." We entered the building together.

Now, Kamela sat across a conference room table from Mel and me, tight-lipped with disapproval. I sat staring into the middle distance and negotiating with my hangover. *Let me get through this without puking and I'll go right back to bed, I promise.* The night in jail might well have been a death sentence—a slow, sloshy death sentence.

The senator burst into the room, brandishing a tablet. "What the hell is this?"

Mel looked at me. I shrugged.

"What is what, sir?" asked Mel.

Kamela winced as Endicott slammed the tablet onto the table. He pointed at the screen, which featured a YouTube video entitled "Senator Pervert."

I had expected to see the video from yesterday, but this was an edited version. It was like the trailer from *Fifty Shades of Grey*. It had been cut and tailored to hide the senator's identity, but to show you exactly what you'd see the senator do if you watched the full show. The video featured a gray-haired back, a moan, a clinking of handcuffs, a flash of a pink nightie, a gasp. No faces. The video promised to be released tomorrow.

The senator shook a finger at Mel. "You were supposed to suppress this filth!"

She looked like I felt: gray and ready to puke. "I'm sorr—"

"Do you know anything?"

Mel shook her head, "No, we—"

I interrupted. "We know who has the video. He told me that he's going to post it online tomorrow."

The senator leaned in on me. "You know who has it?"

"Yes."

"Who?"

"Xiong Shoushan."

"And why hasn't this Xiong Shoushan been arrested?"

Kamela said, "I thought he had been arrested."

Mel said, "There were procedural problems."

"What kind of procedural problems?" The senator pointed at Mel. "Did you screw up the arrest?"

"The point is," I said, "arresting him may not solve your problem."

"He may have set up the video to publish itself automatically," said Mel.

"What?" boomed the senator.

The senator's volume splashed my brain around in my head, causing my eyes to lose their tracking and rattle like marbles. I couldn't take much more of this. Nor did I have to.

I stood to leave. "I really need to get home." Stumbled a bit.

The senator asked, "What is wrong with you?"

Kamela said, "Tucker spent the night in jail."

"Jail?"

"It was a prank," I said. "I got swatted by the Boston Police Department."

"Swatted?"

Mel said, "He was arrested by a SWAT team, but released this morning."

"Oh my God!" Endicott cried. "Kamela, have you *ever* seen such incompetence?"

"No, Senator," said Kamela.

"You two need to fix this!" Endicott pointed at us.

I had been dragged after a sleepless, hungover night into this conference room by a powerful man who was stupid enough to make a video of himself screwing his wife and then let it get into the cloud. A powerful man afraid to face the music at home when his wife found out that her deepest fears about the video had been realized. A man who had, to put it bluntly, fucked up. And now this man was yelling at me like *I* had done something wrong?

"Why two?" I asked.

"What?"

"Why should I help you?"

"Because I asked you to!"

I looked straight into the senator's eyes. "I don't give a shit."

"If you do it for me you'll have a powerful friend."

"I don't need a powerful friend," I said. "I need a nap."

"Or a powerful enemy."

I took a step toward the senator. Mel stood, put a hand on my arm.

"I've got powerful enemies," I said. "I spent the night in prison because of them."

Mel tugged at my arm. "C'mon, Tucker."

I shook my arm free.

"We should go," she said.

I pointed at Endicott. "Don't blame us, you horny idiot."

Mel said, "I'm sorry, sir."

Endicott's face flushed red under his white hair. He raised his finger, started to say something, but turned and pointed the finger at Kamela. "Fix this," he said, then stalked out of the room.

I said to Kamela, "Give me one good reason that I should risk my ass for that joker."

Kamela said, "For Betty."

"What?"

"Betty," Kamela said. "Betty Endicott. The senator's wife."

"Hmmph."

"I've been following #TuckerGate."

"I hear it's great entertainment."

"I'm thinking you don't like it much."

"Of course I don't."

"But you understand it, don't you? You know what's happening to you and why."

I crossed my arms.

Kamela continued, "Betty isn't from this time, Tucker. She grew up in a time when reporters would have considered this little sex video a private domestic matter between the senator and his wife."

"It wouldn't have been in the newspapers," I said.

"And it wouldn't have gone viral."

I thought about the woman in the video.

Landon, you're sure nobody will see this?

I asked Mel, "What do you think?"

"Doesn't matter what I think. It's my job. It matters what you think."

"I do feel bad for Betty."

"So will you help?"

"Yeah."

"We should get out to see Xiong," said Mel.

"I've got something I need to do," I said. "I'll meet you in your office in two hours."

"What do you need to do?"

"Give PwnSec my condolences." I flipped my phone open, texted Dorothy. Can we talk?

A delay, then: Yes.

Where?

Dorothy texted back a location. I showed Mel.

"Really?" she said. "You're going to go there?"

"I probably deserve it."

FIFTY-SEVEN

TWO BEASTS, GREAT AND terrible, claw at each other over Boston, battling to supply bitter, overroasted coffee to its citizens. While Peet's yaps at the edges of the struggle, trying to get a word in, and Tim Horton's looks on from its frigid perch in Canada, Starbucks and Dunkin' Donuts roar and wrestle for dominance.

At one point in the battle, Dunkin' Donuts launched an advertising campaign portraying Starbucks customers as effete dandies whose willingness to pay ungodly sums of money for a cup of Starbucks coffee demonstrated their wussiness, as opposed to the toughness of the callus-handed, working-class heroes who drank Dunkin' Donuts coffee, drove pickup trucks, and built skyscrapers.

Dunkin' Donuts customers reveled in the class-warrior glory of the campaign, while the Starbucks customers never noticed. They were too busy texting.

Meanwhile, hipsters, in their unending quest for irony, had gravitated to Dunkin' Donuts as if it were the font of all vinyl records. And so Dorothy and Russell had invited me to their favorite coffee shop. I pushed through the door of the Dunkin' Donuts in Cleveland Circle and spotted Russell's purple Mohawk sitting at a booth in the back. Dorothy sat across from him.

I bought a box of assorted Munchkins and, God help me, a cup of coffee. Sat next to Russell, across from Dorothy.

"I'm sorry about Earl," I said.

"Yeah?" said Russell. "Why? You kill him?"

"You want a Munchkin?" I asked, choosing a chocolate one. I popped it in my mouth, momentarily getting relief from my hangover as a wash of sugar invaded my bloodstream.

"You didn't answer my question."

"Of course he didn't kill him," said Dorothy. "I wouldn't have called him if he had killed Earl."

"Thank you," I said to Dorothy. "Want a Munchkin?"

She chose a jelly one.

I drank my coffee, winced, ate a powdered-sugar Munchkin to kill the taste.

"You should put cream and sugar in that," said Dorothy.

Russell said, "You *still* didn't answer my question."

"For crying out loud, Sherlock. No, I didn't kill Earl."

"Then who did?"

"That's a more interesting question."

"I'm scared," said Dorothy.

"I think we should all be a little scared."

"Why should you be scared?" asked Russell. "You're not in PwnSec."

"You ever have the whole Internet after you?"

"No."

"It's getting a little scary. I got swatted last night, and there's only one way for me to get Anonymous off my back."

"A manifesto?"

"No, not a manifesto! I need to catch this killer, whoever he is."

"The HackMaster," said Russell. "Or you."

Between the hangover, lack of sleep, and Munchkin sugar rush, there wasn't much left of my emotional defenses.

I fixed Russell with a stare. "What?"

"You know what," said Russell.

"Can you believe this guy?" I said to Dorothy.

"Russell, c'mon," said Dorothy. "Tucker didn't kill Earl."

"Yeah? Where were you?"

"I was busy getting thrown out of my cousin's house because of what you wrote on Twitter, you little fuck," I said, poking Russell in the shoulder.

"Ow! Stop it! I didn't write that."

"You started it. You're still telling people that I killed Peter."

"No, I—"

"Is there anyone else you've fucked up, Russell? Anyone else like me or that poor girl out at UMass?"

"I didn't make her kill herself."

"You are a first-class piece of shit."

"Hey, fuck you, dude!"

Heads turned.

Dorothy said, "Children's Hospital."

Russell and I looked at her.

"We attacked Children's Hospital," said Dorothy.

"You were involved with that?"

Russell said, "Yeah, they took that girl, Justina, away from her family, so we helped Anonymous crash their website."

"How would that get you guys on someone's death list?"

Dorothy said, "Russell wrote a manifesto about how PwnSec was dealing justice."

"It was a good one."

"Jesus, Russell, you're pathetic."

"Fuck you!"

More heads turned. A cop standing in line glanced at us.

I said, "Will you just be quiet for once?"

"I'm so sick of you, man. You think you're such hot shit."

"I am hot shit, compared to you."

"You're a useless old man!"

"And you're just a script kiddie who writes manifestos, *Eliza.*"

"I don't have to take this abuse. Get out of my way."

Russell poked at me, I stood. Russell slid out of the booth and stormed out of the Dunkin' Donuts.

Dorothy took another Munchkin, nibbled it. Sipped some coffee. I drank some more of my coffee. Spit it back into the cup.

"That was smooth," said Dorothy.

"He's an idiot."

Dorothy stood. Headed for the door.

"Dorothy," I said. She turned. I handed her the box of Munchkins. "For your aunt."

"Thanks."

I sat alone in the Dunkin' Donuts staring out at Commonwealth Ave. I thought about checking Twitter, remembered that I only had a flip phone. Decided to call E instead. Immediate voicemail. Texted her. Good morning.

Shouldn't you be saying that to your FBI girlfriend?

It's not like that. Want to talk?

I stared at the phone, waiting for E's response.

It never came.

FIFTY-EIGHT

I emerged from the glass obelisk that is the Government Center T stop. Looked up into the gray April sky to see low clouds scudding by, portending rain for tomorrow's race. Heading across the plaza toward Mel's office, I saw two things that stopped me in my tracks. Two people, really.

One was the self-styled Internet bounty hunter Billy Janks, who went by the name CapnMerica. The other was the senator's hatchet-nosed fixer, Pat Turner.

What caused this unholy matrimony?

CapnMerica and Pat reached me at about the same time. Pat opened his mouth to speak but got cut off.

"Aloysius Tucker, I am placing you under citizen's arrest," CapnMerica said.

Pat said, "Wait. What now?"

"I'm arresting Tucker."

"And who are you?"

I said, "Pat, meet CapnMerica. CapnMerica, Pat."

"Captain America?" asked Pat, looking Billy over. "You're a little shit. Don't you need to take a potion?"

"Shut up! I'm arresting Tucker."

"Yeah? For what?"

"Murder!"

"How about I arrest you for being a dick?"

"He's a murderer!" shouted Billy.

"It's not polite to point, Billy," I said.

"He's working for me," said Pat.

"I am?" I asked.

"Who are you?" asked Billy.

"I'm the guy who's going to punch you in the face," said Pat.

"You guys going to fight over me? That's adorable."

"I might punch you in the face too."

"How about we tone it down," I said.

"You're supposed to be getting that video."

"That's why I'm trying to get to Special Agent Hunter's office."

"Then go!"

I took a step. CapnMerica, brandishing handcuffs, reached for me. Pat made good on his word, punching CapnMerica right in the face. I stepped around the fight. Walked away. Someone would definitely be video recording this baloney, and I had enough problems.

The shouting and scrabbling faded as I crossed the street and entered Center Plaza. Took the elevator to Mel's floor.

Mel met me in a conference room. She had changed into a black turtleneck and jeans that flared into bell-bottoms. She caught me appraising her outfit.

"What? It's casual Sunday," she said.

"I just think you look nice."

"Do you want coffee?"

"My hangover says yes."

"It's one o'clock. You're *still* hung over?"

"Ah, youth."

We moved to a break room, where Mel pointed at a Keurig machine. I operated the machine, got a mug of brown water that had been pushed through a little plastic cup.

Mel said, "We have a problem."

"Yes," I said. "These machines are taking over the landscape."

"Not a coffee problem. An Internet problem."

"Is the Internet broken? Because that would be great. I've kind of had my fill this week."

"You're not going to like it," she said and walked out, expecting me to follow.

We sat next to each other in her office facing a Facebook page on her computer screen.

"You've been life ruined," she said.

"What? I'm not even on Facebook."

"You are now." She pointed.

The page said Aloysius Tucker. The profile picture featured Angry Tucker wearing Guy Fawkes face paint, teeth bared in the altercation that happened in front of my house.

"I didn't make this page," I said. "How did I get a hundred and fifty friends?"

"I think they got a list of your Twitter followers and used them to do friend requests here."

I scrolled down. "So what did I put on my page?"

A photograph of Earl's head looked out at me, surprising me like a punch in the gut. "Jesus!"

"It gets worse," said Mel.

"How can it get worse?"

"4chan.org had its usual shot of the body with *Sic semper contumeliosis* as the caption."

"Okay, so we're getting a pattern."

"This particular shot was not the one from 4chan. It's nowhere else on the Internet."

"This is an original?"

"The killer was the only one with this shot."

"And the killer took the time to life ruin me."

"It's definitely someone you know. And it gets worse."

"Of course it does."

Mel opened another window in the browser, headed over to Twitter. Did a search. The same pictures came up under @TuckerInB0ston. My Twitter doppelganger who had tweeted: `Ima kill me some cops`. Every tweet bore the hashtags #HackMaster and #TuckerGate.

I sat back in my chair, the double gut punch of the pictures and personal violation mixing with the remnants of my undying hangover to suck the energy out of me.

Mel said, "I'm running some searches, trying to see—"

"I've got to catch the HackMaster," I said.

"Actually, *I* have to catch the HackMaster," said Mel. "This is becoming an FBI case."

"You're going to take it from Lee?"

"We're one short of an official serial killer. I'd rather not let it go that far."

I drank some brown Keurig water. Sighed. "I don't even know where to start."

"I did some research," said Mel. "Some Latin research."

"It doesn't mean 'Thus ever to the insolent'?"

"It can. Latin doesn't have that many words, so they do a lot of double duty."

"What else could it mean?"

"'Spiteful,' for one."

"'Spiteful'? Shit. That could describe the entire Anonymous collective."

"I don't know. I'm still trying to figure it out."

I reached for the keyboard. "Let's bring up these—"

As I spoke, another picture popped up on the @TuckerInB0ston feed. The photographer had stood across the street from my house during the protest. He must have been wearing a Guy Fawkes mask and had snapped a picture just after the police sirens had sounded.

Five people clustered on the three steps leading to my front door as I worked the lock: Dorothy, Russell, Earl, and E holding my arm, beaming up at me. @TuckerInB0ston had modified the picture, placing a red X over Earl. The associated tweet told the rest of the story:

@TuckerInB0ston: One down. Three to go. #Hack-Master #TuckerGate

FIFTY-NINE

THE PICTURE POPPED UP on faux-Tucker's Facebook feed next. Five people stood on my steps. One was dead. Four were left. Three to go.

Which three?

Mel pushed me aside, started clattering at the keys. I closed my eyes, resting a brain that had processed too much information on too little sleep after too much alcohol. I slipped into the moment, hearing the keys clicking, feeling the hard plastic chair, rolling the past few minutes around in my mind.

Three to go. Three little pigs. Three blind mice. *Three Days of the Condor.* Three had to be one of the best numbers out there: the first prime number, if you don't count two, and who counts two? Three kills makes a serial killer. Lee would tell me it was three days till Christ rose. Three to go.

Mel shook my arm. My head drooped to the side. A warm trail of drool graced my shoulder. My muscles, which had recently lost all tone, protested against the hard plastic of the chair.

"I found the picture," she said.

"Where?"

"It started on—"

My flip phone chirped a text message. "It's Xiong," I told Mel.

"What does he say?"

"'Help me.'"

"Help you?"

"Xiong is asking for help."

I texted, `Where are you?`

We waited. No answer. I called Xiong's cell. It went to voicemail after a while.

"Took long enough to go to voicemail," I said.

"So?"

"So he didn't answer, but he didn't block the call either."

"What's his phone number?"

I told Mel, she clattered at her keys some more.

"You've got him on GPS?"

"Just because we had to let him go doesn't mean we couldn't surveil him. It was easy to get a warrant."

"Where is he?"

Mel pointed at the screen. A blue dot sat over Xiong Distribution in Chelsea. Mel grabbed her coat and we headed down the elevator to her car. Got the car going, navigated past Faneuil Hall, past the North End, and across the Charlestown Bridge, Sunday's afternoon traffic providing no resistance.

"So the picture of the five of us," I said.

"Yeah."

"Where did it come from?"

"It first appeared on the Internet on CapnMerica's feed."

"CapnMerica," I said. "God, I hate that guy."

We crossed the Charlestown Bridge, the GPS lady guiding us.

"You know, that is what they pictured," I said pointing at the GPS.

"Who?"

"The people who invented the Internet."

"They pictured a GPS?"

"They pictured people being able to access a service like this any-where."

"Did they picture porn?"

"Back then they would have had to upload their own."

"You think he did it?" asked Mel.

"Did CapnMerica kill Peter and Earl?"

"Yeah."

"No idea. Once he put that picture up, anyone could have grabbed it."

We bumped over the railroad tracks on Second Street. Mel parked in front of the warehouse, and we walked through the front door into the little office. It looked the same as before: same crappy desk, same creepy paneling. The computer at the desktop sat with its Windows desktop exposed. I tapped a key a few times to keep the screensaver from kicking in, then checked its settings.

"This is supposed to lock the computer if it's left alone for a half hour."

"How long had it been sitting there?"

"Less than a half hour."

"Duh."

"Duh yourself," I said, disabling the screensaver so the screen wouldn't lock. "We might want to look at this later."

We opened the door to the back room. Slipped inside. Lights were on, nobody was home.

Mel saw me about to shout Xiong's name. "Shh!"

"We don't want to find him?"

"We don't want to be found. I have a bad feeling."

We moved to the door leading to the warehouse. Cracked it open. Lights glared over rows of tchotchke-laden shelves. We slipped into one of the rows. A box of South Boston commemorative plates had been pulled off a shelf and smashed to the floor. We moved past it, trying to keep from making crunching noises as we walked over the shattered china. We failed.

"Shh!" Mel and I hissed at each other. Somewhere in the warehouse metal clanged on metal. Something had touched one of the shelves. A sword? We ran to the end of the row, peeked around the corner at row upon row of shelving. Saw nothing. Stepped out. Mel motioned that she would walk down this row and I should walk down the next.

"Split up?" I mouthed.

Mel nodded. Pulled me close, whispered in my ear, "Can't shoot both of us."

Great.

We walked down the row, me staying level with Mel by watching her through the spaces in the shelves. Walked past the Italian section. We reached the end. Continued our peeking and walking exercise for a few more rows: Portuguese, Spanish, Croatian. Never Chinese. One more row and I hit the Manchester United paraphernalia, then Liverpool, then on to baseball. I stopped us at the next row.

I whispered to Mel, "I think we're alone."

"Can't assume."

Mel took the next row, I took the one after that. That was when I saw it.

This row had holiday lawn ornaments. I could tell because several pink flamingos wearing Santa hats lay in the row. Several had their little Santa-hat heads cut off. Farther down the row, a giant inflatable snowman lay deflated in a pile. The pile formed a puffy barrier across the row.

I shouted, "Over here!" to Mel. Ran down the row to the deflated snowman. Pulled at the material as a shadow fell across me. I looked up, expecting Mel. Instead, I stared down the barrel of a black gun, its barrel rock solid.

Behind the gun stood Jael Navas.

"What are you doing here?" she asked.

Mel rounded the corner, gun drawn. "Drop the gun!"

Jael didn't waver, didn't jump. "What are you both doing here?"

"Drop the gun!"

Jael executed a quick movement and suddenly the gun had disappeared, probably into her handbag. She raised her hands, looked at Mel's gun, then pointedly at Mel. Mel kept her gun out, finger along the barrel.

I said, "Can we stop now?"

"Why is she here?" asked Mel.

"More important question," I said. "Who is that?"

A body lay outlined under the snowman. I grabbed the snowman fabric, pulled.

Xiong's head appeared. Then the rest of him.

"Shit," Jael said.

SIXTY

WE REPLACED THE SNOWMAN fabric and stepped away, careful to avoid the pool of blood.

Mel said to Jael, "You know him?"

"Yes."

"How do you know him?"

Jael took a deep breath, looked back toward the body. "Football."

"Football?"

"You call it soccer."

"How do you know him from soccer?"

"He was a midfielder. He was quite good."

"You play soccer?"

"Striker."

"How did you wind up playing soccer with a Chinese spy?" I asked.

"It is a friendly game."

"That doesn't really answer the question," Mel said. "How did you even find each other?"

"He texted me that he was in danger," Jael said.

"No, I mean to play—"

"Me too," I said. "He asked for help."

"Wait a minute. I'm still trying to figure out how they know each other," Mel said.

"Soccer," said Jael.

"You just randomly play soccer with a Chinese spy?"

"He said one of his assets had gone mad," Jael said to me.

"Assets?"

"Someone he had recruited. Someone he worked with."

"What was he working on?"

"I do not know."

"How can you not know?"

"We never talk about our work."

I said, "You never talk shop at the soccer game?"

"Correct."

"Is this a spy soccer game?"

"If it were a spy soccer game, I would not admit it."

"So it *is* a spy soccer game."

"He must not have expected to be killed," Jael said. "Or he would not have met the person."

Sirens sounded in the distance, a response to Mel's call for backup. I needed to check something on the Internet. Pulled out my phone … *Friggin' flip phone!* Dialed Xiong's number.

An old fashioned ringer sounded out in the office. We followed the sound to drops of blood and followed the blood to a closet. Opened the door. Full of computer servers, the phone rested on the floor, next to Xiong's hand.

"He must have run in here to hide," Mel said.

I fiddled with the door. "It had no lock."

"Shitty hiding place," said Mel.

The servers blinked at us from their rack.

"Why would he have these?" I wondered. "Everybody uses the cloud."

"Except spies," said Mel. "How is it that you play soccer with spies?"

"I do not."

"You just said you did!"

I said, "She told you that if she played soccer with spies, she would not admit it."

"I swear, if I have to arrest you, Jael, I will. How do you know him?"

Jael pursed her lips. "Let us leave the crime scene."

We walked out into the front office just as Everett police came through the door, followed by EMTs and a medical examiner. Mel pointed them in the right direction and they headed out.

"Out with it. Soccer," Mel said.

"Do you have gloves?" I asked Mel. "So I can use the computer and not leave prints."

"No."

Jael reached into her handbag of horrors and pulled out gloves. "They are latex. Are you allergic?"

"No." I took the gloves, donned them, and started poking around Xiong's computer.

"Tell me about soccer," said Mel.

Jael said, "You are new to this job."

"Yeah, yeah, I'm twenty-five. Can we get past that?"

"It is a lonely life."

I looked up from the computer. "But you're retired."

"I have a set of skills and some enemies. It is best to stay … disconnected."

"So you play soccer?" asked Mel.

"Do you think Xiong's government will admit his role here?" Jael asked.

I paused, thinking about it.

"They will not. They will say they have never heard of him," she said.

"But we have pictures of him in uniform."

"It will not matter. No government admits the existence of people like Xiong, or like me."

"How does soccer help that?" Mel asked.

I said, "They're in the same boat." I opened pastebin.com. Copied a text file to it.

"Yes," said Jael.

"But don't you spy on each other?"

"We do not talk about work," Jael said. "And I am retired."

"This doesn't—"

"There it is," I said, pointing at the screen.

"What?" asked Mel.

"The senator's video. Right on the desktop."

"So Xiong had it after all."

"Yes, but that doesn't explain how he got it. I've looked through his files here and on the servers. There's no evidence that he knew how to set up a phishing scam and trick Kamela into giving him the password. There's not even any evidence that he uploaded it anywhere."

"So what are you saying?"

"I'm saying that he had a helper. Maybe this mad asset."

"How will you find him?"

I pointed at the file on pastebin.com. "I'll crack these passwords, log in as one of these people."

It was a short list of usernames: xiong, farli, sarah, roger, chao. "I'll bet one of these people is our asset."

We walked back out to the warehouse. The medical examiner called us over. She had pulled back the snowman shroud revealing Xiong's headless body, or bodiless head, depending on how you looked at it.

"Who found the body?" she asked.

Mel pointed at me.

I stuck out my hand. "I'm Tucker."

The medical examiner waved her gloved hand, pointing at the blood on the fingers.

"Right," I said and converted my handshake to a little wave of my own.

She said, "I'm Maura Williamson." Maura stood about five feet tall, brown hair, blue eyes, delicate gloved hands. "So you found him?"

I nodded.

"What happened here?" Mel asked.

"There was definitely a fight," Maura said, pointing at the flamingo. "I guess he was using that as a shield."

"How did he get those cuts on his chest?" Mel asked.

"I've got a better question for you."

"What?"

"Where's his hand?"

"It's in the server closet in the other room," I said.

"With his cell phone," Mel said.

"He called for help?"

"Yes."

"Then he ran out here," Maura pointed around, "and started grabbing things to block the sword."

"Sword?" asked Mel.

"For sure. Probably the same one that killed those kids."

"Same person?"

"I don't know."

"Why?"

"Different MO. None of those kids had defensive wounds. None of them were attacked like this. They were all killed in their homes and were near a doorway. Someone had knocked on the door, stepped inside, swung the sword. This guy had warning."

I asked Mel, "Could you check 4chan for me?"

"Already did," she said.

"And?"

"No pictures of a decapitated Xiong."

"So this wasn't a planned killing."

"No." Mel tapped at her smartphone, placed a call. "Kamela, this is Special Agent Hunter. We've secured the senator's video . . ."

I drifted away from the phone call, walked over to Jael, touched her hand. "Are you okay?"

Jael crouched next to Xiong. Closed her eyes, sighed, looked up at me. "He tried to stop the killer."

Was that a glistening in her eye?

"I know," I said.

"Now more people will die."

SIXTY-ONE

THERE IS NO TECHNOLOGY, no matter how wonderful, no matter how useful, no matter how frivolous, that cannot be turned to evil. Atomic energy can be used for bombs, a video can be used for blackmail, a chia pet can be used as a club. Or in my case, graphics cards intended to make video games go faster can be used to crack passwords.

Contrary to the claims of TV, encrypted information cannot simply be decrypted by wicked smart hackers. "This is military-grade encryption. It will take me twenty minutes to hack," is one of the stupidest things you'll hear during an evening of television. Given a file full of usernames and encrypted passwords like the one I got from Xiong Distribution, the only way to crack the passwords is by guessing. Lots of guessing. That's where my massively powerful guessing engine comes in. You guess a password, encrypt it, and see if it matches the gobbledygook in the password file.

I had created the guessing engine for a start-up called PassHack, whose mission was to show you that your weak password could be hacked. Turned out that nobody wanted to know that their password could be hacked, and PassHack went out of business. But I had kept the password hacking engine. Sort of a combination souvenir and nod to the same technology-hoarding tendencies that cause me to save old power cables. The thing was a little old: it could only make a billion guesses a second, but it still had some game. With that kind of speed I could guess every possible seven-character password, then every password that had ever been cracked, then all the words in the dictionary with the Os converted to zeros, etc.

I sat in my office, the last of my Green Monsta IPAs at my side, and fired up my password cracker. In a few minutes it had started to work on the Xiong password file.

My stupid flip phone rang. No idea who it was; I hadn't bothered to load names into the thing.

"Hello?"

"It's Adriana. Is Maria with you?"

My brain stalled. "What?"

"Is Maria with you?" she repeated.

"With me?"

"Maria's taken off."

"Taken off?"

"What's wrong with you?"

"She ran away?"

"Catherine and I were having a fight, then we called her and she wasn't in her room."

"Maybe she went for a walk."

"She's ten."

"Ten-year-olds can walk."

"We've looked all over the neighborhood."

"Did you try calling her phone?"

"She left her phone here. Why would she do that?"

"She knows we have a GPS on it."

"Dammit!"

"Did you check Caffe Vittoria?"

"Of course we did!"

"Don't yell at me. I didn't do anything."

"Do you think this has to do with #TuckerGate?"

I turned the question over. Internet trolls have done some horrible things, driving people to suicide, forcing them to move, enticing them into sexual liaisons. But I've never heard of them kidnapping a kid as part of an online war. Still.

"It's possible," I said.

"You have to do something!" She hung up.

Do something.

I opened Twitter and looked at #TuckerGate. The same long stream of vitriol and death threats scrolled by. I didn't even process it. Some people seem to be able to make an online fight their raison d'être, waking up every morning ready to do online battle for some obscure issue that has taken hold of their minds.

But I can't. I burn out. The arguments, counter-arguments, threats, insults, memes, and unfiltered meanness rub a raw spot in my brain, raising a blister then forming a callus. After that, I don't care anymore.

I skimmed the scummy discourse looking for any mention of Maria. Headed over to 4chan, and, eyes half shut, ran through the top pictures. I threw together combinations of #TuckerGate and "Maria" and did searches.

Came up empty.

As far as I could see, the writhing mass of trolls was still sure that I was a murderer, perhaps even a mass murderer, but if they had taken their hatred out on Maria, nobody thought to mention it.

What now? Wander the streets yelling her name? Ask these morons for help? Wouldn't that be a heartwarming end to this tale? Internet trolls discovering their inner humanity by helping their target find a runaway girl.

Fat chance.

The rage was back: churning stomach, twitching hands, the fervent wish that CapnMerica would try to arrest me right now so I'd have a reason to pound him into pulp. I sat at my kitchen nook and looked at Click and Clack, who ignored me.

Who has fucking crabs as pets?

Dark images of a smashed crab tank flashed through my mind, followed by horror, guilt, and self-loathing. The hamster wheel in my mind cranked and clattered, spinning in a loop of abuse, slander, and decapitated corpses. I looked up at my cabinet full of whiskey. Pre-game drinking? Maybe sit alone in my kitchen and drink rye whiskey out of a jelly jar? I could just flat out declare myself an alcoholic.

Fuck that. I hate meetings. If I was going to drink, I'd do it in a bar. Bukowski with its craft beer, loud music, and twenty-something vibe would do nicely. I grabbed my coat, opened my newly installed front door.

Maria sat on the steps in my hallway, chin in her hands. She looked up at me with red eyes.

"Can I come in?"

SIXTY-TWO

MARIA WALKED INTO MY dark apartment and climbed onto one of my kitchen stools. She looked at Click and Clack.

"They're sleeping?"

"Yeah."

She looked around. "It's dark."

I flipped on the kitchen lights. They barely pierced the gloom. Maria had been to my apartment before in the context of sleepovers. Those times, the apartment seemed to absorb the happy energy of my preparations. I wiped all the counters, stocked the fridge with fruit and the cabinets with granola bars, my air-blowing popcorn maker taking pride of place on my countertop. Maria had never seen my condo in its mundane state of me just living in it, just eating, just sleeping, just going through my motions. I looked around the apartment through her eyes. What a dreary place.

I pulled out my flip phone.

"Are you calling Auntie Adriana?"

"Yeah, of course. She's worried sick."

Maria pouted.

"You don't want me to call her?"

"No."

"Too bad." I dialed.

Adriana answered.

"She's here," I said.

"We'll be right over."

I flipped the phone shut. "They're coming over."

More pouting.

"What's wrong with you?"

"I'm thirsty."

I got glasses, filled them with tap water. Gave one to Maria, kept one for myself, stood behind the breakfast nook. Tried again.

"Why did you run away?"

"I didn't run away," said Maria. "I came here."

"Why didn't you tell Aunt Adriana where you were going?"

"They were fighting."

"People do that. It's no reason to scare them."

Maria drank some water, looked at the sleeping crabs. Tapped on the glass.

"Please don't tap on the glass," I said. "It disturbs the animals."

"Like at the aquarium."

"Exactly."

More water drinking.

"They were fighting about me," said Maria.

"What about you?"

"About whether I could come see you anymore."

"Of course you can come see me. You didn't have to run away."

"Auntie Catherine says you're dangerous."

Just another kick in the gut. I was getting used to them.

"I'm not dangerous," I said. "That's ridiculous."

"That's what Auntie Adriana said. She says you're family."

"I am family."

"And Auntie Catherine said that you were just another Rizzo. That you belonged in jail."

"They had this fight in front of you?"

"I was in my room. But I could hear."

Great. Just fucking great. I didn't know what I was supposed to do with this. So I punted. "You want to watch Netflix?"

Maria nodded. We moved to the living room, where I threw on the Powerpuff Girls. Maria and I had made a pact to only watch the show with each other. It picked up where we had left off. That nut Professor Utonium had left the girls alone for an afternoon, and hilarity ensued.

"I used to think you were like him," said Maria, nodding at the flat-screen monitor on my wall.

"Who? Utonium?"

"Uh-huh. You know, because you're like a scientist."

"But you don't anymore?"

"Professor Utonium doesn't get mad, but you do. So I don't think you're the same."

"If he had to deal with a bunch of hackers, he'd be mad too."

Maria nodded. "Yeah, he also doesn't listen sometimes."

"I listen." On the screen, the Powerpuff Girls were beating up a goofy monster.

"Yeah, you do sometimes."

"When don't I listen?"

She said nothing.

We watched cartoons until the doorbell buzzed. I walked to the door, worked the intercom.

"It's us," said Adriana.

I buzzed them up, opened the door to my apartment. Went back into the living room and paused the show.

"I was watching that," Maria said.

"I know, but your moms are here."

Maria crossed her arms and sulked on the couch. Adriana and Catherine walked through the open door.

Catherine said, "You should put in a peephole, so you don't have to leave the door open."

"And a Happy Unsolicited Advice Day to you too," I said, leaving the door open.

"Jesus, are we going to start already?" Adriana said. She went to Maria on the couch. "You get over here!"

Maria didn't move.

"You see what I put up with," Adriana said to me.

"What *we* put up with," said Catherine.

"Yes. Yes," said Adriana.

"I'm surprised you two came alone," I said.

"Why?" asked Catherine.

"Seems bold, seeing as how Maria's been told I'm dangerous and all."

Catherine looked away. Adriana said to her, "I told you Maria was listening."

"It's true."

"Because you heard it on the Internet, right?" I said. "What are you? A child?"

"You haven't been able to explain any of it!" Catherine said.

"I don't have to explain it. It's lies."

"Not the videos."

"The videos show me—"

"Show you beating people up."

"That's not a beating."

"You can't go around hitting people. You're a bad influence on Maria."

"Leave me out of it," said Maria with preternatural maturity.

"You, young lady, are in big, big trouble," said Adriana. "What got into you?"

"Your fighting," I said.

"We're fighting because of you," said Adriana.

"Because Catherine says I'm a bad influence?"

"I'm not wrong," said Catherine. "You're just as bad as the rest of them."

"The rest of what?"

"The rest of the Internet trolls."

"I'm not a troll. I was just minding my own business."

"You started this whole thing!"

"Peter started it."

"And what if you had let it go?" Catherine said.

"What?"

"What if you didn't have to be the big man on the Internet?"

"He would have—"

"He would have gone and picked on somebody else, and Maria would have gotten off with a suspension. But you had to go after him."

"He deserved it."

"And what do you think the #TuckerGate people are saying about you?"

I had had enough of this. I stalked over to Maria. "You need to go now."

Maria remained unmoved. "I don't want to go!"

Adriana said, "C'mon, honey. We've got to go home."

"No!"

This had an easy solution. I picked Maria up.

"Put me down!" she shrieked.

"Put her down, Tucker," said Adriana.

"Just put her down," said Catherine.

I carried the squirming Maria to the open door of my apartment and placed her in the hallway. "It's time for you to go home."

Maria looked up at me, eyes narrowed. "I hate you!"
They all left. I closed the door behind them.
"That makes two of us."

SIXTY-THREE

EARLY, WAY TOO EARLY, on the morning of April 19, 1775, a group of wannabe soldiers stood around on the Lexington town green waiting to confront troops, fellow citizens of the British Empire, who had come to take away their guns. The battle, such as it was, went as poorly as encounters between armed troops and angry citizens always go. From the Boston Massacre to Kent State, hair-trigger tension and the slip of a finger have the same result. Five killed at the Boston Massacre, four at Kent State, and eight at Lexington Green.

The difference was that Lexington launched a war. We don't talk about the Lexington Massacre. Instead we talk about the Battles of Lexington and Concord, and how those battles triggered enough rage across the Colonies to drive a revolution, *the* Revolution, the birth of the United States.

Today, in Boston, we celebrate Patriots' Day with reenactments (at the same cock-crowing early hour), pancake breakfasts, and the Boston Marathon. At the moment, I was celebrating Patriots' Day by tapping at my tablet, drinking a cup of coffee, and enjoying a hangover-free brain.

About twenty-five miles west, the elite women marathon runners were starting their race toward Boston. I, on the other hand, was engaged in no such healthy behavior. I was poking through Twitter trying to make sense of Catherine's comments last night. I wasn't a troll. Was I?

The picture of Dorothy, Russell, Earl, E, and me continued to make its rounds in the darker corners of the conversation. The picture had been turned into a meme, with *One Down Three to Go* superimposed over the shot in Impact font. Bets were being made as to who'd be next.

Not surprisingly, Epomis (E), NotAGirl (Dorothy) and Eliza (Russell) had gone to ground, after Eliza had gotten into an all-caps shouting match over whether Tron (Earl) had gotten what he deserved because of his life ruins. The conversation ended with the tweet from my online doppelganger:

`@TuckerInB0ston: I guess you're next, Eliza. #TuckerGate`

I'd had enough of Twitter for a lifetime. I turned on the TV, watched as the women ran down Route 135 in Hopkinton. They'd just started. Then, sitting in front of the TV, I checked out the results of my password cracking. The results were acutely disappointing. Worst passwords ever.

Xiong's password was *xiongspassword*. The username *sarah* had opted for the ever popular *qwerty1234*, and *roger* had showed his team spirit with *GoRedSox!* At least he had thrown in some capitals and special characters. These passwords were cute, adorable even. But the password for *farli* told the whole story: *di3hack3rsdi3!!*

I flipped open my phone, called Mel.

"Meet me at Xiong's."

"Why?"

"Our killer works there."

I threw on clothes, ran downstairs, debated Uber vs Zipcar. Tried the Uber app; the city was already at peak demand. Patriots' Day traffic would have the Uber drivers milling about like ants in a smashed colony. Better to drive myself.

A half hour later, I was sitting on the hood of a Zipcar Honda Civic named Zesty in front of Xiong Distribution.

Mel pulled alongside me. "What's up?"

Mel unlocked the front door. We stopped at the front desk with its crappy PC and I logged into the server as *farli* using the *di-3hack3rsdi3!!* password. Started poking around, but didn't have to poke far. A folder of pictures sat on *farli*'s desktop. The first was a picture of five people in front of my house. A picture without an X over any of us.

Mel said, "The original."

"Yeah."

Ten other pictures filled the folder. Pictures of headless bodies: Peter and Earl.

"These are also originals," said Mel. "These shots aren't out there."

One picture was different than the others, a Photoshopped merging of Peter's head and Earl's head into a meme with Latin on the bottom.

Dies ultimus.

"Who dies?" I asked.

"It's Latin," said Mel. "*Dies* is 'the day.'"

"*Ultimus*?"

"The last day?" she guessed.

"Oh no."

I jumped into the browser, started to type 4chan.org. The browser had been there before, filling in the URL for me. I hit return. The meme sat at the top of the page. Anonymous comments scrolling down as the 4chan denizens tried to decipher it.

"They're all targets," I said.

"You too," said Mel.

"I'm not worried about me. I know where I am." I dialed a number on my phone.

Dorothy picked up. "Can you get out of the house today?" I said quickly. "Go see the marathon or something?"

"No," said Dorothy. "My aunt and I are watching it on TV."

"Don't show her 4chan, and don't let anyone in."

"What's on 4chan?"

"I gotta go." I dialed Russell. "Did you see 4chan?"

"No," said Russell. "But there's a new picture on Twitter."

"*Dies ultimus*?"

"That's the one."

"Stay inside," I said. "I'll try to get the four of us to a safe place. Don't let anyone in."

"What am I supposed to do inside?"

"Seriously? You have a computer and a ballgame starting at eleven. Figure it out."

Hung up, called E. It rang. It rang some more. It rang a little bit more and went to a voicemail message that repeated the number back to me.

I texted E: We need to talk.

No answer.

I had a bad feeling.

"C'mon," I said to Mel. "We've got to get to E's house."

"Do you think ... ?"

I didn't answer, just moved.

SIXTY-FOUR

ZESTY THE ZIPCAR WOULD have to sit in Everett until I got back to it. Mel and I buckled into her car, and she pulled out.

"What's the address?" asked Mel.

"I don't know," I said.

"Never been to her house?"

"I didn't say that."

We had walked down a street near the Beehive, E's hand in mine, stopping on the front steps of a brownstone.

"So you have been to her house."

"Yeah."

"But you don't know where it is."

"It was late."

"I see ..." said Mel. She looked forward, continued driving. "I'm heading for Boston. Is that at least in the right direction?"

"Seriously?"

"Because, you know, maybe she could live anywhere in New England."

"We had breakfast."

"Yeah? Did you call her or nudge her?"

"Nudged her," I muttered.

"What?"

"Are you jealous?"

"I'm just surprised that you're a little bit more whorey than I imagined."

"We ate at the Wholy Grain." I took Mel's phone, typed in the address. Looked at the map. "And her house is on Hanson Street."

"Hanson Street."

"Across the street from a playground."

"That's a start, I guess."

"Seriously, are you jealous? Why?"

Mel pursed her lips and drove. I flipped open my stupid phone, called Jael. Told her what was happening, where we were going.

"Across the street from a playground?" asked Jael.

"I don't know the address."

"I will see you there."

Hung up with Jael, called Lee. Told him the same thing.

"On Hanson Street," said Lee.

"Yes."

"Across the street from a playground."

"Yes."

"You are calling to tell me about a potential murder and you don't have a better address than 'across the street from a playground.'"

"On Hanson Street!"

"On Hanson Street."

"Are you coming or not?"

"Of course," said Lee. "I have to see this playground on Hanson Street."

"It's no joke. She's going to get killed."

"I will be there."

Mel, following the GPS, drove us up onto the Zakim Bridge and down onto Storrow Drive, where traffic ground to a stop.

316

"I thought this thing was supposed to take us around traffic," I said.

"It's all traffic," said Mel. "It's Patriots' Day."

We inched past the Hatch Shell and the Esplanade. The day had turned on us, a splattering of raindrops hitting the windshield. Somewhere west of Boston the second and third waves of thirty thousand runners were being unleashed upon the 26.2 miles from Hopkinton to Boston. Their friends and family were jamming the city now, looking for parking, filling the public transit, finding a spot where they could watch the race. College students were pre-gaming a day of drunken cheering, cops were adjusting crowd control barriers, the elite runners were getting into their stride, and the great mass of weekend athletes were inching their way toward a starting line in anticipation of their big day.

None of this was helping us get to E's apartment any faster.

Mel drove, silent.

"Can I use your phone?" I asked.

"Don't mess up the GPS."

"I won't."

I opened the browser, jumped to 4chan.org/b/. The only thing at the top of the list was a poll asking whether you're a homo for getting off on a transwoman. Horrible, as usual, but at least it wasn't a picture of E's head staring into the camera. Nerves and fascination caused me to scroll down a couple of pages, but I saw only more of the same. E was safe so far.

Mel pulled off of Storrow, navigated Arlington, driving between the Public Garden and the Taj Hotel. We hit every red light, caught no breaks, and watched helplessly as mobs of crowds crossed the street in front of us.

"Doesn't this have a siren?" I asked.

"Don't you think I'd be using it?" Mel said.

I blew a sigh. "Maybe I should walk."

"Don't be stupid."

"Are you *mad* at me?"

Mel shook her head.

"Because as far as I know, we were never dating."

"I just expected a little more from you, is all."

Welcome to the club.

The traffic opened up as we got onto Tremont Street, allowing us to scoot down the street and park on Hanson in front of the playground. Lieutenant Lee and Jael stood in front of the playground, looking at three brownstones.

"One of these?" asked Lee.

"You didn't check?"

"I don't see anything happening."

"It may be too late," Jael said. "Which building is it?"

I thought back. E and I had stumbled up the stairs from the Beehive, walked down this street, and . . . and . . . nothing. I remembered making jokes. I remembered the feel of her back under my hand. I remembered her giving me a boozy kiss at one of these three doorways. I could not remember which one.

"Do you remember which floor?"

That I could remember.

"It was the first floor," I said. "I made some comment about not having to take the stairs."

Mel said, "Lieutenant Lee, you take the one on the left. I'll take the one on the right. And Tucker and Jael can check the middle one."

We split up. Jael and I climbed the stairs on the middle building. Rang the bottom bell.

"You're probably going to have to pick the lock," I said.

Jael reached into her handbag, pulled out a packet of tools.

A text chirped on my stupid flip phone.

The door started rattling.

"Or not," I said.

Jael put the tools back, kept her hand hidden in her handbag.

The door opened and a bald guy stood before us, arms crossed against the cold sprinkling rain. He sported a three-day-growth beard, a T-shirt displaying a Boston terrier wearing glasses, and plaid pajama bottoms.

"Is E here?" I asked.

"Who?"

"E. It's her nickname."

"What's her real name?"

"Um."

Jael said, "He does not know."

"E stands for Epomis," I offered

The guy crinkled his nose. "That's disgusting."

"Maybe she lives next door? Asian girl. I was visiting her a couple of days ago."

"Asian, huh?"

"Yeah."

Guy called over his shoulder. "Honey, can I use your phone?"

Mel and Lee saw that we were having some success and joined us on the front stoop. Meanwhile, a woman appeared over the guy's shoulder, brown hair sporting a wisp of gray. She wore a long sleeping T-shirt with a matching terrier. She handed the guy an iPhone. "What do you need it for?"

"I want to show him a picture."

The guy poked at the iPhone, brought up a picture, showed us. E.

"That's her," I said. "Where is she?"

"No idea. I don't know her."

The woman said, "She was our guest a couple of days ago."

"And you don't know her?"

"Ever hear of Airbnb?" the guy asked.

I blinked at him. Airbnb. I thought back to the iPhone charger, and my dead phone. Remembered that E used a Samsung. So why was there no charger for me? E didn't have a charger here because she didn't live here. She'd rented this house—

"This was her plan," Jael said.

"Yeah," I said.

"She intended to seduce you and she needed a place."

Stupid!

The guy asked, "You called her Epomis?"

"Eww," said the woman.

"Pretty disgusting nickname," said the guy.

"Why?"

The guy poked at his phone some more, showed me a video.

In the video, a frog stood in a wide beaker. Sand covered the beaker's bottom. A beetle sat across from the frog. The beetle waved its antenna catching the frog's attention. The frog twitched its head toward the beetle, took a step. The beetle, oblivious to the danger, kept moving, attracting attention. The frog stepped forward, the beetle took a step. The frog leaped forward, mouth wide, but missed. The beetle was suddenly on the frog's back, hanging on as the frog thrashed to get it off. The frog flopped on its side, scrabbling at the beetle with its hind leg, flailing and rolling. The beetle remained in place, burrowed its head toward the frog, started chewing.

"Gross," said Mel.

The video began flashing forward in time. The beetle chewed through the frog's back, disabling the powerful legs, and the frog was left waving its little front legs as the beetle ate it alive in time-elapsed horror.

I stopped watching when it reached the eyes.

"I think I'm going to be sick," I said.

"The larva do the same thing," he said, and ran another video. "Grab the frogs when they try to eat them."

The frogs thrashed and rolled, flailing their legs, jumping, unable to escape an inch-long beetle larva locked onto their throats. The time lapse always moved to an immobile frog being sucked dry by the bristly larva.

"That's an Epomis beetle," the guy said.

"E's nickname," said Mel. "Epomis."

"What's her real name?" I asked.

"Far Li."

SIXTY-FIVE

THE COUPLE CLOSED THEIR apartment door. Lee and Mel had joined Jael and me.

"What is Airbnb?" asked Lee.

I said, "It's a website that lets you make some extra money renting out your apartment."

"These two rented that apartment to her?"

"Yeah. They went away for the weekend, rented the place to Far Li."

"And she brought you there to have sex with you?"

"Yeah."

"Why?"

"What do you mean, 'Why?'"

"You are too old."

"I don't think—"

"He was the frog," Jael said.

"What?"

"The frogs in the videos. They are tempted, drawn toward the beetle."

"I'm the frog."

"Yes, you are the frog. She tempted you and trapped you."

"Then how come I'm not dead?"

Jael said, "Because she did not want to kill *you*. She trapped the others as well."

Mel, silent until now, tapped her phone. Called Bobby on speaker. "Bobby, have we got anything on a Chinese national named Far Li? Any record? Anything in the database?"

"Let me look."

We waited.

"You do look a little green," Mel said.

I stared at her, eyes unfocused, suffering a flash of insight. Not the good kind, not the kind that pulls all the pieces together, solves the puzzle, and suggests that you're a genius. This was the shitty kind, the kind that pulls all the pieces together, solves the puzzle, and tells you that you are a cornucopia of incompetence.

"I got something," Bobby said. "Far Li is here on a work visa. She works at Xiong Distribution in Everett."

"That makes sense," I said.

"Her sister was Shu Li."

"Oh, shit."

"Who is Shu Li?" asked Jael.

Lee said, "Shu Li was a student at UMass. She was here on a student visa."

Mel said, "She committed suicide last year because of online bullying."

And the last piece of my stupidity dropped into place.

"Russell or Dorothy is next," I said.

Mel said, "E's going to his house."

"How do you know?" Bobby asked.

"PwnSec," Mel said. "Far Li blames PwnSec for her sister's death." I remembered the text. Flipped open my phone.

Russell had texted: E's safe. She's coming over.

SIXTY-SIX

I TEXTED RUSSELL BACK: `E is the HackMaster!`

Waited.

Got nothing.

I called Russell, went to voicemail. Called Dorothy. Went to voicemail. Left them both warnings about E, knowing that kids never listen to voicemail. Texted Dorothy. No response.

"We have to get moving."

There is no better way to screw up traffic in a major American city than to run a marathon through it. The elite runners would have already finished the race by now, but the great center of the bell curve would follow them. Thirty thousand marathoners had started winding their way through Boston, dividing the city, forcing you to be on one side or the other. Fortunately we were on the same side as Russell.

Mel drove, Jael in the back, and me riding shotgun, though *drove* is a strong word for what Mel was doing. There wasn't much driving to be done. We were clogged in traffic caused by drivers realizing that they'd never reach their destination on the other side of the race. A homeless person pushing a shopping cart zoomed past us.

"We'd be faster on foot," I said.

"No. It'll free up," said Mel.

"Let us do both," said Jael. She opened the door, stepped out, and started walking, her long strides taking her around the corner and out of sight.

"Do you think she'll beat us?" asked Mel.

"If she does, she might save Russell."

"Far Li will have a sword."

"Sword in a gunfight."

We inched forward a bit more.

"*Sic semper contumeliosis,*" said Mel. "I'll bet it wasn't 'Thus ever to the insolent.'"

"You said you did some research, that it has several meanings."

"Yeah."

"We had *the insolent* and *the spiteful*. What else could it mean? "*Abusive.*"

"That's got to be it. 'Thus ever to the abusive.' Because of Shu Li committing suicide."

"Why would Far Li blame PwnSec?"

"Because Russell, as Eliza, gave a blow by blow of the life ruin. The idiot was actually proud of it."

"I'm amazed she didn't kill them sooner."

"She would have, but she had to dox them. It was tougher than I made it look."

Mel said, "The traffic clears up after this light."

"Let's see if we can beat the shopping cart."

The traffic moved forward, and we made ground on our shopping-cart nemesis. The light turned red, and the shopping cart pulled away. The light turned back and Mel finally zigged around the shopping cart, down the street, and into the tail end of another line of cars.

I said, "Doxing can be tough if you don't have a place to start. That's why E launched the Epomis beetle plan. She'd make sock-puppet accounts on 4chan and Twitter, create a fake woman and create a fake guy to hate her."

"Then she'd get PwnSec to life ruin the woman."

"And they'd inevitably ask for a picture. A picture that she had spiked with a virus."

"And so she'd take over their computer and figure out who they were. But why did she use Peter's computer to steal the senator's video?"

"Two birds with one stone. She worked for Xiong, so she needed the video. Making Peter's computer do it would get Peter arrested."

"And doxed."

"Right."

"None of this explains the weirdest part."

"What?"

"Why did she hook up with you?" asked Mel.

"I guess we're agreeing it wasn't my good looks?"

"Yeah, let's just agree to that."

The traffic loosened up. Mel shot past Wentworth, got on Huntington, and zoomed toward Russell's house.

"Because I was better at doxing PwnSec than she was. When I got pissed off, I doxed Peter almost immedi—"

And then the whole thing revealed itself. I stared out the window, seeing nothing but a gigantic plan swirling like a hurricane on satellite radar with a tiny pin that said *You are here*. Sure, she'd played me. I was the frog. Not so hard to get a healthy single guy interested in hooking up with a healthy single woman. Guys are like that. But tricking me was only the start.

"Son of a bitch," I said.

"Who?" asked Mel.

"E played us all."

"Who did she play?"

"The Internet."

"What are you talking about?"

I thought back to the five of us standing in my apartment.

Earl pointed at E. "Who's she?"

"She's E."

"Why didn't you dox her?"

"She didn't piss me off."

"She knew I'd do it when I got angry."

"Do what?"

"Dox PwnSec."

"She needed to get you angry."

"So she started #TuckerGate. Made a bunch of different sock puppets online, started the fights, got the trolls trolling. The whole time she played up PwnSec, put them in a leadership position. Inflated their egos."

"And when they went after you—"

"I went after them, and E played 'Let's you and him fight.'"

Mel said nothing.

"Then she staged the Anonymous rally in front of my house. She knew that PwnSec would come, because they were leading #TuckerGate."

"She got all the suspects together."

"And then she got us into my apartment."

Mel said nothing, drove.

I whacked myself in the forehead. "Idiot!"

"Don't worry," said Mel. "We'll get there."

Mel pulled right, off Route 9, shot down Buckminster, then down Clinton. Russell's house was a big brick place fronted by winter-choked ivy. Mel stopped the car. We opened the door.

Mel's phone rang. She put Bobby on speaker.

"I'm looking at 4chan," said Bobby.

"And?"

"Call the medical examiner."

We ran to the house, pushed open the unlocked front door. Russell's head looked up at us from the doormat.

SIXTY-SEVEN

RUSSELL'S FACE, EVEN IN decapitated death, seemed to say, *See, I told you so.* His head rested on an oriental rug, blood oozing between the wool fibers and staining his Mohawk. His body had dropped straight down. It rested against the wall, a tangle of arms and legs.

"Oh, no," said Mel.

"Yeah," I said.

"It just showed up on 4chan," Bobby said over the speakerphone.

The smartest guy in the room, that's me. Unless there's a twenty-something girl around who, against all odds, thinks you're hot. Then not so smart. *Here. Here are my secrets. Here are the people who anger me. You want their real names? You want to know where they live? Sure! Why not! You're purty!*

I had set them up like bowling pins.

I called Dorothy. No answer. Texted. No reply.

"How long ago?" I asked Mel.

She crouched next to the body, touched it. "It's still warm," Mel said. She picked up a floppy arm, dropped it back into place. "No rigor. So less than three hours."

Bobby said over the speaker, "Backup is on the way."

329

"Nothing to do but wait for them," said Mel.

"I have to go," I said. "I need to get to Dorothy."

"Far Li has only ever killed one a day."

"*Dies ultimus,*" I said.

"The final day."

"She knows she's blown. She's got to do it today. Call Lee. I'm going."

My flip phone had no map. I jogged down Clinton toward Chestnut Hill Ave. Came upon a path cutting between two houses. Heard sirens approaching. Brookline Police would be here soon, wanting to talk to me. Get my insights. Sit with chins resting on their cupped palms, enthralled as Mr. Super Hacker told them how the whole thing had fit together.

Confessions of stupidity could wait.

I trotted down the path. It slipped between a pair of houses, forming a no-man's-land of easement, then it came upon railroad tracks and Green Line trains. Then the path dove, forming a tunnel beneath the tracks. I ran into darkness, taking in the miasma of a recent urination.

The tunnel rose on the other side of the tracks. As I emerged I heard cheering ahead of me on Beacon Street. I followed the sound, a constant whooping, punctuated by cowbells and cries of "You got this!" "You go, Mike in the orange hat, you go!" "Woo!"

The Boston Marathon in full swing.

Cops had set up barriers across the street, funneling me through a checkpoint where a cop looked at my empty-handed status and waved me through. The whooping grew louder with each step, and soon I was standing behind college students who leaned over the barrier to shout encouragement at the runners who streamed past.

I turned up Beacon, heading toward Cleveland Circle. It was one o'clock. The elite marathoners were long gone, running their twenty-third mile faster than I could run any single mile. The runners passing were the nameless masses. Athletes who were still chugging along, burning off eight- or nine-minute miles. This group had been running for three hours, and they were almost home.

I reached Cleveland Circle and stopped. Marathoners filled Chestnut Hill Ave, running between barriers separating a sea of happy spectators. The runners reached the bottom of the hill and turned wobbly knees toward the finish line, four miles away.

Had E come here, merged with this crowd? How could she possibly have done it carrying a sword? She was resourceful, but the cops were wary. Maybe I was wrong. Maybe she'd decided to wait for another day, a day with fewer cops. I looked across the race toward Dorothy's house.

Most runners wore bib numbers as their only identifying feature. Others had written their names on their jerseys. All received the enthusiasm of Bostonians who pressed against the barriers, cheering, waving, providing a corridor of encouragement and adulation. Together, the runners and crowd created a joyful space that celebrated spring, freedom, and triumph over adversity.

The image of Russell's head flashed at me, his eyes sneering even in death, his Mohawk tipped in blood. It roiled my stomach, reminded me of how I'd been duped. The marathon receded into the background as I replayed my missteps. My first tryst with E. My need to tweak the Anonymous protesters with my clever makeup. My flaring temper. The Twitter mob was out there, doing their thing, tearing down their sacrifice of the day, and one day it was me. I hadn't needed to participate in #TuckerGate, but I just couldn't resist.

A college girl next to me in a BC hat and sweatshirt called out to the runners. "You're almost there! You got this! Go, fuzzy hat, go!" Her calls of encouragement brought me back into the moment. Reconnected me with the danger.

I looked out across the stream of runners. Saw a girl with the name Miranda written across her tank top. The college girl yelled, "You got this, Miranda! You go, girl!"

Miranda gave a tired smile and a thumbs-up. She had this.

She found another runner. "You go, clown guy!" The guy, whose clown makeup had sweated off long ago, smiled, too tired to take his eyes off the road and make eye contact. A guy next to me rang a cowbell. One runner ran down the line, hand raised, high fiving the crowd.

Then I saw it, across the river of marathoners, behind the crowd of well-wishers, moving toward Dorothy's apartment: a tube, one of those tall portfolio tubes carried by art students. It surely would have been inspected if it had gone through a checkpoint, but a cursory glance probably wouldn't have caught what was hidden inside.

I knew what was hidden inside because I saw who was carrying it.

Far Li, aka Epomis, aka E, turning from the crowd, stepping over the MBTA tracks, and heading for Dorothy's apartment.

SIXTY-EIGHT

I PHONED MEL. "SHE'S here."

"Where?"

"Dorothy's. Get help."

I hung up the phone, stood on tiptoe, and tried to concoct a plan that would get me across the churning crowd of runners. The Boston Marathon was now a river at full flow as the bell-curve bulge of midspeed runners took the turn into Boston.

Two problems prevented me from getting across and stopping E from finishing her revenge tour.

The first was the police who lined the raceway, a nod to increased security since the bombing years ago. I might get one leg over the fence edging the road, but there'd be a cop on me right away, pulling me back.

The second was the runners themselves. Exhausted, chugging out eight-minute miles with cramping legs and grinding knees, they'd be in no shape to dodge some asshat who tried to run sideways across the race. They'd trip on me, fall, create a pileup. In the end I would not only have shattered their dreams and wasted their months of training, I still wouldn't get to Dorothy's house before E's sword finished the job.

I jogged down Beacon Street in the dripping rain, looking for a gap in the barriers, a spot where a mad dash could get me across before I collided with anyone. Then I saw an enormous gap in the police barrier, a gap filled with ten people who stood with an unobstructed path to the road. These people ran from table to track handing out cups of water in their capacity as Boston Athletic Association volunteers, the yellow-jacketed backbone of the event.

I needed one of those jackets.

The volunteers hustled back and forth between the crush of runners and a stack of green cups filled with water. The runners pelted by as the volunteers matched their stride, handed them the water, and ran back for more. One of the volunteers delivered her water, peeled away from the table, and headed for a blue port-a-potty behind me, giving me an idea. I had one shot at this, but I'd need some social engineering to pull it off.

I turned, entered the port-a-potty, and in a nod to authenticity, unzipped and used the facility, letting the sound of splashing water show that there was, indeed, a man at work inside. Then I waited another moment, undid the latch, and stepped out.

The woman in the BAA jacket waited in front of the john. I stepped down, closed the door behind me, and shook my head at her.

"It's a disaster in there," I said.

She crinkled her nose. "Really?"

"It's gross. I'm glad I didn't have to touch anything."

"But I have to go."

"Yeah, just giving you fair warning."

The woman fingered her BAA volunteer jacket, clearly thinking about how to avoid soiling it.

"I can hold it for you," I said.

"But you'll miss the race."

"It's gonna run for a another couple of hours."

She pulled off the jacket, handed it to me. "Thank you! Thank you!"

"Good luck in there," I said.

She climbed into the port-a-potty, closed the door, and latched it. I donned her jacket. It pulled across the back but made a fine disguise. I ran back to the water table, ignoring the cop monitoring the entry point, counting on my new yellow jacket to get me to the roadway.

It worked.

I looked across Beacon Street. The art tube holding E's sword bobbed in front of Pino's Pizza as she made her way toward Dorothy's apartment. Dorothy had been safe behind her nickname of "NotAGirl" and the fact that nobody knew where she lived, until I had given E all the information she needed to finish off the last member of PwnSec. I grabbed a cup of water, started running, matched stride with the next runner. A woman wearing an orange and blue checked top with the words *Children's Hospital Boston* above her bib number.

I held out the cup. "Water?"

She shook her head and panted, "No thanks."

I continued running. "You sure?"

"I'll throw up."

I dropped back to her teammate, a bald guy sporting a sheen of pate sweat. "Water?"

"No," he puffed.

"You're sweating."

"I know. No water."

I let him go. Behind him a short thin woman in a crop-top running bra fixed me with a gaze, shook her head.

"You sure?"

She ran on. I reached the end of the open stretch. More runners ran past. I looked toward the port-a-potty. A runner grabbed the cup from my hand when I wasn't looking. The woman whose jacket I wore had emerged and was searching for me. I turned away before she could make eye contact, and saw E's art tube winding its way past the deli, the thick crowd slowing her progress.

I ran back to the table, grabbed another cup of water. Matched pace alongside a guy in a white-sheet toga who now understood why marathon runners had been shirtless Greeks instead of togaed Romans. Two rust-colored stains ran down the front of his toga showing that his nipples would never be the same after twenty-some miles of chafing.

I offered the cup. "Water?"

"No, man."

"You sure?"

"Jesus, it hurts."

I slipped into the race running behind him, came up on the other side. "You look like you could use it."

"Should you be on the course?"

"No," I said. I drank the water, tossed the cup to the ground, and kept going. Looked over my shoulder. I'd have to pick up the pace a bit to get across, so started running harder. Came up on a guy pushing a kid in a wheelchair. Ran past, slid in front of him with plenty of room. Kept running.

Someone in the crowd noticed me. "You can do it, yellow guy!"

"You go, BAA volunteer!"

I ran diagonally away from the wheelchair pair. Ran past a guy with no shirt, wearing red-white-and-blue running shorts, his bib clipped to the front of his shorts. The guy was ripped. Women hooted at him. "You go, hot dude."

"Go! Go! Go!" the crowd yelled.

Though the cheers weren't for me, I took them in anyway, letting them fill me with goodwill and energy. I could see how you could do this for twenty-six miles, as long as your knees held up.

Shirtless Guy looked at me. "What are you doing?"

"Crossing the street."

I veered toward the barriers protecting the race course. Race fans raised hands for high fives. I looked behind me, saw a runner slapping palms, ran away from the barrier to make room, slowed, then stopped in front of the fence and threw a leg over.

"A little help!" I called.

Two guys in BU sweatshirts grabbed me, pulled me over the fence. One said, "Jesus, dude. You coulda killed someone."

"Yeah, sorry," I said. "Emergency."

The marathon had pushed me downstream. I'd have to get back to Dorothy's house.

I looked back up Beacon. Saw E's art tube disappear into Dorothy's entryway.

SIXTY-NINE

MY RUN HAD LANDED me a block downstream from where I had started. I looked back and saw the woman whose jacket I wore, talking to a cop and pointing at me. The cop looked across, spoke into the radio mike on his chest. It was time to get moving. I ducked behind the crowd, pulled off the yellow jacket, hung it on a parking meter, and started across the street.

A line of cars worked their way up Beacon, blocking the path. I looked toward Dorothy's and saw a cop walking toward me, probably looking for the guy who'd stolen the BAA jacket. I'd need to get across. I took a step into the street. A car rolled past. The driver had clearly been trapped in marathon traffic and wasn't giving an inch. I let the car go past, tried another step, blocked by another car. The nearest crosswalk was a half a block back.

Time to start acting like a Bostonian.

I stepped into the traffic. The next car jammed on his brakes, blasted his horn. I gave him the finger. Waved at him to slow down. Ran across his car. Another car came through that lane. Got in front of him. Almost across.

A guy on a bike yelled at me. "Asshole!"

That was fair.

Asshole or not, I was across the street. I started running up the sidewalk, dodging dawdlers left and right, skirting baby carriages, and kids holding hands. E's art tube had been in the apartment building a couple of minutes. It could all be over by now. I ran past the convenience store and turned into the alley that led to the front door.

Ran right into Billy Janks, aka the bounty hunter CapnMerica.

"Got you!" he said, and clamped a handcuff over my wrist. Attached the other one to himself.

I tugged at my wrist, moving his arm. "Get this off me!"

He started walking, pulling me with him. "I'm finding a cop and turning you in."

I stood my ground, stopping him. "What are you doing here?"

"Epomis called me," he said. "She told me you'd be trying to get upstairs."

"Of course I'm trying to get upstairs. She's going to kill Dorothy."

"She told me that you'd say that too."

I raged, whipping my arm back and forth, whipping Billy's arm with it.

"Ow!" he cried.

"I'll break your fucking arm!"

"Stop!"

"I swear you wil—"

And then I stopped. Stopped whipping my arm. Stopped fighting. The rage had taken me again, filling my head with images of dragging Billy's hand to the ground and stomping it until the handcuff came free, reveling in the idea of beating this scrawny loser to a pulp, betraying me once more.

Billy was right. It was time to stop.

I took a deep breath, blew it out, and stood with hands on knees, forcing Billy's head close.

"Look, Billy," I said. "I'm sorry I slapped you."

"You're a criminal."

"But I'm telling you that E is going to kill Dorothy. She's already killed Russell."

"Russell?"

"Eliza."

Eyes wide, Billy said, "No!"

"I'm sorry that I've been a dick this past week. I'm sorry I humiliated you. But we have to get past this."

"I'm going to let the cops sort it out."

The rage tickled my gut, trying to worm its way back into my thinking. I pushed it down. It hadn't helped. It had never helped.

"Billy, how do you think I killed those people?"

"You cut off their heads!"

"With a sword?"

"Yeah."

I spread my arms, carrying Billy's arm with me. "You see a sword?"

Billy looked.

"Did E have a sword?" I asked.

"No."

"Did she have a long tube that could carry a sword?"

Finally, Billy put it together. "She's the HackMaster!"

"Yeah. I can still save Dorothy, but you've got to take these off and go get a cop."

Billy reached into his pants, pulled out a set of keys. I imagined E upstairs, knocking on Dorothy's door, calling out, "It's me!" in a friendly woman's voice. Dorothy opening the door.

Billy dropped the keys. "Shit!"

I thrust out my manacled wrist. "Focus, Billy."

We crouched. He scrabbled for the key, unlocked my cuff.

"Now," I said, "go get a cop. Top floor!"

Billy ran out to find a cop. I turned and ran up the stairs to the front door.

Locked.

SEVENTY

I MASHED ALL THE doorbells next to the door. Listened for a buzzer. Heard a click instead. Realized the buzzer was broken. The click had unlocked the door. Heard another click. The door had relocked.

"Dammit!"

I mashed the buttons again, listened for the click. Got it this time, pushed the door open, and ran into the hallway.

A woman in a faded housedress stood in front of the staircase. "You again! Stop ringing my bell."

I dodged past her. "Sorry. Gotta go."

"I'm serious."

I ran up the steps. "Won't happen again!"

I pounded up the hallway stairs, reached the top apartment. Closed door. Tried the knob: locked. Pounded on the door.

No answer.

I looked for blood seeping into the hallway. None. Pounded again. "It's Tucker! Open up!"

The door swung open. Dorothy stood before me.

"E was just going to show me her artwork," said Dorothy.

Behind Dorothy, E fiddled with her art tube and reached into it.

"Run," I said to Dorothy.

"What?"

Behind Dorothy, E drew a short sword out of the art tube.

"*Run!*"

E yelled, "No!" and raised the sword.

I pushed Dorothy out the door behind me as E charged. I reached down, grabbing the wooden baseball bat Dorothy kept for security. E's sword swooshed. I ducked. The sword clunked into the wooden door. I slammed the door shut, hoping to trap the sword, but E yanked it free.

I ran into the living room, carrying the bat.

"You ruined everything!" E screeched. She turned, raising the sword.

"This isn't helping, E!" I said, holding the bat in front of me. "Your sister is gone."

"No shit!" E said. Swooshing the sword in front of her. "Nothing's going to bring her back."

"So what's the point?"

"The point is to kill them. That's the fucking point."

"Who?"

"You know who. PwnSec." Another swoosh.

"You killed Russell. He's the one who did it."

"They all did it!"

E rushed at me, swinging the sword in a big arc aimed at my neck. I stuck the bat in the air. The sword chunked into it, cutting halfway through, but stopping. I took advantage of my leverage, twisting the bat before E could get the sword free, torquing it out of her hands, and throwing it aside.

I ran at E, reaching down, grabbing her legs, lifting and slamming her to the ground. I just had to hold her here until the police came. E wrapped her legs around me, trying to twist free. I reached for her hands, trying to grab her, immobilize her.

And then ... I don't know what. E grabbed my wrists, pulled my arms toward her and twisted, holding my wrist with one hand and wrapping her other arm around mine. She pulled me down toward her, spun, and suddenly my shoulder was twisting.

"Aagh!" I yelled, trying to yank my arm free.

E held on, twisting her body and pushing. Searing pain shot through my shoulder as I felt the ball lift out of its socket, tendons popping and twisting. I panicked, trying to free my dead arm.

E spun around to my back, wrapping her forearm around my throat, pushing down and cutting off my air. I reached for her with my good arm, couldn't get there. Couldn't stop her. My vision clouded, darkness pooling in from the edges. I looked through the tunnel, spasming and choking, when I saw her.

Dorothy's aunt Ruby sat in her wheelchair, pointing an enormous black gun at us. E, her head burrowed into my back and unreachable, didn't see Ruby fire the gun.

My world exploded. Pain tore through me as all my muscles jammed and clenched into a massive knot of charley horses. I screamed. On my back, E grunted, her chokehold loosening as she screamed alongside me.

The Taser finished the job that the sword, the dislocated shoulder, and the chokehold had started. I saw Dorothy and Billy burst into the room with a cop, and passed out.

SEVENTY-ONE

MY EYES FLUTTERED OPEN. Jael knelt beside me.

"He is awake," Jael said to Mel. "That is unfortunate."

Jael pulled on my ruined arm harder than E ever had. Pain sparkled before my eyes, the joint crackled, the noises twisting my gut. I yelled just as my shoulder snapped back into place.

"I am sorry," said Jael.

"Think nothing of it." I wept.

Outside crowds cheered and cowbells clanged as the marathon continued.

Mel gave me a kiss on the shoulder. "There, it'll feel better soon," she said. "Also, they'll give you drugs."

Across the room E was being yanked to her feet by the cop, wrists handcuffed behind her. CapnMerica videorecorded the arrest. Dorothy's aunt Ruby sat in her wheelchair, her face in her hands. Dorothy knelt beside her, rubbing her back.

Ruby looked up at me.

Mel and Jael helped me to my feet. I knelt next to Dorothy.

"I'm sorry I shot you," Ruby said.

"That's okay."

"I was trying to shoot that girl."

Mel said to me, "The Taser electrodes hit you both."

"Thank you," I said to Ruby. "You saved my life. I'm pretty certain E was going to choke me to death."

"Far Li says you attacked her," Mel said. "She's claiming self-defense."

"The trolls will love that," I said. "It's her word against ours."

"Not so much," Dorothy said. She pointed at the X-Men Cyclops, standing on her mantel looking across the room. "He was watching."

"So there's video evidence," I said. "How long was I out?"

"Only a couple of minutes," said Mel. "We were on the steps with the cop when we heard you get tased."

"So Dorothy doesn't know?"

"Know what?"

"Far Li killed Russell before she came here."

"Who is she?" Dorothy asked.

"She's Shu Li's sister."

Dorothy looked at the ground. "Oh."

Ruby asked, "Who is Shu Li?"

I told her how Shu Li had committed suicide, and how Far Li had wanted revenge.

"But why would she come here?" Ruby asked me. "Dorothy wouldn't bully anyone."

How to answer that. Do I tell her about the incoherent rage? The trolling? The bullying? The way the Internet had turned into a pipeline of raw emotional sewage? The ridiculous alliances, the death threats? Do I enlighten a woman who thinks of the Internet as nothing but a way to get e-mail, buy a book, or read a newspaper?

Should Aunt Ruby know that Dorothy travels the web as NotA-Girl, and while she didn't do the bullying herself, she hung out with guys who did? Would any of this help her make sense of a world where a crazy woman would try to cut off her niece's head?

"Mistaken identity," I told her.

Dorothy hugged me and whispered in my ear, "Thank you. Thank you for everything."

I hugged her back with one arm, the other dead by my side.

I turned to Mel and Jael. "Can I have drugs now?"

SEVENTY-TWO

I STARED INTO MY computer screen, working a hoe made of graphical blocks into soil made of graphical blocks. In front of me lay a green cube representing a melon. I whacked at the melon with a pixelated ax, and it broke into melon slices.

"Have you harvested the melons?" Maria asked.

"I'm working on it," I said.

We sat in Maria's room playing Minecraft.

Catherine, Adriana, and I had gone through a surprisingly rapid rapprochement. I had sat at the kitchen table and had said, "I'm sorry."

Catherine said, "Sorry for what?"

"I'm sorry I brought the whole thing down on us. On you. I'm sorry for not listening."

"I'm sorry too," Catherine said.

We hugged, and that had been that. Families are funny like that. Small hurts can fester forever, while the big hurts, the huge errors, can sometimes be fixed with a simple apology.

Restarting the grief counseling had helped. Maria had resisted at first, but soon looked forward to the visits with her counselor. We all had gone with her at different times and even together. While the picture of Sal and Sophia still graced the wall in Adriana's house, it seemed that we could look at it with fondness now rather than with pain.

Maria had gone through a short Facebook withdrawal. She had pouted and whined, complained about the unfairness of it all, and then, suddenly, stopped. Instead she had asked me about Minecraft. I'd bought the app for her iPad, and soon Facebook was long forgotten, replaced by the need to gather cubicle resources, build a farmhouse, and eventually create a village with her friends. Being a cool, technologically savvy pseudo dad, I had set up a private server in which Maria and her friends built their world, a safe harbor from the ravings of the Internet.

Laughter erupted from the kitchen.

"I think they're watching it again," Maria said.

"They're like children, I swear," I said.

"You should go see."

I left the laptop on the bed. "Leave me some melons to whack."

"I will. I'm getting us some pigs."

"Good."

"Also I'm building a mob farm."

"I don't want to know," I said.

Once in the kitchen, the refrigerator caught my attention. I opened it, pulled out a Harpoon IPA, took a long drink. Walked over to Catherine and Adriana huddled in front of a laptop. When they saw me, they covered their mouths and giggled.

"Are you guys watching it again?" I asked.

"It's just so funny," Catherine said.

Adriana looked serious. "Not funny per se. I mean, you almost got killed."

"Yeah," I said.

"But unexpected, to be sure. Plus people have added background music."

"Really."

There it was on the screen: the viral YouTube video *Tucker Pwned by a Little Girl, Saved by Old Lady #TuckerGate*.

"Yeah," I said, "a little girl with a razor-sharp wakizashi sword."

"Don't forget the Brazilian jiujitsu training," Adriana said.

"I want Maria to learn Brazilian jiujitsu," Catherine said. "I may learn it myself."

On the screen, E tried to kill me with the sword, swinging at me with a martial-arts grace and beauty that had been difficult to appreciate while fending her off with a baseball bat.

They had modified the original video, which had no sound. This version ran at a slightly faster speed while Benny Hill music played in the background. Catherine hummed along with the music.

In the video, Far Li's sword got stuck in my bat and I wrenched it out of her hand. I lunged for her, pushed her to the ground, grabbed at her hands. Far Li grabbed my wrist, wrapped her arm around mine, and wrenched my shoulder out of its socket.

My shoulder twinged. Benny Hill's kazoo played on.

E pressed her advantage, climbing on my back, wrapping her arms around my neck, and cutting off the blood to my brain. We both looked off camera in surprise. Ruby appeared, fired Taser wires into both of us. Then it was all over but for the twitching.

The video had extinguished the fire that was #TuckerGate. It clearly showed that Far Li had the sword and the skills to be cutting off heads, and NotAGirl had made sure that everyone knew the motive. The apparently comical video of me getting my shoulder destroyed by a little girl had sealed the deal.

There was no way this inept pansy Tucker could ever have been a killer.

"I'm going to go help Maria," I said and turned to leave.

"You've already helped Maria," said Adriana. "You're the best dad she could have."

A burning started in my nose, threatened to spill out into my eyes.

"I do my best," I said, draining my beer. "Now I have to go harvest melons."

Catherine stood and hugged me. Adriana joined us and gave me a peck on the cheek.

"To the melons!" I said, sniffling.

I left the kitchen and walked back into Maria's room, where she was pointing into her iPad screen and laughing. "It worked!"

"What worked?"

"I made a mob farm."

"What's a mob farm?"

"It was on a Minecraft hints page."

"What does it do?"

"You know how angry mobs pop up in dark places?"

"Yeah."

"So, I built this dark room like thirty feet above the ground with some flowing water and a trapdoor. The mobs pop up in the room, get caught in the water, fall, and die. See?"

Sure enough, blocky green people were falling out of Maria's contraption onto the ground below. As they shattered, they left treasures such as arrows, pumpkins, and swords. Maria was picking up the treasures, harvesting a mob.

I couldn't think of a better use for the Internet.

THE END

© Lynn Wayne

ABOUT THE AUTHOR

Ray Daniel is the award-winning author of Boston-based crime fiction. His short story "Give Me a Dollar" won a 2014 Derringer Award for short fiction, and "Driving Miss Rachel" was chosen as a 2013 distinguished short story by Otto Penzler, editor of *The Best American Mystery Stories 2013*.

Daniel's work has been published in the Level Best Books anthologies *Thin Ice, Blood Moon,* and *Stone Cold. Hacked* is the fourth Tucker mystery, following *Corrupted Memory, Terminated,* and *Child Not Found.*

For more information, visit him online at raydanielmystery.com and follow him on Twitter: @raydanielmystry, and Tucker's bot: @TuckerInBoston.

OTHER BOOKS BY KENNETH ROBERTS . . .

>─┤◆)─●─(◆─┤─◄

The Chronicles of Arundel

Arundel (I)
Arundel is the story of the American attempt to take Quebec in 1775, a heroic but doomed effort masterminded by one of the most brilliant (and later infamous) of George Washington's officers: Colonel Benedict Arnold.

Rabble in Arms (II)
The second of Roberts's epic novels of the American Revolution, *Rabble in Arms* was hailed by one critic as "the greatest historical novel written about America" upon its publication in 1933.

The Lively Lady (III)
Set in the War of 1812, *The Lively Lady* follows the fortunes of Richard Nason, an American sailing master and privateer who is captured and imprisoned by the British.

Captain Caution (IV)
First published in 1934, *Captain Caution* is the final volume in the Chronicles of Arundel.

>─┤◆)─●─(◆─┤─◄

Oliver Wiswell
In *Oliver Wiswell* Roberts portrays a very different side to the story of the American Revolution, that of the loyalists (those colonists who supported the British monarchy).

(All titles are paperback.)

CHECK YOUR LOCAL BOOKSTORE, OR ORDER
FROM DOWN EAST BOOKS AT 1-800-685-7962